"Your reputation doesn't do you justice, does it?"

Boone's low, intimate voice wrapped around her like a velvet cloak. "You're more than the old-maid busybody everybody takes you for, aren't you, Rose?"

"I . . . I don't know what you're talking about," Rose said stiffly, turning her head away. She couldn't bear to look at him, all silver-gilded and strong and tempting.

"Sure you do." He caught her chin with his fingers and turned her face toward his. "I'm talking about this."

He was going to kiss her; he made his intentions quite clear. And she—she, heaven help her!—stood there stiff as a stump and let it happen. When his mouth at last touched hers, she closed her eyes and let him transport her to another world.

Dear Reader,

There is a lot to look for this month from Harlequin Historicals.

Sweet Seduction by Julie Tetel is the first of two intriguing stories set in Maryland during the early 1800s. Heroine Jane Shaw was raised as a Southern belle, but she is more than a match for the British soldiers who sequester her family's home. And don't miss the sequel, *Sweet Sensations,* coming in July.

Readers following the TAGGARTS OF TEXAS! series by Ruth Jean Dale will be delighted to discover the prequel to the earlier books in this month's lineup. *Legend!* is the story of Boone, the Taggart who started it all by turning the little town of Jones, Texas, on its ear.

Captured Moment by Coral Smith Saxe is set during the California mining days. Straight off the boat from the old country, the impish Rowen Trelarken stumbles into an immediate series of misadventures, dragging an unwilling Alec McKenzie along for the ride.

Frenchwoman Elise de Vire marries Sir Adam Saker as an act of revenge, but the force of the attraction between them places them both in mortal danger in *Beloved Deceiver,* a medieval tale from Laurie Grant.

Four new romances from Harlequin Historicals. We hope you enjoy them.

Sincerely,

Tracy Farrell
Senior Editor

Legend!

RUTH JEAN DALE

Harlequin Books

TORONTO • NEW YORK • LONDON
AMSTERDAM • PARIS • SYDNEY • HAMBURG
STOCKHOLM • ATHENS • TOKYO • MILAN
MADRID • WARSAW • BUDAPEST • AUCKLAND

Harlequin Historicals first edition April 1993

ISBN 0-373-28768-2

LEGEND!

RUTH JEAN DALE

never dreamed, when she began writing about the Taggarts of Texas, that the story would eventually cross three Harlequin lines to culminate here with her first historical romance. Born in the Ozark Mountains of Missouri, Ruth Jean has spent considerable time in Texas; in fact, her two youngest daughters were born in San Antonio. A lifelong student of Western history and a great fan of Louis L'Amour, she lives in a pine forest in Colorado with her husband and a sheepdog named Rocky Bob.

Special thanks to Beverlee Ross,
that lover of batwing doors;
and to all my other friends in the San Diego
Chapter of Romance Writers of America,
including but not limited to Dawn Carroll and
Marian Jones, Karen and Carole and Caro and
B.J. and Cathy and Teresa—well, you know who
you are. For years you humored me when I said I
was going to write a historical, and now I *have!*

Chapter One

"*Virginia Rose Taggart, you are the stubbornest woman in three counties—maybe all of Texas!*"

George Curtis, middle-aged proprietor of the only mercantile and grocery emporium in Jones, Texas, glared at the dark-haired young woman who'd just interrupted his private conversation with Fred Loveless. Fred owned the harness shop and livery stable at the north end of town. Everybody knew the two men met on the boardwalk each morning, regular as clockwork weather permitting, to talk politics and plan their next move in the ongoing civic war with neighboring Crystal Springs.

Fred piped up. "Yeah, Rose, can't you take a hint? Why you always hornin' in?" He cast a glance at his companion, a glance reminiscent of a hound dog seeking his master's approval.

Or so Rose thought, watching Fred's obsequious manner. The scrawny little man was irritating, no doubt about it, but she had no quarrel with Fred Loveless; her business was with George Curtis, and she must press it. She had promised.

"Mr. Curtis," she said, her voice ringing with determination, "you've avoided me long enough. You may as well listen and get it over with because I'm not going away until you do. Whether you choose to admit it or not, Sally is no longer a child. She is sixteen and—"

"I know how old my own daughter is, missy." George's eyes narrowed beneath beetled brows. "I sure don't need you to tell me."

Rose felt the hated flush of color rise in her cheeks, but she refused to be put off by the man's overbearing manner. With Sally's future at stake, Rose tried to moderate her tone. "Yes, of course you do, but—"

"And how old are you, missy?"

His downright rudeness stopped her for a moment. "Why, I'm—" She frowned. "You know how old I am."

George nodded. "Indeed I do. A *twenty-two-year-old maiden lady* is in no position to tell me how to raise my little girl."

Rose couldn't stifle her groan. "That's my point exactly. Sally's not a little girl, she's a young woman, and you've got to—"

"Rosie, Rosie, Rosie—don't you be tellin' me what I've *got* to do." George hooked his thumbs into the armholes of the vest straining to cover his barrel chest and favored her with a condescending smile. "Why don't you marry the marshal like he wants you to and mind his business instead of mine?"

"Yeah," Fred chimed in, "instead of ours?"

Even angry as she was, Rose's air of melancholy slipped easily into place; after five years of rehearsal, it should. She gave a practiced sigh and lifted wide sad eyes to George. "You of all people must surely realize that I will never—"

"—love any boy but Billy." George put the finishing touches on her standard speech. "Yes, yes, the whole town knows that. But jumpin' Jehoshaphat, girl, he was *my son* and I managed to get ahold of my grief a year or two after the good Lord saw fit to take him from us. It's time you done the same. It just ain't natural for a woman your age to be without a man."

"Yeah, without a man." Fred nodded in vigorous agreement. "Besides," he added in a confidential tone, "it'd keep you outa *our* hair."

The two men regarded her with expectant expressions. This was where all Rose's conversations of a serious nature tended to bog down, for their attitude was shared by just about everybody in town. No one seemed able to understand why she held a fine man like Marshal Jack Guthrie at arm's length.

But then, they didn't know her guilty secret. If she had to move heaven and earth, she was determined that they never would.

For the horrible truth was, Virginia Rose Taggart had lost her virtue at seventeen to Billy Curtis, son of this selfsame George and brother to Sally, current subject of contention. On the very day they became engaged, young Billy had convinced Rose that it was perfectly all right to have the honeymoon before the wedding.

Only it wasn't; she knew it at the time but let him convince her otherwise. "No one else will ever know," he'd promised in a voice quivering with sincerity, "as long as you don't get ... *friendly* with no other man. 'Course, *he'd* know—a woman can't fool us men about anything this important."

He'd puffed up his chest when he said it, and she'd been overcome with admiration for the male sex. Billy was so handsome and she was so lucky that he'd chosen her when he could have had any girl in the country. But she shouldn't give in to him; she knew she really shouldn't....

And then he'd added the clincher. "As long as you'r true-blue, you got nothin' to worry about, darlin'. Nothin in the whole wide world."

Of *course* she was true-blue—and there was only one wa to prove it. Since she would never, ever be intimate with an other man, what had she to fear?

Plenty, as it turned out; a couple of weeks later Billy wa thrown by his horse and dragged to death. Rose was left be hind, grieving for her lost love and her lost virtue. In he own eyes, she was ruined forever—as she would be in th eyes of the town, should anyone learn of her lack of mora fiber.

To avoid that disgrace at all costs was her prayer as sh collapsed into deep mourning. She swore she'd be true t Billy as long as she lived, and everyone patted her shoulde and admired her loyalty. They didn't know Rose was als weeping for the future she'd given up for a few minutes o hasty and unsatisfactory—to her, anyway—lovemaking be neath a tree in Diablo Canyon.

The truth was, she'd been infatuated with the handsom young Billy and determined to be a good wife, but sh hadn't loved him *that* much, not enough to give up all hop of achieving a woman's ultimate goal in life: a husband an family of her own. Now no decent man would want her— for matrimonial purposes, anyway—once he knew her se cret.

Nor dared she marry without confessing her sin. He shame had left some mark, mental or physical, which sh could not herself comprehend but that would be readily ap parent to any man she allowed to get close to her—Billy ha told her so, and it must be true. Otherwise, how were me able to separate women into good and bad categories th way they did?

Rose had a position to maintain in this town, and he downfall would affect others as well as herself. Her fathe was a man who'd earned widespread respect. His Rocking T Ranch was the biggest in this part of Texas.

And what about her older brother? James would be forced to defend her honor, however tarnished, against all comers. She wouldn't be able to bear it if anything happened to him because of her.

So, early on, she realized she dared not marry and take the chance of being exposed as a loose woman. She would never be able to bear the disgrace. Perhaps there'd be no public revelation but she knew firsthand what gossip could do to a woman—look what had happened to poor Mary Lou Harris.

Thus it was fear that had made Rose vow to remain forever single, claiming that her love for Billy would never die. After a couple of years of that, her father and brother, not to mention the good citizens of Jones, began to look at her askance. Loyalty was one thing, but life went on.

After four years, even the Curtises—Billy's parents, George and Alice—began to urge her to get on with living. Rose remained adamant while her supporters dwindled until only her sister-in-law, Diana, and Billy's sister, Sally, remained.

Lately even Diana seemed to be wavering.

Now George Curtis, who should have been Rose's father-in-law, had the effrontery to stand there and suggest—

But at the moment, she realized, he wasn't suggesting anything, and neither was Fred. The two men stared past her, into the street, jaws agape and eyes wide. Frowning, she turned to see what had so distracted them.

Down the middle of the wide, dusty street in the harsh summer sunlight rode the hardest, leanest, meanest man Rose had ever laid eyes on. Hat tilted low over his eyes and one hand resting on the revolver strapped to his hip, he slumped in the saddle astride a played-out buckskin.

An image of a wounded wolf she'd once seen cornered on the Rocking T leaped to Rose's mind as she stared at the rider. He had that same gaunt and savage look to him, and it sent a little tremor of horrified awareness down her spine.

Looking neither right nor left, still he gave the distinct impression that he assimilated everything around him. Abreast of the trio standing motionless before the general store, he suddenly turned his head, and his glance locked with Rose's.

The impact of his attention struck her like a blow—so brief and yet so powerful that it took her breath away. His glance flicked down the length of her and then, as if finding her wanting, he looked away again.

Rose felt her heart lurch in her breast, then begin to race. His piercing indifference infuriated her, even as she almost sagged with relief. Whoever this predatory man might be, she neither knew nor cared to know.

Still, she watched him, unable to turn away.

Without seeming to do so, he guided his exhausted mount to the hitching rail in front of the Yellow Rose Saloon, across the street and two doors down from the mercantile. The horse stood with head hanging and sides heaving. The man sat there for a moment as if gathering strength; then he slid to the ground and clung for a moment to the saddle.

He was hurt, Rose realized. And with Doc gone to Wichita two weeks ago for a wedding, it was her duty to offer what assistance she could. But she didn't. The man frightened her. She didn't know why, he just did.

He straightened and stepped away from the buckskin. For a moment he scanned the street like a man used to watching his back trail. Then he turned toward the steps leading up to the boardwalk and the entrance to the Yellow Rose.

At that moment, little Emmett Cox roared around the corner in hot pursuit of a yellow mongrel pup. The dog slipped between the stranger's feet without mishap, but seven-year-old Emmett plowed into the man's midsection.

The stranger grunted and staggered back a step, his hold on the boy's shoulders perhaps keeping him upright. Watching with her heart in her throat, Rose took an unconscious step forward, prepared to rush to Emmett's defense should such be required.

"Gee, I'm sorry, mister!" Emmett tilted his head back to look up into the face shadowed by a hat brim. He tried to squirm away from the hands holding him. "Lemme go, will ya? My dog's gettin' away!"

"Not so fast, sonny." The man released the boy and reached into a pocket, coming out with a coin. He held it up so that it caught the sunlight. "Think you can take my horse to the livery and get him fed and rubbed down?" He flipped the coin into the air.

The boy flashed a quick, delighted smile and snatched the tumbling coin before it could hit the ground. "Sure thing, mister." He pocketed his profit and turned to yank the buckskin's reins free of the hitch rail. "Anything else yawl want done?"

"Not at the moment, son."

"Well, if'n you do, just ask for Emmett Cox—that's me."

"I'll do that," the man promised gravely, but he was already looking past the boy toward the doors of the saloon. Stiffly erect, he limped up the four steps and paused just outside the Yellow Rose.

His shoulders lifted with the force of an indrawn breath; then he plunged through the doors into the dark interior.

Slowly Rose expelled the breath she'd unconsciously been holding. There went a very scary man, despite the fact that he'd been courteous, even kind to the boy. Who could he be and what was he doing in Jones?

George's gleeful chortle brought her swinging around. "That's Clay Allison or I'll eat my hat." The paunchy gro-

cer rubbed his hands together with delight. "Let's see Crystal Springs match *that!*"

Fred shook his head vigorously. "That ain't Allison.
seen Allison once, and that ain't him."

George hauled back in exaggerated surprise. "*You* seer
Clay Allison?"

"Not to talk to," Fred admitted. "But I did see him onc
in Cimmaron. He's a big man but not big as that one. If
had to guess, I'd say that was probably—" he screwed up hi
face, giving it a moment's thought "—John Wesley Har
din—yeah, that's Hardin, all right."

Rose had heard quite enough speculation on the subject
Now that the man was out of sight, she'd already begun t
distrust the sense of danger she'd felt so strongly. "I'm quit
sure that man is simply a cowboy down on his luck," sh
said crisply, not at all convinced herself but feeling dut
bound to bring the two men around to the subject sh
wanted to discuss. "Now getting back to Sally—"

George ignored her. "Who you suppose is worse?" h
queried Fred. "I knew an old boy went up the Abilene Trai
with Hardin back in '71 or '72, and he says the kid gunnec
down twenty men before his twentieth birthday."

A movement behind the two merchants caught Rose's at
tention. Sally stood in the doorway of her father's store, he
big baby-blue eyes pleading. She pointed to her father an
nodded hopefully; Rose shook her head.

Fred had picked up the conversational gauntlet. "Har
din's bad but so's Allison—and a flashy cuss to boot. Yo
hear about that knife duel he fought in an open grave? Som
folks say he's crazy, on account of that."

"He's crazy as a pet coon, but it wasn't the knife fight o
the grave that proved it so much as the fact he done it in hi
birthday suit—beg pardon, Rose. Nah, we're better off if
ain't Allison."

Fred screwed up his face. "I 'spect you're right." He brightened. "Maybe we'll get lucky and it'll be Bill Longley."

"I thought he was hanged for a horse thief a while back," George mused.

"Was, but lived to tell about it. Yep, I'd say we better hope that old boy over there in the Yellow Rose is Longley, or maybe Hickok—"

"Gentlemen!"

Both men looked at Rose as if surprised she was still there.

She gave them her most intimidating schoolteacher's glare. "I can't believe what I'm hearing. After what happened here in this very community only a few months ago, how can the two of you, upstanding businessmen and pillars of the community, *hope* that stranger is some sort of desperado?"

"That's not what we hope, missy." George's smile was sour. "We hope he's some sort of *famous* desperado. And we further hope he shoots somebody—nobody important, you understand. Preferably somebody from Crystal Springs."

The two men guffawed and Fred slapped his thigh for emphasis. "The point is," George went on with exaggerated patience, "we need an edge if Jones is gonna beat out Crystal Springs for county seat. Why, Jones would be famous if a notorious gunman come to town and filled somebody full of lead." His eyes opened wider, as if with sudden inspiration, and he turned excitedly to Fred. "Or if a famous gunman come to town and somebody filled *him* full of lead! George, you suppose—"

Rose gasped in outrage. "Gentlemen, I am shocked and appalled at your callous disregard for public safety. If Jones is ever to grow and prosper—"

"It will be when we wipe that Crystal Springs off the map," George cut in savagely. "And Melville Jones with it."

Automatically Rose's glance lifted to the sign painted on the window of George's store, commonly called the C and J for Curtis and Jones. Only the Jones part had been painted over when the partnership broke up three years ago amidst great acrimony. Melville Jones, founder of Jones, Texas, had moved a few miles away and started another town, calling it Crystal Springs, although it had no springs, crystal or otherwise.

Nobody knew what had caused the partnership to flounder, but since then George Curtis had lived and breathed revenge. As Crystal Springs stole away more and more of Jones's residents and businesses, George fussed and fumed and schemed and counterschemed.

Now, with county seat honors at stake, the rivalry between men and towns had become even more intense. A couple of months ago the Springs succeeded in luring the only newspaper in this part of Texas into relocating, a sure sign that Jones was falling behind.

Rose, who did not care in the slightest which community won out, frowned. "That is not a Christian attitude," she reminded George Curtis primly. "Now, getting back to the subject of Sally—"

"Mornin', Miss Rose. Your brother's lookin' for you."

At the sound of the arrogant youthful voice behind her, Rose stifled a groan. The last person she wanted to show up just now was Tonio Ryan. His presence was all it would take to throw Sally's father into an apoplectic rage.

Not that there was a thing she could do about it, she realized, watching the crimson tide suffuse George Curtis's already ruddy cheeks.

"You!" he flung at the boy. "Don't think I don't know you been sniffin' around my girl again, you young pup. I warned you before and I'll say it just once more. If I ever catch yawl together—"

"You'll what?"

Rose grabbed Tonio's arm just in time to keep him from thrusting that stubborn jaw right into the older man's face. Although Tonio was only seventeen and not full grown, his arm beneath her clutching hands felt hard as an oak limb.

"I'll shoot you, if I have to!" George's hands clenched into meaty fists. "No white man'll ever be convicted for shootin' a mangy Injun or Mex or Mick, and you're all three, boy."

The boy lunged, Rose clinging desperately to his arm. "Tonio, you promised—" She stopped before saying *who* he'd promised, but they both knew. "You say James is looking for me?"

For a moment she thought he'd shake her off and jump the taunting merchant anyway. Instead he pulled back, drawing a quick, hard breath. The angry challenge left his face and he gave her a charmingly crooked smile tinged with mockery.

"Yes, ma'am," he said. "James'll be over to the Jones house long about suppertime, he said to tell you." Tonio tipped his hat, gave the two men a narrow-eyed glance and walked on, his shoulders thrown back and his stride arrogant.

"Damn that little—" George seemed to realize there was a woman present and choked on his words. "I don't see why we let his kind walk the streets of our town. He's a menace to decent women."

"Yeah, decent women!" Fred shook his head and tsk-tsked.

George turned toward his store, then stopped and gave Rose an unfriendly look. "As for you, missy, I'm getting almighty tired of you always bringin' up the subject of my daughter—so tired that I want you to say your piece right here and now and then let the subject drop." He crossed his arms over his massive chest. "I'm waitin'."

"I . . . Why, this isn't—you—" There was no way she could tell him now that his beautiful blond sixteen-year-old Sally fancied herself in love with Tonio Ryan. Lord, Rose couldn't even tell him Sally had discovered boys!

George gave her a withering glance. "You had your chance. Now I want you to quit botherin' me about it."

"Yeah, quit botherin' us about it." Fred followed his leader inside the store.

"Bourbon."

It took no small effort to get the word out, but when the bartender set the shot glass down, Boone knew it had been worth it. Even the fumes gave him strength—strength he desperately needed.

He picked up the glass and tossed down the contents, welcoming that gut-warming glow to be found even in bad whiskey. Not that he was much of a drinker under normal circumstances; he wasn't. But he'd come too many miles, lost too much blood, not to seek quick comfort.

The bartender, a hard-looking man of perhaps forty who sported an impressive mustache, waited patiently, his eyes keen with curiosity. Boone, a stranger wherever he rode, was used to it. He set the glass down carefully. "I'll have another," he said.

While the barkeep poured, Boone looked around the interior of the Yellow Rose, empty at midmorning except for himself, the bartender and a man snoring on a faro table in the back of the room. He'd seen a lot of thirst parlors like this one, from the heavy mahogany bar to the brass rail where a man could hook his boot heels and be comfortable.

Could be comfortable, that is, if he didn't have a bullet hole in one leg, another in his shoulder and a knife wound in the ribs. The bartender corked the bottle and shoved the glass toward Boone, who curved his fingers around it and stared into the murky depths.

Feeling the barkeep's scrutiny, Boone looked up suddenly. "Got a marshal in these parts?" he asked.

The barkeep's eyes narrowed. "Yeah, we got one." He hesitated. "You askin' for peaceful purposes, stranger?"

"I'm a peaceful man." Or tried to be. Boone drank down the second shot of liquor and licked his lips. The last thing he wanted was trouble; he'd be as peaceful as they'd let him. Whether he liked it or not, this quiet little cow town was the end of the line.

Even if he could go on, which he doubted, old Buck was a hard-pressed horse. All heart, the big buckskin wouldn't quit till he dropped, a fate he didn't deserve.

Hell, don't blame it on the horse, he thought with disgust. *He'll last longer than I will. I need a place to hole up until I can mend, and Jones, Texas, is it.*

He straightened. Another wave of dizziness struck him and he gripped the edge of the bar until his head cleared. Then he asked, "Where do I find this lawman of yours?"

"Outside, bear left. There's a sign. Cain't miss it."

Boone nodded and turned away. It took considerable determination to keep putting one booted foot in front of the other when all he wanted to do was close his eyes and surrender to the dark.

Still he managed to keep going and somehow found himself opening the door to the marshal's office, then limping inside.

"You the marshal?" he asked the young man sitting at the scarred and wobbly table fronting the lone jail cell with its single inebriated occupant.

At Boone's question, the man looked up, a smile starting before he even had time to identify the speaker. When he did, the smile slipped, but not by much.

"That's right." He rose and extended his hand, a well-mannered man with an open, intelligent face. Hell of a choice for a lawman. "I'm Jack Guthrie, marshal of Jones. And you're . . . ?"

The marshal was a dude or close to it, Boone decided, looking the other man over. He guessed the lawman to be a shade younger than his own thirty years. With the briefest of hesitations, Boone accepted the proffered hand and found it relatively smooth and uncallused.

But the shake was firm and straightforward.

Jack frowned. "I'm Marshal Guthrie," he repeated, as if he thought maybe Boone hadn't heard him the first time. "And you are—"

"—not looking for trouble," Boone inserted, sure now that his first guess had been correct. This was no local boy. Only an easterner would press a man for his name that way. "I thought it would behoove me to make that known to the law."

The younger man's mouth turned down at the corners. "I guess you heard, then," he said unhappily.

Hell. In the act of turning to leave, Boone halted. "Heard what?"

"About the lynching."

Son of a— "What lynching?"

Jack's face lightened. "Oh, you hadn't heard. Forget I mentioned it." He sat down, his expression one of relief, and began to shuffle through the stack of paper before him.

Boone stood there, trying not to sway too noticeably. If he didn't get out of here and find a place to go to ground soon, he was going to fall flat on his face right here on Johnny Law's floor. But he had to know, so he said through tight lips, "Look, friend, a lynchin's not one of those things you can just mention and then forget."

Jesus, he didn't have time to wheedle the information out
f the man; if he wasn't so damned weak he'd just grab the
arshal and—

Jack looked apologetic. "Sorry. It happened while we
ere between marshals. The Vigilance Committee got a lit-
e excited."

"A *little* excited?"

"That's pretty much the way I took it—had a fit, is what
did. Which is how I ended up with this badge." Jack
anced down at the star on his chest as if puzzled to find it
ill there. "They said—"

He looked at the tall man wavering before him, stopped
ort and cocked his head. "You all right, mister?"

Damn fool question. "I could use a sawbones, if you got
ne." Boone gritted his teeth. What little strength he had
emed to be oozing away with the blood he felt trickling
own his side beneath his shirt and vest.

Jack looked offended. "Sure, we got a doctor."

"Want to tell me where I can . . . find him?"

"Afraid you can't. He's out of town for a wedding."

The disheveled drunk in the cell sat up. "Any chance o'
u two lettin' a man get some sleep?" he demanded plain-
vely.

"Sorry, Junius." Jack lowered his voice and added for
oone, "Like I said, Doc's out of town, but there's a young
dy who often helps him out. She's the local schoolteacher
d—"

I don't care if she's Saint Joan, Boone wanted to shout,
t her in here! But his mouth was so dry he didn't seem able
form the words. A curious sound intruded on his waver-
g consciousness—footsteps, perhaps. Moving as if fight-
g his way through thick molasses, he turned toward the
or just as *she* appeared.

It was the woman he'd seen when he rode into town, th
dark-haired beauty who'd been standing before the gener
store with the two solid, upright citizens. As his presenc
registered, he saw the shock and surprise on her lovely fac
turn to distaste.

A good woman, he thought. What was it they said? ''I'ı
not afraid of anything except a good woman or bein' le
afoot.'' Yeah, that was it. Damned good philosophy, too.

He didn't know how he managed but he finally got h
hand to the brim of his hat. ''Ma'am,'' he said, packing
lot of sarcasm into that single word.

On that triumphant note, he pitched forward onto his fac
on the floor of Marshal Jack Guthrie's office.

Chapter Two

Rose stared down at the man lying at her feet, then across his prone body at Jack. "What in the world—"

Jack came around the corner of the table and knelt beside the fallen man. He'd hit hard; when Jack rolled him over, there was blood on his forehead.

And blood on Jack's hand. "He's hurt," Jack said unnecessarily. "Let's get him up on my cot."

Rose nodded, glancing doubtfully toward the narrow rope-sprung bed against the far wall. The marshal spent the night there when he had guests in the cell. Jack grasped the unconscious man beneath the arms and Rose lifted his booted feet, careful not to scratch herself on his heavy, black-iron spurs.

Working together, they managed to half drag, half carry the man's dead weight across the room. Gasping with effort, they let his body sag to the floor by the cot while they caught their breaths.

"He's bigger than he looks," Jack observed, a dubious expression on his face for the man lying so still.

Rose looked at him, too, but she didn't think she was seeing the same things the marshal saw.

She'd met handsomer men, she realized. Jack Guthrie was handsomer, with his regular features and straight nose. But

there was something about this man's dark, wicked looks
that tightened her scalp and sent little shivers through her.

For sheer, animal attraction . . . Good heavens, what was
she thinking? He was disgusting! His face was too lean and
hard, his strong jaw stubbled with untidy whiskers, as if he
usually went clean-shaven. Dark brown hair, curling slightly,
fell over his wide forehead, bloody now where he'd smashed
into the floor when he fell. Lush dark lashes fanned out over
high cheekbones.

Dark-skinned and asymmetrical, his was quite the most
intriguing face she'd ever seen. It gave her goose bumps just
to look at him. So why did she?

"Miss Rose? I asked, can you help me lift him up there?"

Blushing furiously, she nodded and bent to her task.
Quickly, she removed his spurs. His boots were dusty but
not old or abused, she noticed, high-heeled, thin-soled and
custom-made of good leather. She settled them carefully on
the colorful Indian blanket folded at the end of the cot and
straightened.

His leather vest hung open, revealing the dark blue flan-
nel shirt beneath. A black handkerchief was draped around
his neck, the knot in back. His pants were also dark, some
dusty color between blue and black, and his leather chaps—

His leather chaps were dark with blood. Rose swallowed
hard and looked up to meet Jack's unhappy frown.

"Doc's not here," he announced. "What should be done
for him?"

His plaintive question snapped her to her senses. "You get
him out of that vest and shirt and get his chaps off. We'll
have to cut his pants leg. I'll get water." With action to be
taken, she was in her element again. "He's bleeding. We've
got to find out where and stop it before we worry about
anything else."

Hurrying, she carried the water bucket with its tin dipper
to the cot. Jack had removed the chaps and unbuttoned the

man's shirt; he proceeded to drag it down, along with the vest.

"Jesus!" Jack breathed, looking at the torso thus revealed—a bruised and bloody mass only partially concealed by a dirty bandage sagging around the waistband of his pants. "Sorry, Miss Rose." He gave her a quick, apologetic glance.

Rose excused his lapse briskly. "I quite understand." Without thinking, she lifted the hem of her skirt a few inches, grasped her petticoat and tore off the lower dust ruffle. Jack made a strangled sound and she glanced at him, startled by his red face and embarrassed expression. Merciful heavens, couldn't he see she didn't have time to humor overdeveloped sensibilities?

Dipping the rag she'd made into the water bucket, she knelt beside her patient and began sponging away the blood. George and Fred had undoubtedly been right when they sized up this man as a renegade of one sort or another, she decided as she worked. These were knife wounds, and there—right there on the fleshy top of his left shoulder—a bullet had ripped all the way through.

And she still hadn't checked the bleeding in his leg. She glanced at Jack. "Give me your knife so—"

The look on his face stopped her. Jack was gazing at her with such a worshipful expression that she continued more brusquely, hoping to snap him out of it. "Now!" She held out her hand. He withdrew his pocketknife and gave it to her.

She fumbled with the blade. "I need more bandages. Anything—old towels, tablecloths, whatever you have handy."

"I've got a clean shirt around here somewhere." With a last, lovesick glance, he went in search of it.

Knife in hand, Rose took a deep breath and proceeded to slit the leg of the stranger's pants from ankle to knee. She

worked quickly, automatically. Carefully she uncovered the
second bullet wound, this one in his calf. She couldn't
imagine any altercation that would leave a man shot twice,
knifed who knew how many times and still able to travel.

Dipping her rag into the bucket of water, she laid it over
the bullet wound and turned to the task of removing the
bloody makeshift bandage around his torso. What a mess,
she thought, peeling away the clumsy wrapping.

The man was seriously injured; he might even die. That
probably made it even more sinful of her to stare at him so,
but she'd never seen a body so well muscled. The curling
mat of hair on his chest startled her. Billy's chest had been
smooth and almost hairless ...

"Rose, you—you're wonderful."

Jack's declaration surprised and embarrassed her. If he
only knew what she'd been thinking! But then, Jack had no
idea what kind of woman she really was. If he did, he
wouldn't be so generous with his approval. "Don't be ridiculous," she said curtly. "I've helped Doc many a time."

"But you *are* wonderful." He licked his lips and seemed
to screw up his courage. "Miss Rose—Rose, you know how
fond I am of you. It's no secret, everybody knows. I wonder if—"

"Not another word." She jumped to her feet. "This is
neither the time nor the place for conversations of a—of a
personal nature." She looked around a bit wildly. "Do you
have any alcohol in here?"

"I don't want to talk about alcohol, I want to talk about
us." He took a step toward her.

She took a step back. "No, Jack." She lifted one hand,
palm up in warning. "Don't say any more. You know that
I was pledged to Billy Curtis and that I'll never love another man as long as I live."

Jack's smooth-shaven face, such a contrast to the stranger's days-old beard, tightened. "Don't say that, Rose. I won't accept it. You're too young and too beautiful—"

"Oh, for heaven's sake, Jack, I'm not that young and I'm *certainly* not beautiful—and this wouldn't be the time to discuss it if I was." She planted her hands on her hips, completely out of patience with him. "We have an injured man here who may be dying. I must disinfect his wounds. Whiskey will do if that's all—"

An agonized wail from the incarcerated Junius Cox made her blink in surprise, for she'd forgotten he was present.

"Don't waste any of the good stuff," Junius pleaded. He leaned against the bars, white-knuckled hands clutching. "He ain't worth it. Cain't you see he's just another gun slick?"

Rose frowned and glanced at Jack. "He could be right, you know. Maybe you should check your wanted posters before we go any further."

"I suppose so, but it won't matter—he's still a human being." Jack looked unhappy. "Don't think I'm giving up on you, Miss Virginia Rose Taggart, because I'm not." He walked to a cabinet, opened it and withdrew a whiskey bottle, half-full. Junius licked his lips and groaned piteously, but Jack ignored the prisoner. Pulling the cork from the bottle, he offered it to Rose.

She accepted. "Assuming he lives, what do you plan to do with him?" She hesitated, poised to dribble the fiery brown liquid over the stranger's battered torso. "With Doc in Wichita, there's no place for him to—" She tipped the bottle and the first drops splashed onto his wounds.

A low, animal sound erupted from his throat, and his eyes flew open—gray eyes, she saw in that instant before his right hand flew up to clamp around her wrist.

* * *

Wichita! Drifting in and out of consciousness, Boone was there again. Wichita, where his troubles had begun—or if not begun, sure as hell multiplied. It had been four years since the twenty-six-year-old Boone first pinned on a badge as an assistant marshal in the first flush of that Kansas cow town's glory days.

That was 1872, and the Atchison, Topeka and Santa Fe Railroad had just pushed a branch line into town, an event that would result in the shipment of a quarter-million head of beef through Wichita within two years. The town was wild and the town was woolly; signs proclaimed, "Anything goes in Wichita!"

And it did. Jeremy Edward Boone Smith, a Virginia native who'd run away from military school in search of adventure in 1861 and joined the Confederate Army at the age of fifteen, was delighted to find himself in the middle of it all.

No wet-behind-the-ears kid, Boone came to Wichita after making his way through the West as a cowboy, a gambler and a bounty hunter. By the time he hit Wichita, he was good and tough, and he knew it.

Boone liked being a lawman. His confident way of handling disorderly cowboys was equaled only by his way with the ladies. Cocky and sure, he quickly established himself as an up-and-comer with a bright future, so bright that he began to court the lovely daughter of the local banker.

Things were looking good—until that chilly January night when Booker Wall, a notorious Texas badman, indulged in his favorite pastime: using women as punching bags.

By the time Boone arrived on the scene, no room remained for compromise or reason. The situation called for gun justice, pure and simple. The showdown, a classic confrontation on Main Street, was quick and clean—and for Booker Wall, deadly.

Later that same night, Wall's unsavory friends ambushed Boone, who shot two of them dead on the spot. A running battle with three others ensued; Boone shot two and the third bolted like a jackrabbit in tall grass.

Boone didn't follow; he'd caught a bullet himself. Once up and around again, he found himself elevated to the status of a legend. Snub-nosed, freckle-faced kids looked at him with hero worship in their eyes and followed him through the streets; ladies swept their skirts aside as if to avoid contamination, even while they looked him over with oblique glances. Older boys swaggered past to size him up.

Boone's actions, everyone agreed, had been entirely appropriate to his position and the occasion. Nevertheless, he no longer found himself welcome in the best homes—including his erstwhile sweetheart's. Other men challenged him; more lead was thrown. One of the unsuccessful pretenders to gun glory turned out to be a hulking fifteen-year-old runaway who drew down on the deputy marshal. Boone, already beleaguered with a growing reputation he did not savor, came close to killing the kid.

That pretty much ended him in Wichita. With reputation tarnished apparently beyond recall, he headed west in late '73. He made it as far as Colorado Territory before deciding he'd run enough. Staking his claim on the South Platte, he stocked a few head of cattle and settled down to life as a rancher.

Without success. After three challenges ended in gunplay, he pulled up stakes in 1875 and headed for Texas. There, in a land with more than its share of badmen, he hoped to escape his reputation.

In San Antone, he found out how wrong he was.

"Who are you? Open your eyes and speak to me."

To his surprise, Boone found himself able to comply with the order. An angel leaned over him—or maybe she was just a woman; it wouldn't be the first time he'd mistaken one for

the other. Whatever she was, she didn't smile, but still she
was beautiful....

"Your name," she repeated. "What should I call you?"

"Jeremy..." Boone gave his first name, then hesitated,
trying to swallow. The dark-haired angel lifted his head and
held a cup of cool water to his lips; he drank greedily. "Jeremy Edward—Edwards," he said with more strength, using his first and second names as a familiar alias and
neglecting to mention the rest of it: Boone Smith. He didn't
know if he was being followed, but at the very least, he
wanted to remain anonymous in the sanctuary of this little
Texas town.

"Mr. Edwards." Carefully she lowered his head onto the
pillow, and he found himself sorry to lose the solace of her
touch.

"Where ...am I?" He tried to turn his head to look
around, but the effort was too much.

"You're in Marshal Guthrie's house," the angel answered. "He took pity on you, although heaven only knows
why."

She sure didn't *sound* like an angel, and he wanted to
laugh at her tone as much as her words. Obviously she didn't
approve of the actions of the softhearted law in Jones,
Texas. "Now that you ...know my name," he managed,
"will you tell me yours?"

She remained silent for a long time. She was no longer
within his limited range of vision, and he began to think
she'd left the room.

At last she spoke. "My name is Virginia Rose Taggart.
My father owns the Rocking T Ranch, and I am the schoolteacher in Jones."

Boone knew nothing of the Rocking T, but from the way
she said it, in a slightly pompous and self-important tone,
he figured he should be impressed. He was—with her, not

with any credentials she might trot out. "Well, good for your father," he said softly.

She turned away. He supposed he had offended her, and after she had been kind enough to save his life. He wanted to apologize, to tell her he was indeed grateful, but the mists of pain and exhaustion were settling around him once again.

Besides, she would be there when he awoke.

He was sure of it . . . because he wanted it so much.

"I repeat, I don't *know* anything more about him. If I did, I'd certainly tell you!"

Rose stared morosely at her plate of beef and beans, wishing her brother would stop pressing her for answers she didn't have. She shouldn't be surprised, of course. When James invited her to join him and his wife, Diana, for supper at the Blue Bonnet Café, she should have known.

"Don't get all walleyed about it," James ordered. "He's probably going to die anyway, from what I hear. Then it won't matter."

"He's not going to die!" Rose surprised herself with the vehemence of her outburst. Mr. Edwards would live—for better or worse, he would live, by damn, or she would know the reason why! She'd put in some of her best nursing on him and she wouldn't be denied.

Diana's beautiful blue eyes were pleading as she put one hand lightly on her husband's arm. "James, don't tease your sister. She is merely doing her duty as a Christian woman. It's not her fault that the entire town is abuzz about her patient."

"I suppose you're right." James shoveled a spoonful of beans into his mouth. "But we'd probably all be better off if the mysterious Mr. Edwards—if that's who he really is— cashed in his chips."

"James!" Diana and Rose exclaimed in unison.

"I mean it." James, his sister's senior by four years, took
his role as big brother seriously. Somewhat overbearing at
times for a man of twenty-six, he also took *himself* seriously. "George Curtis thinks he's a notorious gunman."

"George Curtis is a—"

"Be careful, Rose." James's thick mustache twitched as
he fought a smile. "The man was almost your father-in-
law."

Rose glared at him. "Nevertheless—"

"That's not all. Tonio says—"

"Tonio! He's only a boy."

"Tonio is a most observant young man—it's probably the
Indian in him," James said calmly. "Tonio says your Mr.
Edwards—"

"He's not *my* Mr. Edwards," she objected, aghast that he
could suggest such a thing.

"Will you quit interrupting and let me say my piece?
Lord, Rosie, I can almost understand why George and Fred
are so annoyed with you."

Rose clamped her lips together, determined not to say
another word if he begged her.

As if satisfied he could now proceed uninterrupted, James
resumed, "Tonio says Mr. Edwards rode in here on a hard-
used horse lookin' very much like a man on the dodge, ea-
gle-eyed and wearin' nothin' that would reflect the sun or
draw attention to himself."

Diana looked from her husband to her sister-in-law, who
still sat with clenched jaws. So Diana dutifully said what
Rose would have. "That hardly constitutes proof."

James gave his wife a faintly condescending look. "He
packed a double-action Smith and Wesson revolver."

"Jamie, for goodness' sake, Rose is not the least bit
interested in any of this."

"And he carried a high-powered custom-made rifle." He
patted his wife's hand but spoke to his sister. "Rose, the

man is a professional. Chances are excellent that he's just two jumps ahead of some lawman.''

Rose could remain silent no longer. "If that was true," she declared, "the marshal would know. He's gone through every wanted poster in his office."

James reached for his cup of coffee. "There's paper out on him somewhere, you can lay book on it. Maybe it's just not reached this far south—the man is obviously from up north. He straddles a Denver saddle—"

"So Tonio says."

"That's right," James conceded blandly, "but I saw it myself. Also, that buckskin he was ridin' carries a brand no one in these parts has ever seen before."

Exasperated beyond forbearance, Rose threw her napkin beside her plate. "James, I don't care to continue this conversation," she said. "I won't be called to account for the actions of a man I don't even know."

"Or want to know," Diana added. She lifted her small chin and gave her husband a disapproving frown. "For shame, James! You have no call to interrogate Rose about a man who is nothing more to her than a patient."

Oh, if that were true! Rose thought, even as she gave a corroborating nod. The truth was, Mr. Jeremy Edwards sorely tried Rose in many and unexpected ways.

"So how's our patient today?" Jack gestured toward the hallway leading to his spare bedroom, where Mr. Edwards had been installed.

"Fine," Rose said, "as far as I can tell."

"That's good," Jack approved, his cheerfulness undiminished, "because I have to ride over to Crystal Springs tomorrow and I don't want to be worrying about him."

"Well, you'd better," Rose said shortly.

He frowned. "But you just said—"

"Marshal Guthrie, everyone in town thinks that Mr. Edwards is some sort of—some sort of desperado. Do you really consider it wise to give him free run of your house?"

"Free run! But Miss Rose, the man is an invalid, flat on his back."

"Oh, you're such an innocent." Saying that, Rose felt very sophisticated and superior. "Being from the east has made you ... different. You're a fine person, but sometimes—"

"You think our guest is making a fool of me, is that it?"

"Well—" she hedged "—not exactly a fool."

"But close." He thought about it for a moment. "You're wrong, Rose. People are basically good—I believe that with all my heart. Mr. Edwards is no exception. We are right to nurse him back to health. We are right to give him the benefit of the doubt. I'm going to Crystal Springs with a clear conscience."

"Fine, Marshal. You do that." But she sighed, because she knew he was wrong.

So wrong. Any man who made her feel as uncomfortable as Mr. Edwards did couldn't possibly be any good.

"Are you sure you're not strong enough to feed yourself, Mr. Edwards?" Rose held a steaming bowl of chicken soup in her hands while she eyed her patient with suspicion.

"Quite sure," Boone responded, "although I do expect to live, thanks to your excellent nursing, Miss Rose."

"Yes, well..." She sat down on the chair next to his bed, careful not to let her gaze drift to the long length of him beneath the light summer covering. She'd seen quite enough of those mysteries, thank you very much!

She offered him a sip of the soup, fascinated by the way his lips curved to accept the spoon. She swallowed hard and looked away.

"I'm improving every day," he offered, as if he owed her that much.

"I know that, Mr. Edwards."

Rose lifted another spoonful to his lips; the upper was thin, the lower full, and together they created a sensuous whole that greatly disturbed her. She replaced the spoon in the bowl and let out an expressive sigh. "Mr. Edwards, since it now appears that you won't die—"

He gave a hearty laugh. "I never had the slightest intention of dying, Miss Rose."

"Then you are doubtless gratified by the outcome," she said, a snap in her tone. "What I would like to know is, how soon will you be leaving Jones?"

He turned his head on the pillow and looked at her, his gray eyes alight with speculation. The intensity of his scrutiny made her want to shift nervously in her chair, but she held herself perfectly still, the bowl of soup cradled on her lap.

"I kinda like it around here," he said finally. "I may hang around for a while."

"That," she informed him flatly, "would not be a good idea."

She scooped up another spoonful of soup but he shook his head, so she set the bowl aside.

"Why wouldn't it be a good idea, Miss Rose?"

She felt a little shiver run through her at the sound of her name on his lips. He didn't exactly frighten her when he spoke in that low, intimate voice, but he did make her extremely nervous.

Well, she'd opened up the subject on the minds of everybody in town; she might as well press onward. "I think perhaps you've ... misjudged our city, Mr. Edwards."

"How have I done that, Miss Rose?"

She lifted her chin and met his mocking gaze. "Don't be deceived because Jones seems sleepy and dull on the surface," she warned. "What you may not realize is that many of the men are away, driving cattle to Kansas—"

"I know all about the Kansas cattle trade," he assured her. "Are you suggesting that Jones is normally a hotbed of excitement and intrigue?"

"Of course not." She tried to think of a polite way to say what she wanted to say but couldn't come up with one, so she simply blurted, "I'm trying to tell you that we know how to deal with troublemakers, Mr. Edwards."

Amusement crinkled the corners of his eyes. "Is that your gentle way of informing me that you and the entire town have decided I am one—a troublemaker, I mean?"

Now she did shift uneasily in her chair. "Well, the thought has crossed our minds," she admitted. "Uh ... would you like any more soup before I—"

"I would like answers, not soup. Exactly how *does* the town deal with troublemakers? This is simply idle curiosity on my part, mind you." Again there was the hint of a smile in his eyes and around the corners of his mouth. "The fact that I rode into town with a couple of bullets and a few knife slashes in my hide doesn't mean a thing, you understand. So tell me, how does Jones handle troublemakers?"

He was teasing her, she realized; well, let him! She'd tell him what kind of town this was in short order. "We hang them," she said, favoring him with her most beatific smile. "Whenever troublemakers come to town, we hang them, Mr. Edwards."

Chapter Three

Hanging—something tugged at the edges of Boone's memory, eluding all his efforts to drag it forth. Hanging was no joking matter, not in any man's book. Up till then, he'd been enjoying himself mightily watching Miss Rose Taggart attempt to elicit information from him. Now all of a sudden, he wasn't.

Rose sprang from her chair but he caught her wrist with his hand, wincing a little at the sudden movement. The parts of him not cut or shot were still sore as the devil.

"Care to elaborate on that?" he asked, no longer smiling.

"Certainly—just as soon as you take your hands off me."

He could see he had frightened her, at least a little, but instead of cowering or crying, she stood straighter and looked him right in the eye. She had beautiful eyes, dark and sparkling with intelligence.

The rest of her wasn't bad, either. If she were another kind of woman... Abruptly he released his hold on her arm.

She let out a relieved sigh and rubbed at the red marks on her wrist. Sitting down in the chair, she thrust out her full lower lip and glared at him.

"You mentioned a hanging," he reminded her.

Her expression didn't soften. "That's right. He was a horse thief—a lot of that goes on around here, with marshals so hard to come by and all. Folks naturally get upset. Otherwise the men would never have formed the Vigilance Committee.''

Vigilantes—damn it to hell. Amateurs were a hundred times worse than professionals. ''Where was Marshal Guthrie while the good citizens of Jones were out hangin' horse thieves?''

''He wasn't Marshal Guthrie then, he was Jack Guthrie, esquire—he'd only been in town a few months. He'd put up his shingle and was trying to practice law, which isn't easy when so many people simply shoot their legal problems.''

Boone recognized a good point when he heard one. ''Then how did he end up with a badge pinned to his chest?''

''I'll tell you how, if you'll answer a question or two for me first.'' She met his surprised glance boldly.

So she wanted to bargain, did she? The girl had sand. Boone hid his admiration while he considered. ''I expect I owe you that and more,'' he said finally. ''You can ask, but I don't guarantee an answer.''

She nodded. ''That's fair.'' She took a deep breath and spoke in a rush. ''Are you a famous outlaw? Nobody believes your name is really Jeremy Edwards. Are you really John Wesley Hardin?''

He stared at her in astonishment. ''*That's* what everybody thinks?''

''Yes. Mr. Curtis, who owns the C and J hopes you're either Hardin or Clay Allison. Are you?''

''*Hopes?*'' Boone shook his head in befuddlement. Maybe he was sicker than he thought.

''Please answer my question.'' She gripped her hands in her lap, twisting her fingers together. She seemed far more upset than the situation warranted.

''No.''

''No, you won't tell me?''

"No, I'm not Hardin and I'm not Allison. In case word hasn't yet reached this hamlet, those are two of the roughest hombres around. Why would anyone with the brains of a grasshopper hope they'd show up here?"

She shrugged, but he didn't believe her innocent expression for an instant.

"Oh, no reason," she said. "It was just a silly idea." She stood up and looked at Boone with that prissy schoolmarm expression. "So the marshal won't find any reward posters on you?"

"I'll be very surprised if he does," Boone said. He'd be surprised but not astonished. Strange things happened every day. No telling how the authorities in San Antone would view the recent shenanigans there. "Any more questions?"

"Are you married?"

He could tell the question had just popped out, to her instant and obvious mortification. A wave of color washed over her cheeks, and her big brown eyes went wide and panicky. It was all he could do to keep from reaching out and—damn it, no! He wasn't going to let himself start thinking about her that way. She was a good woman, and he'd learned the hard way to avoid that kind at all costs.

"No, I'm not married," he said roughly, "although why you'd ask—"

She rushed to explain. "B-because if you had a wife—well, I'd want to write to her and tell her you're all right. I mean, you're not all right, exactly, but you will be."

She was lying through her pearly white teeth. She'd asked the question because she was interested, keenly interested in him. He'd seen enough interested women over the years to know.

Damn! If he thought he was in trouble before... "I kept my end of the bargain," he said roughly. "Now it's your turn. Tell me about the lynching."

She flashed him a look he took for gratitude, probably because he'd let her save face.

"Yes—well, the marshal we had before Jack wasn't all that good anyway, but he was better than nothing, I suppose. Then he quit and went to work in Crystal Springs and the horse thieves became very bold. After a while the whole town was in an uproar. That's when the men got together and decided to form the Vigilance Committee."

"And Jack Guthrie was among them?" He didn't seem the type to Boone, but you never could tell about people.

"Oh, heavens, no!" She looked appalled at the very idea. "Marshal Guthrie is a man of law, a peaceful man. He would never violate the law—never. He advised them against it—he warned them against it. But they wouldn't listen, and then they caught one of the thieves red-handed."

She shivered despite July's oppressive heat. He was sure—fairly sure, anyway—that she wouldn't have seen any of what she was reporting, only heard the tales. Well, Boone *had* seen a hanging, and it wasn't anything he ever cared to participate in. A bullet in the brain was more humane.

He shifted uncomfortably on the lumpy mattress. "So they caught a horse thief and hung him to the nearest cottonwood," he supplied. "How'd the town feel about that?"

"I...I think what they'd done scared them, especially when Jack heard about it. Let me tell you, he didn't mince words." Her dark eyes glowed. "He was wonderful—talked about the majesty of the law and the rights of the accused to a fair trial and all kinds of things."

Boone didn't like the admiration he saw on her face. Guthrie wasn't *that* good. "You still haven't told me how he got to be marshal," he reminded her brusquely.

"Why, they were so impressed they told him they'd disband the Vigilance Committee if he'd pin on the badge. He didn't want to at first, but Mr. Curtis—"

"The same Mr. Curtis who thinks I'm Clay Allison?" Boone's lip curled with contempt for the man's intelligence. "He was part of that lynch mob?"

"Yes, most every man in town was, except Jack." She looked distinctly uncomfortable. "But of course, none of them thought of it as a lynch mob. Anyway, Mr. Curtis pointed out that marshaling was about as close as Jack was likely to get to the law if he stayed in Jones. At least if he took on the job, he could see that everything was done properly from there on out."

"Give 'em a fair trial and then hang the guilty bastards," Boone muttered. He glanced at her and added, "Sorry."

"I am familiar with the word," she said with dignity, but nonetheless she looked a little shocked at his language. "So that is how Jack Guthrie became marshal of Jones. He must have been right—about respect for the law, I mean—because there's been no trouble of that kind since. And he doesn't even have to wear a gun to do it."

She picked up the cold soup and walked out of the room. Boone watched her go, enjoying the swing of her rounded backside beneath the blue flower-sprigged dress.

Yeah, he could well believe there'd been no trouble since, but he wouldn't attribute it to an unarmed lawman interested in guarding the rights of the accused.

Amazing how a public hanging served as a deterrent to crime.

Rose consulted her shopping list to be sure she hadn't forgotten anything. Everything she'd need to prepare supper at her little house tonight for James and Diana was here.

"I'd appreciate it if you'd have the boy deliver these things," she told George Curtis.

"Sure 'nough, Rose." George glanced around, then shoved aside a jar of peppermint sticks so he could lean across the counter on his elbows. "How's the gun slick doin'?" he asked in a conspiratorial tone.

"Very well, thank you." She turned to leave.

"But I heard—now slow down, Rose, I want to talk to you about—"

Stifling a smile, Rose gave him a wave of one hand. "Sorry, Mr. Curtis, but I'm much too busy today," she called. Now there was a change; a few days ago she'd been begging *him* to talk.

Which was something she'd still have to do, and soon. Pausing at the door, Rose saw Sally hovering in one corner of the store, randomly arranging bolts of calico on a shelf. Sally darted the older woman an anguished glance before turning back to her task.

Subdued by the realization that trouble was still building in that quarter, Rose stepped outside. Instantly Marshal Guthrie appeared, dragging his hat from his head and smiling broadly.

"Howdy, Miss Rose," he said politely. "I've been waiting for you."

Her smile felt tight and insincere. Why, oh why, wouldn't Jack take no for an answer? It was the only answer she'd ever be able to give him. Even if she'd never met the mysterious stranger— *Oh, don't think of him in those terms. Don't think of him as a man who might stand between you and other men,* she scolded herself. *You know very well that you made your own bed and now you must lie in it—alone. Alone forever.*

Jack didn't seem to notice anything wrong. "I was hoping," he began, turning his hat brim between his smooth lawyer's hands and shuffling his feet nervously, "that is, if you don't have other plans, I'd be most pleased and honored to escort you to the Blue Bonnet for dinner."

"Now?" Confused, she frowned at him.

"No, ma'am, tonight."

He appeared equally confused, and then she remembered that Jack called the evening meal *dinner* while everybody else in town referred to it as *supper.* Which gave her a perfect excuse to turn him down.

"I'm sorry, Marshal Guthrie, but I've invited my brother and his wife to dine with me this evening. I'm on my way to your house to check on our patient and then I must hurry home and begin preparations."

"Oh." His head drooped; then he brightened. "Perhaps some other time?"

"Perhaps." She nodded and turned away.

"Tomorrow?"

"We will discuss the subject at some later date." A social promise, nothing more, and surely the man must realize it, she thought. Walking away quickly to avoid encouraging further familiarity, she wondered again why Jack, by far the most eligible young man in town, insisted upon such a single-minded pursuit of her.

She sighed. If things were only different... If Billy Curtis hadn't had a silver tongue... If Mr. Edwards had never ridden into town...

Quietly Rose let herself into the marshal's house through the unlocked back door. Crossing the kitchen, she turned down the short hallway, moving with care not to disturb the patient should he be sleeping.

The door to his bedroom stood slightly ajar before her. Hesitating, she geared herself up for another unpleasant encounter. Her breath came a little faster, and she balled her hands into fists to warm her icy fingers.

No wonder he affected her so, she rationalized, soothing her jangled nerves. She felt only the natural revulsion any well-bred woman would feel for a man of his sort. The sooner he was recovered and gone from here, the better.

Filled with fresh resolve, she pushed the door wide—and found herself staring down the barrel of a pistol. The fierce expression on Jeremy Edwards's face frightened her more than his artillery. She had never seen a face so cold and hard as the menacing one before her.

She gasped and fell back a step, one hand flying to press against her breast. She fully expected him to shoot her; instead he uttered a fearsome oath and flipped the pistol over his wrist and into the holster anchored around his lean middle.

At that point, several things registered with Rose at once. He was out of bed and on his feet; he wore denim pants and a gun belt and nothing more; and the dark and dangerous intruder she'd surprised was changing into a man whose apologetic smile and raw masculinity staggered her.

He sucked in a deep breath, his bare chest rising and falling before her mesmerized eyes. "I beg your pardon, Miss Rose. You surprised me," he said, his voice calm and unruffled.

"Then we are more than even, sir!" She straightened, lowering her fluttering hand to her side. Anger surged through her, making her speak rashly. "I abhor violence, Mr. Edwards."

"As all decent people do," he agreed with an edge to his voice. He picked up a shirt lying on the foot of the bed and pulled it over his bruised and scarred torso.

Immediately she felt less threatened, but no less angry. "You, sir, are a violent man."

He paused in the act of buttoning his shirt, cocking his head to one side to gaze at her long and hard. At last he said, "And if I am, Miss Rose, who do you suppose made me that way? Since you yourself are obviously without sin, feel free to cast a stone—although it won't be the first one."

Without sin? How dared she judge him? Wide-eyed and ashamed, she pressed the fingers of one hand against her slightly parted lips. He frowned and took a step toward her.

"What is it, Rose? Surely you're not still frightened of me. Even hard, violent men respect the sanctity of a good woman."

She recognized sarcasm when she heard it, and her blood ran cold. Was he making fun of her? While she tended his wounds, had he somehow come close enough to divine her horrible secret? "Oh, God," she whispered. "God help me!"

Taking two steps backward, she flung herself around and ran down the hall and out the door through which she'd entered, leaving Boone standing there staring after her.

What the hell had he said to make her golden-brown eyes fly wide with such consternation? Bad enough he'd drawn down on her, but somehow, in trying to apologize, he'd made matters worse.

Limping over to the window, he pulled aside the lace curtain, hoping to see her again. In that he failed, but he did see that half-breed kid slip just a second too slowly into the stand of trees separating the marshal's house from his nearest neighbor's.

Ryan, the marshal said his name was; Irish, Mex and Indian. *And I thought I had troubles,* Boone told himself—just before he remembered where the kid worked.

At the Taggarts' Rocking T.

Rose Taggart lived across from the one-room schoolhouse, in a white frame cottage on the southern edge of town. Her small doll's house, with its neat white-picket-fenced yard and flower beds beneath all the windows, suited her needs perfectly.

Still, it was not a house where a man felt comfortable, even a brother. At five feet ten inches tall, James was not exactly a giant, yet he always seemed like a bull in a china shop when he entered his sister's domain. As a result, he tried to tend to his business and get out as quickly as possible, regardless of how his wife might feel on the subject.

Therefore Rose was not surprised when James set about shoveling down the supper of fried chicken and potatoes boiled in their jackets. She herself wasn't hungry and merely moved the food around on her plate.

Serious thinking often took away her appetite.

Diana, wielding knife and fork with delicate grace, gave her sister-in-law a chiding glance. "Rose, dear, you're not eating this wonderful meal you worked so hard to prepare. Is anything wrong?"

James glanced up curiously, chewing stolidly while awaiting Rose's answer, an answer she was loath to give.

"Everything's fine," she prevaricated. "It's just that..." She looked up from her plate suddenly. "I'm thinking about taking a trip."

"A trip!" Diana laid her knife carefully across the edge of her china dinner plate. "This is the first you've mentioned such a possibility."

James frowned. "No time for that," he said autocratically. "School will be starting before long and you have students—"

"I don't think I'll be teaching in the fall," Rose interrupted. "I...I may not be back. From my trip, I mean."

James stared at his sister as if she'd lost her mind. "J.D. know about this?"

J.D. was Jesse Daniel Taggart, James's and Rose's father, known far and wide and even to his children, for the most part, by his initials. Miserably Rose shook her head.

"Oh, Rose!"

Diana's soft wail expressed welcome concern, but Rose was more worried about her brother's reaction; she spoke directly to him. "James, I can't stand it here any longer. I've been thinking about leaving for a long time and I've decided. I want to go away—permanently, if I can manage it. Perhaps I could start with a visit to Great-Aunt Marie in New Orleans and then—''

"Absolutely not." He shook his dark head decisively. "J.D.'ll never stand for it. When he gets back from the drive to Kansas—" James said the word *Kansas* with contempt. If he hadn't broken his arm just before the trail drive started, he'd be on his way there now instead of his father.

"By the time he gets back, I can be gone," Rose cried. "Don't you see, there's nothing for me here any more, except the humiliation I bring on the family by remaining unmarried."

Diana and James exchanged startled looks. Then Diana leaned across the small table to pat her sister-in-law's hand. "Rose, dear, just before your father left he—" She darted her husband a helpless glance. "You tell her, James."

He had no apparent trouble doing so. "He said when he gets back he *will* see you married if he has to pick the bridegroom himself. There'll be no spinsters in the Taggart family—that's what J.D. said, and he by damn meant it!" He glanced at his wife. "Sorry, hon."

Rose hadn't thought her heart or her spirits could droop any lower, but both did at his words. She'd been well aware of her father's increasing displeasure with her unmarried state but she hadn't dreamed he'd go to such lengths. Now she realized she should have. He'd been shoving her at Jack Guthrie ever since the man arrived in town.

James pushed back his chair. "Good chuck, Rosie. Hate to eat and run but Di and I have to get back to the ranch."

Diana stood more slowly. "Sometimes," she said severely to her husband, "you can be an insensitive lout."

James shrugged and gave her a cocky grin. "Fortunately that's not all I can be." He turned toward the door; the table and chairs were located in the middle of Rose's kitchen.

"I'll wait for you in the buckboard, honey. Don't be too long."

He sauntered out.

Diana watched him go, pursing her lips. Then she turned to her sister-in-law. "Rose, whatever is troubling you? No—don't say nothing is. I can tell. You haven't been yourself for days. You know I want to help you if I can."

Rose forced a bright smile. "I know you do, Diana. And I thank you—you are more dear to me than any sister could ever be. Let me think about all that's been said here and then we'll talk."

Diana frowned. "You're sure? You're sure there's nothing you want to say to me now? Because you know you can trust me—I won't even tell James if you ask me not to."

Rose draped her arm over her smaller sister-in-law's shoulders and together they moved toward the door. "I know that, and I love you for your loyalty." With a final squeeze, she released Diana. "Don't worry about me. As you can plainly see, I'm fine."

"I suppose." With a doubtful smile, Diana turned and ran lightly down the wooden steps to where her husband waited under a stand of cottonwoods, already in the seat of the buckboard with the reins in his hand.

And talking to Tonio Ryan. The boy turned with a smile at Diana's approach and gave her a hand up to the wooden seat beside her husband. He stood watching until they had driven away, then trotted over to where Rose waited. He looked up at her with eyes half-closed, a questioning smile on his wide and sensuous mouth.

What a handsome boy, Rose thought with admiration, gesturing Tonio to enter the house before her. No wonder Sally spent so much time pining for him.

Once in the kitchen, he picked up a drumstick remaining on the platter in the middle of the table and spun around

He reminded her of a young wild animal; she could hear her father saying, *The wilder the colt, the better the horse.*

Tonio had a chance to become a very fine horse indeed, if the gentling process didn't break him entirely. And then she suddenly wasn't thinking of Tonio at all but of Mr. Edwards. What kind of colt had he been? She thought she knew what kind of horse he had become—an outlaw horse, from the looks of him.

"I wasn't expecting you tonight," she said, stacking plates in the tin tub she kept for washing dishes. She shoved the cast iron teakettle to the back of the banked cookstove, where she knew embers still glowed.

Tonio's mouth glistened with grease from the chicken leg he was eating. "I told James you were giving me another reading lesson."

"But that's not why you're here?"

He shook his head and tossed the chicken bone on the empty platter. His Indian-dark eyes glittered. "He's practically keeping her a prisoner."

"Need I ask who he is?"

"Sally's pa." Tonio wiped his greasy fingers on the side of his faded denim pants and half sat on the edge of the table. "Sometimes I just want to grab that Mr. Curtis by his fat neck and—" He stopped short, his lips curling over even white teeth, which contrasted starkly with his dark skin.

Suddenly his expression turned pleading. "What are we gonna do, Miss Rose? Me and Sally—we love each other!"

Rose felt her heart constrict in response to his misery. She couldn't bring herself to tell him the truth, that she saw no future for the relationship, not only because George Curtis was a bigot but because the would-be lovers were much too young.

But with him looking at her with anguished eyes, she had to find some way to comfort him without telling an outright lie. "Tonio..." she began.

A pounding on the front door made her jump and brought her young visitor to his feet.

Rose held up one hand in warning. "Wait here," she ordered, "and don't make a sound, you hear me? Not a sound. I can't imagine who that is but I'll send them on their way. We really need to talk about this, Tonio."

He nodded, but she couldn't see any real hope in his expression that she'd be able to offer a solution to his problem. Closing the kitchen door carefully behind her, she hurried to the open front door.

George Curtis stood there, Sally by his side. Rose couldn't have been any more surprised if it had been—if it had been Mr. Jeremy Edwards.

"Good evening, Mr. Curtis." She glanced at Sally. "Is anything wrong?" She made no move to invite them inside.

Which didn't bother George Curtis in the slightest; he walked in anyway, Sally straggling along behind him. The girl glanced at Rose and rolled her eyes in resignation.

In the small parlor, George turned to Rose. "I need to speak to you privately," he announced, glancing over his shoulder as if he expected to find someone lurking there. "I only brought Sally along because—well, because it wouldn't be seemly for me, a married man and pillar of the community, to call on a lady, even you, without a chaperon."

"Oh, for goodness sake." Rose clenched her hands in the folds of her skirt, crumpling the yellow muslin. She resisted glancing behind her toward the kitchen. If Tonio realized Sally was out here—

George turned to his daughter. "Sally, run along to Miz Rose's kitchen and find yourself a drink of water or something. Just don't come back till I call you."

"Aw, Pa." Sally shuffled one foot in its high-buttoned black kid slipper. She appealed to Rose. "I didn't want to come but he made me."

Rose wondered if all the color had fled her cheeks or if it merely felt that way. She grabbed the girl's arm. "James and Diana were here for supper and I haven't cleaned the kitchen yet. There's no need for Sally—"

George's face set in jowly but determined lines. "Sally, go clean up Miz Rose's kitchen," he said bluntly.

"Aw, Pa! Do I have to?" Sally, notoriously lazy, looked on the verge of tears.

"I won't allow it! George Curtis, you can't come into my house this way and—"

The bulky grocer hauled himself up to his full and portly height. "Virginia Rose Taggart, don't you take that tone with me," he warned. "You were very nearly my daughter-in-law and I still deserve a little respect."

He turned his displeasure on his daughter. *"Do as I say, girl, and hop to it."*

"But—" both Rose and Sally chorused.

"Females!" George roared. "I won't be sassed! You—" he pointed to Rose "—sit down! And you—" he pointed at Sally "—*skedaddle!*"

With a last, defiant glance at her father, Sally did. Watching the girl slip inside the kitchen, Rose could hardly keep from groaning.

Chapter Four

George Curtis stomped around Rose's small parlor, gesturing broadly while he speculated aloud. "He's a gunfighter, I'm sure of it," the grocer declared. "The question is, who? Is he famous, or just some two-bit road agent?"

"Mr. Curtis!" Rose fought to keep herself from glancing toward the kitchen. There hadn't been so much as a squeak since Sally closed the door behind her. Rose knew she had to keep her mind clear when dealing with her portly guest, who had a habit of catching her off guard anyway. "I really don't understand why you're so determined that Mr. Edwards isn't exactly who he says he is," she protested.

George stopped pacing and faced her, his small eyes narrowing into slits. Despite the heat, he wore the heavy dark suit he'd had on all day, now wrinkled and shapeless. "That's exactly why I'm here. Who does he *say* he is?"

"You know very well—you've questioned me enough about it. He says he's Jeremy Edwards, and we have no reason to believe he's not telling the—"

"Don't be such a ninny, Rose. Has he said what he's doing in Jones, given you any hints as to his real reason for being here? He's no businessman, I can tell you that. And he sure ain't a regular ol' cowboy driftin' through. How'd he explain gettin' hisself filled full of lead? Answer me that, missy."

"Well, he—" Rose stopped short, biting her lower lip. While delirious, Mr. Edwards had said all sorts of things, most of which she couldn't understand; what mutterings she had discerned had made very little sense. Mostly his ramblings had gone in one ear and out the other. "He didn't explain," she said lamely.

"You must at least know where he's from. He must've said something sometime!" George regarded her with scorn.

"I have no idea where he came from," she insisted, feeling defensive before such grim determination. "He did mention San Antonio but he was out of his mind with fever at the time and I didn't get the feeling that was his home, exactly."

George's eyes brightened. "San Antone, huh? That'll give me someplace to start, anyway. Good work, Rose, good work." He patted her shoulder as if for a job well done.

"Don't get the wrong idea, Mr. Curtis." She shifted away from him, as uncomfortable with his approval as she had been with his scorn. "I'm not the least bit interested in spying for you." In fact, she almost felt as if she'd betrayed a trust when all she'd done was throw out a crumb to sidetrack the grocer's inquisition.

He winked at her. "Of course not." He rubbed his big hands together gleefully, as if they'd just come to some important understanding. "I gotta good feelin' about this, Rosie. The minute I saw him I knew he was some kinda famous shootist. The question is, if he engaged in gunplay here in Jones, for example, would it bring fame or shame to our fair city?"

"Shame on you for asking!" Rose tangled her hands tightly in the fabric of her skirts. "We have law and order here now, in case you've forgotten. Marshal Jack—"

"Yes, yes, I've got the utmost respect for Jack Guthrie." He dismissed the marshal with a wave of the hand. "But I'm getting the cart before the horse. What if a famous gunman died here? Would a headstone in the cemetery with his name on it bring Jones the attention and respect we deserve? That's my question, girl—would all them stump suckers over to Crystal Springs be able to match that?'' He glanced at her hopefully. ''Maybe we won't have to turn a tap. He looked to be in bad shape when he rode in—maybe he's already dyin'. Why, we could put up a special marker! We could—''

''Are you out of your mind?'' Rose stared at the man, appalled. ''Mr. Edwards is improving every day. He's not going to die—''

A crash from the kitchen made them both jump with surprise. Rose held her breath, afraid to speculate on what Sally and Tonio might be doing in there. When she made no move to investigate, George gave her a curious glance.

''Sounds like Sally's just as handy to have around here as she is at home,'' he observed with uncharacteristic humor. ''Maybe I should go tell her to have a little more care with your breakables.''

''No!'' Rose stepped between him and the kitchen. ''I mean, what's a little broken crockery compared to conversation about a man's death?''

''Only you said he ain't dyin'.'' George turned morose again. ''I don't know why you're takin' up for him the way you are. Surely you don't still think he's just some innocent cowpoke?''

''Yes—no.'' She shook her head with frustration, trying to concentrate on countering his arguments while thinking about what might be going on in her kitchen. Tonio was a randy young buck and Rose knew it, whether Sally did or not. The girl was a tease, plain and simple, and if she baited the boy too far—

''Which is it, yes or no?'' George followed her glance toward the kitchen.

"All right, I'll admit I don't approve of him." To distract the man, Rose walked past him to stand by the window. As she'd intended, he turned with her, until his back was toward the room where his daughter was doing God only knew what with a boy he despised. "He does appear to be a hard and violent man, but I can't allow you or anyone else to stand in my house and wish ill for another human being—at least not without better reason than spite and ambition!"

"Spite and ambition!" George howled in protest. "This ain't personal, Virginia Rose Taggart! I'm thinkin' about what's good for the town, not what's good for me personal. Jones was here long before Crystal Springs was even thought about. We deserve to be the county seat, and that's the pure and simple truth of it."

Listening to him launch into a recitation of the myriad reasons his position was the correct one, Rose began to relax slightly. When George Curtis got started like this, he could talk for hours without taking the slightest notice of anything going on around him.

Which was exactly her intention, because what was going on around him—or at least, in the next room—was something he'd be better off not knowing.

And that probably goes double for me, she admitted privately, suppressing a slight shiver of apprehension . . . and maybe just a trace of envy.

"If you love me, you will," Tonio breathed against the silken tendrils of golden hair shielding his true love's dainty ear. "Sally, Sally, you're driving me crazy!"

"Oh, Tonio!" She clung to his shoulders weakly, as if too overcome with emotion to stand on her own. "You make me feel so . . . funny."

He groaned. There was nothing funny about the way *he* felt. If he didn't find some relief soon, he thought he might explode. It had been ten days since he'd had a moment alone with Sally, a chance to hold her in his arms and feel her nipples tighten into hard little pebbles pressing against his chest.

He ran one hand down her side and grabbed her bottom, barely able to discern female flesh through the layers of fabric. This was about as far as Sally ever allowed him to go—a few virginal if fevered kisses, a furtive touch here or there. Once she'd let him slide a hand inside her bodice to caress her warm female flesh. He still dreamed about those brief moments.

But a few stolen kisses and caresses were no longer enough, damn it! He was tired of getting all lathered up and having to visit Libby over at the Yellow Rose to find relief, when it was Sally he loved.

Sally *would* meet him tonight—he'd make sure. With one hand he cupped her chin and turned her dreamy face toward him. Her eyes were closed, her luscious mouth curved up in a gentle smile, as if savoring sweet dreams.

He spoke in a low, ragged voice. "Do you love me, Sally?"

"Oh, Tonio . . . you know I—"

He kissed her open mouth before she could finish. Without giving her time to protest, he plunged his tongue between her lips in the kind of kiss he'd never before dared give her. At the same time, he thrust his hips against her and backed her up against the table.

She was helpless, her struggles as ineffectual as the wing beats of a captured bird. He ignored her strangled bleats of panic and plundered her mouth, knowing what he was doing and despising himself for it but unable to control the lust that drove him on.

He loved her, but he was a man at seventeen with a man's needs. Why the beautiful blond daughter of the town's leading citizen had ever looked twice at him he didn't know.

But she had, and looking, touching and yearning were getting mighty old mighty fast.

There was only one way her pa would ever let her marry a mixed breed like Tonio Ryan, and it was a way that appealed mightily to the lusty young cowboy, even knowing full well that he ran the strong risk of being shot or hung before a preacher could be summoned. But as her mouth opened wider beneath his and he heard her whimpers change from fear to need, he thought it would be worth it. Once he'd plunged into her soft body, he could probably die happy.

"Tonight," he grated, his teeth nipping at her full lower lip. "I know a place—"

"You never kissed me like that before, Tonio." She opened passion-glazed eyes and her tongue darted out to touch his mouth. "Do it again—oh, God, Tonio, do it again!"

"Tonight. Come outside after they're asleep—" A bargaining chip, he argued with himself, wanting to lift her up onto the table and throw her skirt over her head and ram into her. Desire choked him.

"I'm afraid."

He caught one of her breasts in his cupped hand and squeezed. "It'll be worth it, I promise. Say you'll come."

"I...I want to but...I..."

He cut off further protests with a kiss, thrusting his tongue deeply and intimately into her hot, hungry mouth. He had her now, he thought exultantly. Tonight she'd lie naked and wanting in his arms, and tomorrow she'd belong to him forever.

She loved him. It seemed like a miracle, but it must be true, for she was a nice girl—the nicest in town. Sally Curtis couldn't be writhing against him the same way that whore Libby did unless she loved him as much as he loved her.

* * *

Jack paused on Rose's back step to glance down at the bunch of wilting wildflowers in his hand, then at his companion. "Sure you're up to this, Jeremy?" he inquired. "This is the first time you've been out in over a week."

Boone grinned, wondering how much was honest concern and how much was a desire to be alone with his girl. In truth, Boone was feeling a shade wobbly, but the only way to get his strength back was to get up and start moving around. He was still a bit stiff and sore but he didn't deceive himself that he'd been lying abed for a solid week because he had no choice.

He'd had a choice, all right. Had there been a need, he could have ridden away days ago. He'd decided not to rush it this time, however.

The fact that he was being nursed by just about the prettiest little piece of calico he'd ever run across had nothing whatsoever to do with it. "I'm not ready to run any foot races but I'm not complaining," he assured the marshal.

Jack nodded seriously. "Well, if you're sure. Guess we might as well see what Miss Rose is up to this fine summer evening."

The marshal rapped sharply on the door, then pushed it wide. "Rose!" he called out cheerfully. "Surprise—you got company."

But it was the company that got the surprise. The two men stopped as one, staring at the embracing couple half reclining on the kitchen table.

At first Boone thought it must be Rose, and he took a quick step forward, fists and temper rising simultaneously. But no—this woman had blond hair. And the man holding her in his arms—*boy,* he corrected—was the Ryan boy who worked for the Taggarts, the half-breed boy who'd been watching Boone.

Youngsters, both of them, but their embrace had already gone well past the preliminary fumblings of young love,

Boone realized with amusement. The boy had her arched back over the table, his knee thrust between her legs while he fumbled at her skirts, and she was clawing at his shirt as if it were on fire.

Jack exploded—a most uncharacteristic reaction, Boone thought. "Sally? Tonio! What in the name of thunder—" He sounded more shocked than alarmed.

His mistake, Boone thought as the young lovers sprang apart at the same moment the inner door flew open and Rose hurtled into the room—backward, propelled by George Curtis, the storekeeper. Obviously she'd been trying to hold the man at bay, and just as obviously had been swept along before him like dust before a broom.

Curtis took in the scene with a sweep of his head, letting out a roar that all but rattled the windows. "What in the name of Hades is goin' on out here?" He started toward Tonio. "You little half-breed bastard, slobbering all over my girl like some damned animal. If you've hurt her, you're a dead man!"

Boone saw fury flash through the boy's slender frame. "I'd never hurt Sally!" he cried. "I love—"

"Papa!" Sally's shriek sliced through all the other voices, and she began to sob hysterically. Throwing herself against her father's chest, she clung to him like a burr, effectively halting his lumbering advance. "Take me home, Papa! Please take me home!"

Rose clutched at George's arm. "Don't do anything you'll regret," she begged. "This is all a misunderstanding. Sally's not hurt—"

He shook her off and grabbed his daughter by the arms, practically lifting her off her feet. "Are you, Sally? Is this the first time that damned Injun's tried to force himself on you or have there been other times, times when I wasn't there to stop him?"

If looks could kill, Tonio would have dropped dead, Boone thought. And vice versa; although at his age the boy was doubtless used to racial slurs, it was obvious they still stung.

Tonio lunged forward, and Boone surprised himself by reaching out almost casually to lay an iron hand on the kid's forearm. After a startled glance, Tonio subsided to glare at his beloved's father.

Sally sobbed harder. "I didn't do anything, Papa, I swear it. I came in here like you told me, and *he* was here and—" She choked off.

George hauled her against his chest, still glowering at the boy. "You don't have to go on, honey. Anyone could see what he was up to. Men have been hung for less." He turned on Jack. "Well, marshal? You gonna let this half-breed terrorize decent girls or you gonna do somethin' about it?"

Jack looked pained. "To tell you the truth, George, it didn't look all that one-sided to me."

"What!" George reared back as if he had been subjected to a deadly insult. "Are you suggestin' my girl would take up with that kind of trash of her own free will?" He looked astounded at the idea.

Jack's glance met Boone's and Boone suppressed a laconic smile. That little girl's free will had been freely engaged when they walked in, and not in fighting for her virtue, either. But looking at her now, it was plain to see that she'd even scream rape if she had to to get out of this mess with her father.

Jack, however, was a man of principle. He squared his shoulders. "George, I'm satisfied nothing really happened here."

"Nothing! How can you call it nothing when he was all over her—"

"Shut up, George!" Jack's voice crackled with sudden authority. "You think he was about to have his way with her right here on the kitchen table with her pa in the next room? Think, man! They're kids—they lost their heads for a moment but no harm's been done.''

"I'm pressin' charges,'' George insisted grimly.

Rose's shoulders sagged. "Oh, don't do that!''

"No,'' Boone agreed softly, indifferently, "because if you do, everybody in town will know and it's your daughter who'll suffer.''

"What's it to you, you damned gunfighter?'' George had found a new target for his ire. "I know this yella pup and you don't.''

Boone shrugged. "That's true. But even if you're right about the kid here and it was all his doing—and I'm not sayin' you're wrong—but even so, who'll this hurt most if it gets out? Not him, I double-damn guarantee you. It won't hurt his reputation a bit to be known as the man who seduced—''

"Don't talk dirty!'' George roared. "There's women present!''

"Sorry.'' Boone held up his hands in a soothing gesture, glancing at Jack in a signal to take up the cause.

"He's right, George.'' Jack stepped forward to pat the older man on the back. "Take your girl on home and forget this ever happened. I'll have a talk with the boy and make sure—''

Tonio started forward again. "What the hell am I, a stick of wood? Yawl are talkin' about me like I'm not even human. The truth is—''

"—not the issue,'' Boone inserted. "We all *know* what happened here, so why don't you shut up and sit down.''

Rose added her exhortations to his. "Yes, please do, Tonio. Don't make things any worse.''

Muttering under his breath, the boy did as they suggested, although his every move clearly indicated it went against the grain.

For a moment George Curtis hesitated. Then he let out his breath in a disgusted snarl. "I'll let it pass this once, but if he ever so much as looks at my daughter again I'll—I'll horsewhip the young scalawag within an inch of his life!"

Tonio bounced to his feet. "Who you threatening, you old windbag?"

Boone shoved the boy back down into his seat none too gently, and Tonio found a new target for his fury. "Well, I ain't afraid of him!" he shouted. "He treats me like dirt, always did, and I'm gettin' fed up—"

"See?" George glanced around triumphantly. "He's no better than an animal." Shoving the still sobbing Sally ahead of him through the door, he paused to fix a gimlet eye on Rose. "And you, missy—I'm mightily disappointed in you. You stay away from my daughter or I'm going straight to your pa the minute he gets back from Kansas. May do that anyway."

He shook his head meaningfully at Jack. "This is what happens when old maids got nothin' wholesome to occupy their minds. Why don't you marry her and keep her barefoot and pregnant for about fifteen years?"

He made his exit accompanied by Rose's sputtering protests.

For a moment the four of them stood in silence. Then Rose sighed mournfully. "I'm sorry," she said, wringing her hands. "This is all my fault."

Three pairs of eyes turned toward her in surprise. "Your fault?" Jack echoed. "How is it your fault?"

She shrugged. "I knew Tonio was here. When Mr. Curtis sent Sally out of the room—" She shuddered. "I didn't know how to stop her without making matters worse. I am so sorry, Tonio. You shouldn't have had to go through that."

"He's nothing but an old hypocrite." The boy started from his chair and once more Boone slammed him back down with a warning glance. Tonio was growing angrier by the minute. "Sally loves me—"

"Tonio!" Rose shot a warning glance at the two men, which of course was pointless since the cat was out of the bag—if indeed it needed the boy's declaration.

"I don't care who knows!" Tonio flared. His strong young face looked pinched and tight with strain. "What's the difference who knows? Her old man will never let her marry me now."

"Kid," Boone said patiently, dropping a heavy hand on Tonio's shoulder, "you didn't have a Chinaman's chance *before,* and after this... Why not cut your losses and move on? There's plenty of fish in the sea."

Rose looked at him with disapproval, wondering what would make a man so cynical. "Will you kindly mind your own business, Mr. Edwards?" She turned to the boy. "I didn't know they were coming or I'd have... I don't know, warned you, sent you away."

"Why *did* George Curtis come?" Jack asked, pulling out a chair to sit at the table. He still clutched his bunch of wildflowers.

Rose was loath to respond with an outsider present. Mr. Edwards stood slightly behind Tonio, looking much too healthy and much too sure of himself. She didn't like answering questions in front of him, especially questions such as the one Jack had just posed.

Boone grinned. "If I were a gambling man, I'd wager that our fine upstanding storekeeper came by to question you about a certain suspicious stranger in your midst," he drawled.

"Well..." She bit her lip and searched for a plausible lie. None occurred to her. "Yes."

"What did you tell him?"

Legend!

She rolled her eyes. "Let's forget about Mr. Curtis and this whole unfortunate incident, shall we? Would anyone like something to drink? A cup of coffee, perhaps? There's plenty left from supper—"

Tonio leaned forward, a sneer on his lean face. "Come on, Miss Rose. Tell us what the big man wanted."

They were all looking at her expectantly. She swallowed hard and tightened her lips for a moment, but they did not seem at all deterred. "Oh, all right!" She gave in ungracefully. "First he wanted to know if Mr. Edwards might die of his wounds."

"That must explain why he looked so disappointed to see me here," Boone suggested dryly.

"Hell," Tonio scoffed, "once he saw *me* he didn't even notice *you.*"

"You could be right." Boone sat down—in her brother's chair, Rose noted, at the head of the table. "How'd he take the bad news?"

"What bad news? Oh, you mean that you're well on your way to recovery?" She made a face. "Like a trooper. He's still hoping you'll turn out to be some famous gunfighter who'll somehow end up six feet under in the local cemetery."

The corners of Boone's eyes crinkled with laughter. "Hope he can learn to live with disappointment because I've got no intention of obliging him."

"I can't say I blame you," she conceded, about to turn away—until the saw the avid interest burning in Tonio's eyes. The boy leaned forward, staring at the man.

"Who are you *really?*" It was the blunt question on the minds of half the people in town, none of whom had the courage to ask it.

Chapter Five

The very air in Rose's kitchen seemed to grow still and heavy, waiting for Boone's response. He sighed gently and leaned back in his chair as if resigned to their rapt attention. When he spoke, his tone was soft and elusive as smoke.

"I'm nobody, kid—nobody you'd know."

Tonio looked disappointed. Glancing at Jack, Rose saw the marshal give a little nod of tacit approval. He'd maintained all along that Boone was innocent until proven guilty—of anything, including a bad reputation.

Tonio's dark eyes narrowed. "There's folks hereabouts say otherwise. There's folks thinkin'—"

"That's enough, young man." Rose couldn't let such a flagrant breach of etiquette pass unchallenged. "I know James set you to watch Mr. Edwards but— Oh!" She clapped a hand over her mouth, mortified at implicating her brother.

Boone shrugged. "I knew."

Tonio frowned. "Who told you?"

"Nobody had to tell me. I saw you. You're too impatient, kid, too hot-tempered. A combination like that can get you killed."

"What the hell you know about it?" Tonio flared. An embarrassed flush darkened already dark cheeks, as if he realized he wasn't on firm ground here.

Jack leaned forward with his forearms on the table. For the first time Rose noticed the cluster of flowers drooping from his fist. He spoke earnestly. "Tonio, he's right. George Curtis is an important man in this town and he can make your life pretty doggoned miserable. You shouldn't have lost your temper with him that way."

Tonio ducked his head. "Ah, what's the difference? I couldn't have made it any worse. You think he'd ever get over a dirty half-breed even touchin' his precious daughter?"

"*Touching?*" Boone glanced at Rose, then at Jack. Some silent understanding seemed to pass between the two men. "What we walked in on was more than *touching*. If Curtis had seen that instead of just two red-faced and guilty-lookin' kids—"

Rose's alarm grew with each word. "What *were* the two of you doing?" she demanded of Tonio. She pressed her palms against her cheeks, aware of the heat there. "Sally is an innocent and genteel young lady deserving of your respect. You told me your feelings were deep and—and honorable!"

"They are. I want to marry her. You can't get much more honorable than that!" Tonio sprang to his feet.

Suddenly Rose realized how much he'd grown since he went to work at the Rocking T almost two years ago. He wasn't a boy any longer, no matter how others might perceive him. He was a young man who'd known more than his share of hurt and betrayal, and he was a young man in love.

"Nobody understands," Tonio blurted, his face twisting. "Not even you, Miss Rose—"

The boy bolted from the kitchen. Rose called his name and started after him, only to be stopped by a command from Mr. Edwards.

"Let him go. He's got a lot to think about."

"As do we all." She looked pointedly at the two men sitting at her table as if they had every right to be there. "Jack, perhaps you can talk to Sally's father and calm him down a little. I'd hate to see him make Tonio's life miserable."

Jack shook his head, obviously doubtful. "It won't be Sally's father who does the dirty work. It'll be Sally herself."

Rose frowned. "Sally? I don't understand." She glanced from one man to the other. "What *was* going on in here?"

"Miss Rose, where that boy and girl had their hands, you don't *want* to know. Then two minutes later, Sally's all set to deny everything and let Tonio take the blame alone."

"Sally's not like that," Rose declared, shocked at the implication.

"Yeah, she is. But in her defense, what could she do? If her pa thought those two had been carrying on behind his back, no power on earth could have prevented a shooting."

"Oh, dear God." Rose sank down in a chair, wondering how she'd ever got involved in this mess. "I thought . . . I hoped . . ."

Jack looked sympathetic but not optimistic. "If you've got any influence with the boy, now's the time to warn him that George Curtis would see his daughter dead before he'd let her marry a half-breed. Sally knows that, even if Tonio doesn't."

Boone's lips curved in a cynical smile. "Love rarely conquers all in real life, Miss Rose," he observed. "Everything the marshal here says is right as rain. You may consider Romeo and Juliet's story romantic, but don't forget that they both ended up dead."

Rose's mouth fell open and she stared at the big man across the table. A gunfighter conversant with Shakespeare? "Who are you—*really?*" she whispered.

Boone found her way of speaking before she thought completely charming, even when she asked questions he had no intention of answering. It was none of her business that he'd attended one of the finest military academies in the south, or that he'd studied the classics and much more before leaving at fifteen to join the Confederate Army.

"I'm nothing more than what you see," he said lightly. "Jeremy Edwards, a poor wandering cowboy."

Her cheeks flamed but she kept her head high. "With two bullet holes in your hide?"

He laughed. "I'll have to be more careful about the way I handle firearms."

She tossed her head, shaking loose a dark strand from the mass pinned at the nape of her neck. She shoved it back in place. "You should also be more careful about barging into people's private homes uninvited," she suggested, her tone tart.

"That's my fault," Jack said quickly. "I do beg your pardon, Miss Rose. But I was on my way to bring you these flowers." He offered them, by now so overcome by the heat of his fist that they hung over like so many strands of string.

When she stared at his tribute with consternation on her pretty face, he rushed on. "Anyway, Mr. Edwards expressed a desire to see a little of our fair city so I invited him to join me."

Some invitation; Boone had more or less invited himself along once he knew where the marshal was headed. Nevertheless, he nodded in agreement as if it were the gospel truth.

Rose sniffed with haughty disdain, but Boone could tell she wasn't really angry, just going through the motions. "Do you always walk in unannounced?"

"Of course not. I knocked first." Jack glanced at Boone for confirmation, which was forthcoming. "I guess nobody heard me, which is understandable considering you were in the parlor and . . ." He trailed off uncomfortably.

"It's that *and* that worries me," she agreed dryly. She took the wilted posies from his hand. "Poor little things," she crooned, laying them out before her on the white table-cloth as if preparing them for burial. "Wildflowers are so delicate. They never live very long once you've picked them."

Jack stared at her with such hunger and longing that Boone felt uncomfortable even seeing it. He shifted unhappily in his chair but couldn't seem to look away. He was glad he hadn't when she glanced up with a wide, sparkling smile curving those soft pink lips.

"Oh, well," she said, "it's the thought that counts. I'm sorry I was so ungracious."

Jack swallowed hard. "Y-you could never be ungracious, Miss Rose. I wonder—" He glanced at Boone as if remembering all at once that they weren't alone.

Rose looked at Boone, too, from beneath half-lowered lashes, but he had the very strong impression that, unlike Jack, she hadn't forgotten his presence for a moment. He grinned. "Don't mind me," he suggested. "I'll just be a fly on the wall."

Rose shot to her feet. "Not on *my* wall, you won't," she declared indignantly. "I think it's time for the two of you to run along—but through the front door, please." She pointed with an extravagant gesture. "If James thought I was receiving callers at the kitchen door he'd have a fit!"

"James is her brother," Jack offered, rising obediently.

"I know." Boone stood up more slowly, letting just a touch of arrogant disregard show through. "I also know she doesn't mean just callers, she means gentlemen callers."

"I mean no such thing." Rose flounced through the parlor and out the front door.

The two men followed, pausing beside her on the small porch. Jack grinned; he seemed to be getting into the spirit of the occasion. "We are callers," he teased, "and I don't see how you can suggest we're not gentlemen, Miss Rose."

"Oh, no?" She glanced pointedly at Boone but her eyes shone with mischief. "I'll concede you're callers, but the jury's still out on the gentlemen part."

"Let us prove it," Jack suggested in an eager voice. Then as if realizing that he was to include another man in his long-standing efforts to ingratiate himself with this woman, he corrected, "I mean, let *me* prove it. There's a pie supper coming up soon at the church and—"

"Marshal! Marshal!"

At the breathless cry, the trio on the porch turned as one. A man shuffled rapidly toward them, red-faced and sweating. It took but a moment for Boone to place him: skinny little Junius Cox, frequent resident drunk of the local hoosegow.

Jack stepped off the porch to meet the wheezing man. "What is it, Junius? What's the trouble?"

"It's that cowboy—" Junius sucked in a great gasp of air, doubling over with the effort. "That Mase Williams, you know, from the Box C. He's raisin'—" the little man glanced uneasily at Rose. "—raisin' Cain over to th' Yella Rose, threatenin' to shoot up the place. Max sent me to fetch you quick!"

Jack glanced at Boone, frowning. "If Max is worried, I'd better get on over there," he decided. "It's not like him to ask for help. Don't recall he ever did before."

All the flirtatious byplay of a few moments ago had evaporated; Rose might as well not have been there for all the attention she received. Boone rested his hand on the holster slung low around his hips and spoke to Jack. "You want me to cover your back?"

"That won't be necessary," Jack declined. "I know Mase—he's not a bad sort. He takes a nip or two of John

Barleycorn now and again and thinks he can tree a bear with a switch.''

"It ain't no *bear* he's beatin' on this time, Marshal," Junius interjected. "It's—" Again he threw a surreptitious glance at Rose.

Boone understood, whether or not the others did. There was a drunken cowboy at the saloon beating the hell out of a prostitute and threatening worse. "You sure you don't want help?" he asked Jack again.

"No, but much obliged."

"Marshal, you're not packin' any hardware. What're you plannin' to do, ask him politely to dance?"

Jack laughed. "Now there's a thought." He shook his head. "I appreciate your good intentions but I don't approve of the way men go around armed to the teeth in this country. The day I need a gun to do my job is the day I find a new job." He tipped his hat to Rose and set off toward town with Junius at his side.

Boone watched the two men hurry away, one tall and straight-backed and determined, the other hopping along gnomelike. "There," Boone said, tamping down admiration, "goes a man who's a few bricks shy of a load in the good sense department."

Rose glanced at him with a frown on her face. "You've no call to say such a thing. If the marshal says he can handle it, he can handle it."

"Maybe, but in case he's wrong, I think I'll trail along to the Yellow Rose and watch the show."

She bit her full lower lip, a habit he already recognized as a way of battling her impetuous nature. He started down the two porch steps leading to the street but she reached out unexpectedly to touch his arm.

Lightly, ever so lightly, but he felt the jolt as if she'd jabbed him with a dinner fork. He stopped short and turned toward her sharply, a question in his eyes. She caught her breath with a gasp and swayed away from him, her eyes level with his since he stood on a lower step.

"I think—" She swallowed hard and her long lashes swept down to cover honey-colored eyes, then up again so she could confront him bravely. "I think I'll go along as far as the door, if you don't mind...in case somebody gets hurt."

He felt a knot form in his gut, felt it tighten. Tendrils of desire wafted through him like wisps of smoke, elusive but all-pervasive.

Looking deep into her guileless eyes, he nodded. "Come as far as you've a mind to," he said softly. "It'll be my pleasure."

Almost running, Rose lifted her heavy skirts a few inches and struggled to keep up with the long-legged strides of Jeremy Edwards. She supposed she could slip her hand through the crook of his elbow but she'd be damned if she'd deliberately touch *that man* again.

The way he'd looked at her a few minutes ago on the steps—she'd have shuddered at the memory if it were possible to do so while dodging potholes in the street. The boardwalks didn't extend this far from the center of town and walking could be downright hazardous. With a little squeak of alarm, she hopped over a pile of something ominous square in her path.

Mr. Edwards glanced at her, the deadly serious set of his features softening for an instant. "Sorry," he said, grasping her elbow firmly. "Let me assist you."

She wished he wouldn't. Although his momentum tended to pull her along with considerably less effort on her part, she still wasn't sure that was a fair trade-off for the tumultuous emotions surging through her at his touch.

They reached the south end of town and the feed and grain store, where the boardwalk began, and he hurried her toward it. "What can you tell me about this cowboy, Mase?" he asked as they struck more secure footing.

"Nothing," she panted. "I barely know who he is."

"Nothing stands out, huh?"

"No. Just that he's—" she dodged Emmett's puppy, sleeping in front of the C and J "—left-handed."

They'd reached a spot directly across from the Yellow Rose and he stopped short, swinging around to face her. Even through the dusk and with his hat pulled down, she could see his frown.

"That could be important. Why would you think to mention a thing like that?" he wondered.

"W-why—" She stared at him, confused. Now that they were here, why didn't he release her arm? Why didn't she insist? "You asked if anything stands out and that's all that sprang to mind. The first time I saw Mase was at the Blue Bonnet Café and he was eating with his left hand—sloppily, I might add." She bit her lip. "I'm sorry if that sounded facetious but it was entirely unintended."

He tilted his head to one side and pushed back his hat. "You know," he drawled, "I forgot women like you existed." The smile slipped away. "And I was better off before I remembered." He jerked his head toward the saloon. "You fixin' to come any closer?"

She lifted her chin. "I can't see anything from here, can I."

"Suit yourself." He escorted her across the dusty street. "Looks like a crowd's startin' to gather. Better stay clear of the door in case there's a stampede."

She didn't make any promises, just watched him elbow his way through the men and boys loitering near the short swinging doors. He favored one leg, she noticed, doubtless the lingering aftermath of the bullet wound in his calf. He'd moved so quickly on the walk to town that she hadn't even noticed a limp.

He disappeared inside the Yellow Rose and she let out a breath, sagging against a handy post. The man was magnetic, no doubt about it. Now that he was up and about, she felt herself being swept along by the strength of his personality.

Dangerous, very dangerous. She must make it a practice to avoid him at all costs.

And she would...just as soon as she found out what was going on inside the Yellow Rose. Resolutely she turned toward the window.

Boone shouldered his way inside the saloon and stopped short to get his bearings. At the far end of the room, Jack leaned over a poker table, speaking in a low voice to a young cowboy. The boy was so drunk he was weaving in his chair.

Boone might have felt some sympathy for the kid if he hadn't also seen the woman in sleazy green satin and feathers crouched near the stairs in back with her hands covering her face. Her shoulders heaved with the force of her sobs, but no sound emerged.

Tight-lipped, Boone drifted to the bar to stand beside Tonio. The boy didn't look around; all his attention was focused on the trio in back. He spoke in a low, tense voice. "I reckoned you might show up."

"Yeah, well, he told me not to, but what the hell? Nothin' better to do." Boone jerked his chin toward the woman. "You know her?"

"Yeah, I know her." The kid sounded mad as a hornet. "Name's Libby. This ain't the first time Mase beat her up but it's the worst. I don't know why the hell she puts up with it but she does."

"Maybe she doesn't feel she's got a hell of a lot of choice," Boone suggested softly, watching Jack lean closer to the mean-drunk cowboy. "Know what started this?"

"Max—" Tonio indicated the bartender "—says that Mase come in on the prod. Libby was dancin' with another hand from the Box C and trouble commenced. That other ol' boy ducked out first chance he got but Libby wasn't fast enough."

Boone glanced coolly around the room, noting a half-dozen or so men studying their drinks and ignoring the by-play. "None of these fine gentlemen willing to step in to help a lady?"

Tonio gave him an astonished look. "Libby's no lady, she's a whore."

"Some of the finest ladies I've ever known have been whores," Boone shot back. "Respect can be earned horizontally as well as vertically."

"Huh?" Tonio blinked, then frowned.

Boone leaned an elbow against the bar. "What the hell's wrong with the marshal? Why doesn't he just arrest the bastard and throw him in jail?"

"Because," the boy said under his breath, "Mase's got a sawed-off shotgun on his lap under that table, and it's aimed straight at the woman."

"Son of a bitch." Boone turned away in disgust. "Bartender! Bartender, let's have a beer here."

The mustachioed Max looked startled, then moved to comply. Jack glanced over with a frown, saw who was creating the commotion and seemed comforted. Boone picked up his beer and walked boldly toward the threesome at the back of the room.

The young cowboy stiffened and came half out of his chair but Boone ignored him, walking past him to stand in front of the weeping woman. Deliberately he blocked the cowboy's view with his back.

"Libby," he said urgently. "Libby, look at me."

At his tone of command, she jerked her head up like a pup on a leash and stared at him with dark, bruised eyes.

Mase had done a real job on her, Boone thought, feeling a killing rage building in his chest. Her face looked as if it'd been used for a punching bag.

Boone had known another prostitute once who'd suffered the same fate. He'd killed the man who did it, and Boone's life had never been the same.

"Who are you?" she whispered between split lips. "I don't know you . . . do I?"

"That's not important. I'm here to get you out of this. When I turn around, I want you to stand up and run like hell up those stairs. You understand?"

"But—"

"Hey! What the hell you sayin' to my woman?"

It was the drunk with the shotgun. Boone didn't turn around, just waved him off with one hand. *"Do you understand?"* he demanded urgently of Libby.

She nodded quickly, and he could see her tense as she prepared to follow his orders. She'd do her part. Now Boone must do his.

"All right—*now!*"

She moved with the lighting speed of a rabbit who knows there will be only one chance to evade the fox. Satisfied, Boone crouched and whirled, the arm holding the beer stein whipping around to release the foaming mug in a violent path straight at the drunken cowboy's face.

Mase saw it coming but there wasn't a hell of a lot he could do to avoid the bone-crushing impact. Yowling, he yanked the trigger of the concealed shotgun just as Boone threw himself to one side. The load of shot tore into the stairs where Libby should have been but wasn't.

Mase didn't get a second chance. Before Boone could reach him, Jack yanked away the shotgun and pulled the boy's revolver from his holster.

The cowboy swore horribly, pawing at the beer and foam in his eyes and threatening everybody concerned back six generations. Jack looked across the table at Boone and gave him a grim smile.

"Much obliged," he said.

Boone shrugged. "I don't like men who beat up on women."

"Neither do I."

"I'll kill that little whore," Mase howled, surging to his feet. "So help me God, I'll—"

Boone backhanded the man. He wanted to do more but he simply backhanded Mase, knocking him ass over teakettle to land facedown on the sawdust-strewn floor.

Jack looked shocked. "Do you really think that was necess—"

"*Shut up.*" Boone strode to the groggy badman. Heaving the cowboy onto his back, Boone grabbed a fistful of shirt and hauled the supine form halfway off the floor.

The kid stared up without comprehension. "Why'd you go and do that for?" he whined, fumbling at the fist that held him prisoner. "She ain't nothin' no way, just another little whore—"

Boone hit him. Bruised his hand something fierce but he figured it was worth it as he released the drunk to bounce onto the floor. Leaning over, Boone spoke into the shocked silence. "She's worth twenty of you, little man."

Straightening, he cast an unfriendly glance around the room. Finding no one willing to meet the challenge, he turned his back contemptuously—and ran smack into one very angry lawman.

"What the hell did you do that for?" Jack yelled. "You can't beat on an unarmed man who's in my custody!"

Boone started around the marshal but Jack grabbed an arm and hung on, the momentum swinging him around until his back was toward Mase. The cowboy was sitting up groggily and wiping blood from his mouth.

Jack continued to rant and rave but Boone wasn't listening. Something was funny here. Mase was trying to pull together his faculties, shaking his head and focusing his eyes on the marshal's back.

And then the cowboy leaned down and made a grab toward his boot with his left hand, pulling out a—

Boone hooked the heel of one hand beneath Jack's chin and shoved, at the same time drawing his revolver. It slid out with practiced ease, and he knew Mase Williams was a dead man.

Boone acted on instinct, certain the man was reaching for a hideout gun concealed in his boot. In the unlikely event that he was wrong, it would mean he'd just killed an unarmed man.

In which case, there'd be hell to pay in Jones, Texas.

Chapter Six

The bullet smashed into Mase's shoulder, slamming him back into a tangle of chair and table legs. A double-barreled Remington derringer flew from his fingertips and clattered across the floor.

Boone sucked in the familiar acrid scent of burning gunpowder and wondered what the hell had happened. He'd only winged Mase Williams—fancy shooting, had that been his intent.

It hadn't. At the last possible instant, he'd pulled his shot. A softheaded impulse like that could get a man killed.

Damn it, this was Rose Taggart's doing, Rose with her overt disapproval. Scowling, he spun around and stopped short.

Before the report of the single shot had echoed away, pandemonium erupted. Whores screamed, men and boys shouted and surged through the swinging doors, some seeking entrance and others seeking escape. Tonio still stood at the same spot at the bar, his mouth hanging open and his eyes uncharacteristically wide.

Boone knew that look, a combination of respect and fear and speculation. He'd seen it on many men's faces.

"Damn *you!*" The marshal grabbed Boone's arm and swung him around. "Why'd you shoot my prisoner?"

Boone shook the other man off impatiently. "Your prisoner? I'm not real sure he knew that."

"The hell he didn't! Why'd you do it?" Jack looked almost apoplectic with rage.

"Because he grabbed for a hideout gun, you dumb son of a—"

"He grabbed for a gun because you hit him!" Jack fairly trembled. "And you shot the poor bastard before you could even be sure *what* he was reaching for. You had no call to do that, Edwards."

The entire confrontation struck Boone as ludicrous, so ludicrous that bafflement replaced anger. "I've been bushwhacked enough times to trust my instincts. Besides, you'd be dead if I'd waited to be sure. He was aiming at me, but to get to me he had to go through you—square between the shoulder blades, Marshal."

"He wouldn't shoot an unarmed man," Jack declared. He'd gone white around the mouth, Boone saw. "You had no call to—"

"Marshal, what'a you want us to do with 'im?" a voice interrupted.

Glancing around, Boone saw the bartender, Max, and several others kneeling beside the wounded man. Mase groaned and began to thrash around on the floor. He pressed one hand to his shoulder and howled with pain, all the while shooting murderous glances Boone's way.

"How bad's he hurt?" Jack wanted to know.

Max shrugged beefy shoulders. "Don't appear to be too bad."

"I'm dyin'—he's kilt me!" Mase howled. "Look, I'm bleedin' to death!"

Jack ignored that outburst and spoke to Max. "Then have some of the boys haul him over to my office and I'll see if we need to ask Miss Rose to take a look at him," he decided. "I'd just as soon not get her involved in this kind of thing if I can help it."

Four or five men hoisted the wounded cowboy. He cried out with pain but nobody seemed inclined to care.

"Carry him out the back door," Jack suggested, and the little knot of men changed direction as one in order to comply. "No sense upsetting any ladies who might be passing by out front."

He turned to Boone. "And as for you—"

Before he could go on, Max stepped forward.

"Marshal, if you don't mind me sayin' so, the stranger saved your bacon. Mase drew his time earlier today at the Box C, and he come in here lookin' for trouble. There was just no talkin' to him, and I know 'cause when he started beatin' on Libby, I tried."

He offered his hand to Boone. "I'd say Mr. Edwards here done us a real favor, clippin' that bird's wings. I'd be proud to buy you a drink, if you'll step up to the bar."

Boone glanced at Jack, his triumph at Max's vindication plain. "You got anything else you want to say to me, Marshal?" he asked coldly.

Jack's mouth tightened and he hesitated. "Yeah, but not here," he said at last. "Have your drink and then come over to my office. By then I should know if Mase Williams is gonna live or die."

"I'll do that," Boone said brusquely, turning away from the unhappy lawman.

Outside on the boardwalk, Rose stood on tiptoes trying to see past the throng that had shouldered her aside from her spot at the window. If she were a man—

George Curtis backed out of the wriggling mass, chortling and rubbing his hands together. He saw her and a broad grin made the tips of his mustache quiver.

"Did you see that?" he demanded. "The man is greased lighting with a gun!"

A cold fist of fear clenched around her heart. "Who?" she demanded. "I heard a shot but I couldn't see a blasted thing. Did somebody get hurt?"

"Somebody got *killed,*" George corrected. "This is a great day for Jones, Texas, yes, sirree, a great day."

Fred Loveless hurried up the boardwalk and skidded to a stop, his skinny frame quivering with excitement. "What's goin' on in there?" he wanted to know. "That kid Emmett said—"

George nodded eagerly. "That gunfighter showed hisself this time," he crowed. "Just shot that cowboy Mase from the Box C."

"Drunk, I bet," Fred suggested sagely. "He's a bad one, that Mase. He come into the livery last week and got mad at his hoss. He beat the livin'—"

"Nobody cares about him or his horse, neither," George roared. "It's that gunfighter, that Jeremy Edwards—ha! We just *gotta* find out who we're dealin' with here. Rose, you sure you don't know?"

Torn between relief that Jeremy Edwards apparently hadn't been injured and horror that he'd shot a man whose only crime appeared to be drunkenness, Rose clenched her hands into fists. "Did the marshal arrest him?"

"Arrest who?"

"Mr. Edwards, of course!"

"How would I know? Wait a minute." George glanced toward the big front windows of the saloon. "Crowd's just startin' to thin out. Let's belly up front and see what we can see."

He started to do so, then hesitated. Looking at her through narrowed eyes, he placed a heavy hand on her forearm. "Wait a minute, missy. I just recall as how I got plenty reason not to be any too happy with you at the present time.''

She flinched before his disapproval. "Now, Mr. Curtis, I can explain. That was all a mistake earlier with Sally and Tonio, what happened in my kitchen. I didn't—"

"I know you didn't. Sally told me, and my little girl wouldn't lie.'' He shook his head sadly. "That Ryan whelp is no good, Rose, no good at all. Sally told me you been tryin' to teach him to read but I gotta wonder why you're wastin' your time. Don't you know you can't teach his kind nothin'?''

"Yeah,'' Fred echoed, "cain't teach 'em nothin'.'' He glanced from one to the other, frowning. "What happened earlier in Miss Rose's kitchen?''

"None of your business.'' George shouldered aside a man standing in a choice spot before the window. The crowd had diminished considerably, with most of the onlookers moving inside now that the danger was past.

So it was that Rose found herself peering through streaked and dirty glass at Jeremy Edwards, standing at the bar with Tonio Ryan. The boy was doing a lot of talking but Rose spared him hardly a glance.

Instead, she stared at the woman standing on this side of the gunman—for Rose now admitted such he must be. It was easy enough to identify his companion, even from the back. Libby Bowman, her name was. Quiet and pretty and self-effacing, but generous, too—she'd given some old clothing to Rose for distribution to a group of squatters and their families who'd camped east of town a few weeks ago.

Libby wore green satin, and three plumed feathers drooped from her upswept hair. There was something infinitely sad about those feathers, Rose thought, and about the weary set of the other woman's shoulders.

When they occasionally met on the street, Libby always ducked her head and mumbled an embarrassed greeting, which Rose stoutly returned. Had Libby pursued some other line of work, Rose thought they might have been friends. Looking at her now, Rose felt more curiosity than anything else for the woman who had probably witnessed the whole awful confrontation.

Until Libby leaned forward to press a quick kiss on Jeremy Edwards's lean cheek. Then all of a sudden, compassion was the last thing on Rose's mind.

Libby rose on tiptoe to whisper in Boone's ear. "If you'd like to come back later, I'd be pleased to entertain you, mister. It's little enough to repay you for what you done for me."

Her gratitude embarrassed Boone, but her offer to sleep with him embarrassed him even more. Still, he didn't want to wound her with an inadvertent insult. She was offering the only thing she had of value, her body. It was not a gift to be lightly refused.

"Much obliged," he said gruffly, "but I may be spendin' the night in the hoosegow, looks like. Maybe some other time, Miss Libby."

When he called her miss, her blue eyes widened in her battered face and she smiled. "I don't blame you," she said ruefully. "I must look a sight." She touched one cheekbone gingerly and flinched. "But it never lasts long—in a few days I'll be good as new. Maybe you'll come see me then."

"Maybe."

She looked down shyly, at the hands she clenched at her waist. "There's some . . . men . . . who tell me I'm very good at what I do," she murmured with a kind of hesitant pride. "If you ever change your mind . . . or if there's ever anything else I can do for you . . ."

"I won't forget," he promised.

She smiled and stepped away from the bar. Although the place was full now, the drinkers and watchers had left a respectful circle around Boone, Tonio and Libby. She grinned past Boone at the boy, who'd been drinking a beer and listening to the exchange with overt curiosity.

"I haven't seen much of you lately, Tony. I'm beginning to wonder if you've got yourself another girl."

Boone's jaw dropped; he'd have to quit thinking of the kid as just a kid.

"Aw, Libby." Tonio stared down at his boots, his cheeks turning a darker shade. "I been busy. With J.D. pushin' them cows up to Kansas and James on the warpath over bein' left behind, there ain't been time—"

She cut him off with a flirtatious little laugh that said she knew an excuse when she heard one. "There's always time for some things," she scolded. "Whoever she is, she's a lucky girl—and I oughta know!"

With a flounce of her skirt, she walked away, pausing at the first table she reached to exchange pleasantries with the two cowboys sitting there. Business as usual, Boone thought. Hell of a life.

"Seems like a nice woman," he observed.

"Yeah," Tonio muttered. He looked both embarrassed and defiantly proud to have been singled out by her.

"And as she said, you oughta know." Boone plunked his whiskey glass onto the bar and straightened.

"Yeah," Tonio said again. "I oughta know— Where you goin'?"

"Thought I might drop by the marshal's office and see if he's still riled up."

"I'll go with you." Tonio gulped down the last of his beer and he, too, stepped away from the bar, swiping at foam on his mouth with his forearm. He gazed at Boone expectantly, ready for anything.

Boone sighed. "Look, kid—"

He bit off his words. He'd be talkin' to hear his head rattle, as his dear old granny used to say, if he warned the boy away. The forbidden was always so much more attractive. Maybe if he didn't make an issue of it, Tonio would tire of following him around that much more quickly.

If he didn't make an issue of it or shoot somebody else. Damn! He was a fool for following Jack Guthrie to the Yellow Rose in the first place. But he had, and in so doing, he figured he'd paid the debt he owed the lawman for taking him in when he first rode into town and fell on his face.

So now they were even. Boone started for the back door, the one through which they'd carried Mase, all too aware of the wide berth and guarded glances he received. Tonio swaggered along at his side, obviously enjoying the attention. Boone wanted to grab the kid and beat some sense into his hard head.

But he didn't, just strode along to the marshal's office and banged inside without so much as a by your leave. Marshal Guthrie sat at his worktable, his face grim. Mase Williams was nowhere to be seen.

Boone frowned. The cowboy couldn't have died—not from that scratch. "So what'd you do with him?" he demanded.

"Tied a bandage on him, put him on his horse and told him to make tracks out of here," Jack said.

"Ha!" Boone pulled out a chair and sat down while Tonio moved over to stand near the lone window that looked out onto the main street. Smart kid, Boone thought with approval. "I told you I barely scratched the little son of a bitch," he said, returning to the argument.

"And I told you—" Jack choked on his anger and tipped his chair back, his face red and unhappy. "You could have killed him."

"Hell, I *meant* to kill him. Right up to the last minute—" No need to confess that at the last minute he'd heard Rose's voice castigating all those who resorted to violence.

Jack's eyes narrowed. "I *hope* that at the last minute you realized there are better ways to settle arguments than with a fast gun."

"I got news for you, friend. That wasn't a fast gun you saw back there—not when I had to take time to shove the marshal out of the way before he got his ass shot off by a drunk with a hideout gun."

Jack's jaw jutted out. "I told you, he wouldn't have shot me."

"And I'm tellin' you I saved your hide, pilgrim." Boone shot to his feet, frustrated by Jack's complete inability to see and acknowledge the obvious.

Then in a flash, it dawned on him what Jack was doing with that pile of dodgers on the table. He was looking for a reward poster with Boone's description spread all over it. "Jesus Christ, man!" Boone exploded. "You're not only ungrateful, you're plumb loco. You're lookin' for paper on me."

"So what if I am?" Jack's hands clenched, crumpling an already wrinkled sheet of paper. "I'm beginning to think George Curtis is right—Jeremy Edwards is no more your name than my name is...Jesse James! But if you're not Jeremy Edwards, who are you?"

"Well, that does it." In his righteous indignation, Boone didn't stop to consider that Jack was entirely right on that score, that the name Boone might mean considerably more to the law than his first two, completely unknown, monikers. "You and me have split the blanket as of now."

Jack lunged up, leaning forward with his hands braced on the tabletop. His anger matched Boone's. "What the hell's that supposed to mean?"

"You saved my life, I saved yours! We're quits!"

"Fine!"

"I mean it!"

"I said, fine!"

"Don't depend on me the next time you get into trouble!"

"I didn't depend on you this time, you gun-loving— Ah, what's the use?" Jack sat down hard, waving one hand vaguely toward the door. "Talking to you is like talking to a hitching post. Get out of here before I decide to throw you in jail."

Boone scowled, rocking back on his bootheels with his hands resting on his gun belt. "On what charge?"

"Disturbing the peace—hell, I'm a lawyer. I'll think of something." Jack looked down at the posters, then up at Boone. "You sure there's nothing you want to tell me be—"

"Uh-oh!" Tonio braced himself away from the wall just as the door flew open. Miss Rose Taggart stood there, her fine bosom heaving with the force of her labored breathing.

"You!" she cried, pointing one quivering finger at Boone. She swung her disapproving glance toward Jack. "Marshal, why haven't you arrested this man? I demand you do your duty!"

It wouldn't have taken her so long to get to the marshal's office if there hadn't been so many people on the street, all eager to talk about what had just happened in the Yellow Rose.

"I seen it, I seen it," Junius Cox declared when young Emmett pulled his pa out of the saloon. "It was over that whore— Oops!" He looked at Rose, discomfited, but went on anyway. "It was over that woman, Libby. He done it in cold blood, if'n you ask me. Took Mase's rifle away and then drew down on him, that's what that stranger done."

"So where'd they take Mase?" Rose asked, craning her neck to look around. "To Mr. Black's?" Mr. Black was Dudley Black, the undertaker.

Young Emmett piped up. "Over to the marshal's office, Miss Rose. He was bleedin' like a stuck pig but Marshal Jack told me not to bother you." The boy nodded wisely. "Guess they figured he was gonna die anyway."

Rose didn't wait to hear any more. Picking up her skirts, she ran. And what did she find at the marshal's office? That killer, gun still cinched around his hips, and the marshal, yelling at each other so loud she could hear them a block away!

At her precipitous entry, Tonio jumped forward to stand between her and her intended target. He touched her hand lightly, anxiously. "This is no place for a lady, Miss Rose," he said anxiously. "Why don't I escort you home?"

"Kindly do not put your hands on me, Tonio Ryan." She shook him away. "I have come to find out for myself why this—this *gunman* shot down an innocent unarmed cowboy!"

"Huh?" Boone and Jack uttered in unison.

"Where's the body?" She looked around; all she saw out of place was a pile of bloody bandages on the floor near the marshal's cot.

The same cot where they had ministered to the man who'd done this awful thing. She tightened her lips with disapproval and glared at Jack. "Well, what are you waiting for? Arrest him!"

"Now, Rose, I'm not going to arrest anybody." Jack held up his hands in a gesture meant to be soothing.

It failed miserably. "Why not?" Her lip curled with scorn evenly distributed between the two men. "Because he's fast with a gun? I can fix that!"

Without giving herself time to think about what she was doing, Rose marched right up to Jeremy Edwards. Glaring into his face, she reached out with her left hand and pulled his pistol from its holster. The weight of it dragged her arm down to her side but she had it, she thought triumphantly.

She glanced at Jack. "Where would you like me to put—*umph!*" Her arrogant words died in a grunt of alarm as Boone clamped his hands around her upper arms and lifted her off the floor until only her dangling toes retained contact with solid ground.

He tossed an angry glance over his shoulder at Jack. "This your woman?" he demanded in a hard voice.

Jack gulped. "I sure do hope so."

Rose found her voice. "You brute! You beast! You can't do this to me! *Let me go before I—*"

"She's got a big mouth," Boone said.

Yanking her hard against his chest, still holding her by the upper arms, he brought his mouth down on hers. Stunned, she felt the pressure of his chest against her breasts and the corded muscles of his thighs against her legs, and then she forgot all those peripheral distractions before the onslaught of sensations originating at that point where his mouth joined with hers.

It was a fast, hard kiss meant to punish, and in that it failed miserably. Too surprised to resist, Rose hung suspended like a rag doll. A devastating rush of excitement shot through her from the tips of her toes to the roots of her hair and all points in between, leaving fire in its wake. This was a kiss? She'd had no idea!

And then it was over. Before she could even begin to understand what had happened, it was over. He slammed her down on her own two feet and glared into her eyes as if to say, *So there!*

She stared at him with utter disbelief, still holding his revolver in her hand. Weakly she murmured the first words that came to mind. "Oh, dear!"

"Here now!" Jack jumped up behind his worktable, knocking over his chair in the process. His face was red and his expression horrified. "You can't molest women here!"

"Where can I molest them, then?" Boone's mood seemed to have miraculously improved. "Over at the Yellow Rose? That seems a likely place, since you were willing to look the other way when Mase Williams tried it."

Jack came around the table, fire in his eyes. "That's a damned lie!" He choked on the swear word and added, "Beg pardon, Miss Rose." He looked ready to jump Boone. "You can't molest women anywhere in this town!"

Boone leaned forward and slipped his pistol from Rose's numb grip. Flipping it over his hand, he settled it snugly into his holster. "Says who?" he inquired mildly.

"Me, the marshal! That's who! You can't go grabbing women around here and kissing them."

Boone's smile was almost beatific. "So what you gonna do about it?" he challenged. "Shoot me?"

Whistling, he sauntered out the open door.

After a shocked second or two, Tonio followed.

Chapter Seven

Jack's wild glance settled on the rifle rack against the far wall opposite the jail cell. His hands clenched, and for a moment Rose thought he really would have shot Jeremy Edwards if he'd been near enough to grab one of the neatly displayed weapons.

Instead, the marshal took a step toward the door, his face hardening into a mask of resolve.

"Don't," she said in a thick voice. Jack was a man of law, not of violence; she would not be the one to drive him to abandon his principles. She sat down heavily in the chair Mr. Edwards had vacated. "It's—I'm all right."

"Oh, Rose—Miss Rose." Jack whirled and dropped to his knees before her. Picking up her hands, he cradled them between his. He stared into her face, his own twisted with remorse. "I can't tell you how sorry I am that you were subjected to such an outrage. I would have shot that gunman myself the day he collapsed here, had I but known what kind of man he really is."

Rose felt the blood begin to flow through her body again, bringing with it a disturbing glow. She sucked in a deep, shaky breath. "Please don't say such things, Marshal Guthrie. *You* are not that kind of man, even if *he* is."

"You're too kind."

For a moment he stared down at their linked hands, his head bent as if in supplication. She longed to reassure him further but was still too stunned by what she'd just endured to think of suitable words.

What *had* she just endured at the hands of that ruffian? She'd have to sort that out later. At the moment, all she knew was that her lips still trembled with the remembered imprint of his, and she got goose bumps just thinking about the way he'd put his hands on her and hauled her against his strong, hard body—

Jack cleared his throat and she started guiltily, a hot blush staining her cheeks. "Yes?" she whispered.

He faced her with determination. "Miss Rose, surely you must know... I mean, it's no secret that I..." He swallowed hard and squeezed her hands more tightly still. "Miss Rose, the time has come when I must speak what is in my heart. I realize that my courtship has not been—"

"Courtship!" Oh, dear—this was going in the wrong direction entirely. She tried to tug her hands from his but he wouldn't let go.

He looked confused. "My intentions are most honorable, I assure you. I could aspire to no higher honor than to have you for my wife."

It was too much—mauled physically by a gunfighter, then mauled emotionally by the marshal. "Oh, no, it's out of the question!" she cried. Seeing his stricken expression, she tried to temper her outburst. "Please don't misunderstand me, I know you're an honorable man. But this is hardly the time—"

"It's the perfect time, in light of what has happened." He lifted her hands to his lips and kissed them, despite her evasive response. "Forgive me if I presume, but my most cherished ambition is to offer you the protection of my name. I promised your father I would not speak until he returned from Kansas but—"

"My father?" She stiffened. What had James said? *"J.D. says there'll be no old maids in the Taggart family."*

"You can't imagine I'd overstep the bounds of propriety by proposing matrimony without your father's blessing?" Jack looked nonplussed. "Miss Rose, he knows that I respect and honor you above all women, that I love—"

Appalled, she yanked her hands free and clapped one over his mouth. "Don't say it!" she cried. "You hardly know me! Although I hold you in the highest regard, I couldn't possibly consider such a declaration. Surely you know that I was pledged to another."

She felt his smile beneath her fingers and hastily jerked her hand away.

"No one admires such loyalty more than I. I know I'm rushing you but under the circumstances—" He frowned toward the door. "Once we are betrothed, I'm sure you'll have nothing further to fear from men of that stripe."

"I'm sorry, but I can't listen to any more of this, not tonight." Shaking her head forcefully, she jumped to her feet. "All I want to do is go home and put this whole unfortunate incident behind me."

His face fell, but he nodded. "I understand," he said in a dejected tone. "But I'm not giving up, Miss Rose. When you think about what happened here tonight, I hope your thoughts are of me and my steadfast devotion, not of *him*."

"I assure you," she said grimly, "I won't give *him* another thought."

But she was lying. Even as she said it, she knew she'd be able to think of little else. What she didn't imagine was that Jeremy Edwards would even invade her dreams.

She worked in a saloon, a place much like the Yellow Rose. She wore a sleazy satin gown like the ones she'd seen through the window earlier that evening, and she was picking up drinks at the long mahogany bar.

In the mirror behind the pyramided glasses, she saw her own reflection and stopped to stare. Three marabou feathers decorated her high-piled hair, and her gown was cut daringly low. Her breasts were rosy spheres threatening to spring free of their flimsy covering, but Rose didn't feel the shock and horror such immodest exposure should have occasioned. In fact, she felt nothing, nothing at all . . . except some vague sense of anticipation.

Without knowing why she did so, she moved listlessly from table to table, serving drinks and trying to remember to smile. But all the time she was watching the doors, watching and waiting. . . .

Waiting for what? She had no idea until suddenly the doors flew wide and Marshal Jack Guthrie stood there, his badge gleaming dully. Moving as if in a trance, Rose approached him. He smiled and opened his arms and she slipped into them, pressing her cheek against his leather vest.

I am safe now, she thought. *Billy is dead but Jack loves me and will take care of me.* Closing her eyes and gathering strength to act, she lifted her face for his kiss.

His mouth touched hers . . . and her blood ran cold. Jack had never made love to her but she knew this was not the lawman's kiss; it was *his*—that gunman, Jeremy Edwards. She would know it anywhere, among a thousand others, for he had already branded it on her very soul.

She wanted to resist but was helpless to do more than simply stand there straight and unmoving. But then something very strange and very frightening began to happen to her, for this was not simply a replay of the kiss in the marshal's office; no, that had been just a tiny indication of what a kiss from this man could really be.

Her lips softened and parted beneath his. What was happening to her? She had never been kissed like this; surely no one had, for such infinite delight could not be borne outside the magic boundaries of a dream.

His lips withdrew from hers and for a moment she simply stood there, reeling. She felt the touch of his hand on her cheek and with a great effort of will forced her heavy eyelids to open. Jeremy Edwards smiled down at her, his eyebrows arched in a question.

A question she didn't understand, and yet she nodded because it was not in her power to do otherwise. His gray eyes darkened with satisfaction and suddenly he was gone—gone. She whirled around in pure panic, spotting him almost at once.

He stood at the foot of the stairs leading up to a second floor obscured by swirling smoke or fog—Rose couldn't be sure which. He did not move so much as a muscle, didn't lift his hand to beckon her, yet she felt his pull as strongly as if he'd dropped a loop over her shoulders and was hauling her in like a calf at roundup.

She had no choice. Or did she? His holster was empty; she held his pistol in her hand but this time it was light and warm to her touch, not heavy and cold and awkward as it had been in the marshal's office. She could do anything she wanted with it, she realized, her mind moving sluggishly to that conclusion. She held his fate... and her own... in her hands.

Don't go.

Jack's voice sounded in her mind, coming out of nowhere, the words signifying nothing. Like a wraith she moved between the tables and the shadowy men seated there, concentrating only on he who waited. Would he kiss her again? She wanted him to kiss her again, and go on kissing her, and never stop.

She reached the stairs and halted before him, waiting for him to tell her what came next. He smiled and heat surged into her stomach; her knees trembled so badly she had to put out a hand for support.

He touched her cheek with warm, steady fingers, trailing them lightly down her throat and across the agitated swell of her breast, on past the curve of her shoulder and down her arm. At last his hand grasped hers and she closed her eyes, giving in completely to the desire that surged through her veins. Without a word, he turned to the stairs.

She followed his lead willingly, anticipation surging through her as they ascended to...what?

Rose sat bolt upright in her bed, trembling, her cotton nightgown clinging to a body damp with perspiration. Shame clogged her throat, shame at her own weakness— she'd succumbed to the man even in her sleep! But mixed with the shame was also fear, fear that she would never know what bliss might have awaited her at the top of those stairs.

George Curtis and Fred Loveless were also afraid—afraid the mysterious gunfighter would leave town before they had a chance to find out who he really was. The two men met late that night in Fred's "office" at the livery stable—the front stall, straw cleaned out and wooden boxes positioned as furnishings.

"I reckon I'll have to write a few letters," George groused, not pleased with that prospect. "I got friends all over the state and beyond. Somebody's bound to know something about a man that quick on the trigger."

"Quick on the trigger," Fred agreed.

"But I wish there was some other way. I purely hate to write my name, let alone a bunch'a letters."

"Bunch'a letters." Fred nodded understandingly. "Maybe the missus or Sally could give you a hand."

George harrumphed. "This is no business for women," he said darkly.

Deflated in his zeal to help, Fred slumped on his apple-box chair. "I gotta agree with you there." He brightened.

"Doc should be back from Wichita any day now. He met a lotta men while he was doctorin' back in Kansas a few years ago. Maybe he'll—"

"That old rum pot?" George tended to scorn any idea not his own. "We'll be lucky if'n he knows his own name, let alone—" He stopped short and peered into the shadows beyond the wide double doors. "Somebody out there?" he inquired sharply. "Show yourself!"

A tall, lean figure stepped forward, although managing to stay well out of the small circle of light cast by Fred's lantern. A bedroll was hoisted over one shoulder, and he carried his warbag in the other hand. A pistol rode low on his hip.

Both men knew exactly who he was before he uttered a single word.

"I'm lookin' for a place to bed down for the night and I don't much fancy hotels. Mind if I make myself at home in your loft?"

Fred jumped to his feet. "Whatta you mean, sneakin' up on a man thataway? Hell, no, this ain't no—"

George, still seated on his own box, grabbed the other man's coattail with one substantial hand and jerked him back down. "Help yourself, Mr. Edwards," he invited. "Fred's a hospitable man, long's you don't startle him plumb out of his manners."

The tall man stood there for a moment longer as if to give the proprietor an opportunity to disagree. When he spoke, his simple, "Much obliged," was touched with wry humor, which was not missed by George Curtis.

"Now why'd you go and do that?" Fred demanded after the gunman had climbed out of sight up the ladder leading to the dark loft. "I don't need no murderin' coyote right under my nose at night, waitin' to murder me while my back's turned."

George grunted with satisfaction. "Don't get a bee in your bonnet, Fred. If that ol' boy wanted to murder you, he could do it to your face without workin' up a sweat."

Fred looked crestfallen and George laughed, then relented. "What better way to know where he's at and what he's doin' than to have him sleepin' in your own livery stable? If he fixes to leave town, who'll be the first to know? Cheer up, Fred. This'll work out fine, yes, sirree, just fine. Now about them letters..."

Rubbing his meaty hands together, George Curtis set about talking Fred Loveless into secretarial duty.

Boone slumped against his bedroll, staring morosely through the open hay doors at a sliver of moon. Out of habit, he'd positioned himself so he could see anyone coming or going through the double doors below. The murmur of voices had long since ceased, and he'd watched the dark shadows of Curtis and his flunky, Loveless, part company in the middle of the street.

He was alone...almost.

The kid Tonio had shadowed him from the marshal's office to the marshal's house. Boone had made short work of packing up his few possibles, intent upon getting out before Jack showed up to resume the quarrel.

Something Boone was not eager to do, for this time he would be hard-pressed to defend himself. He'd been right to follow Jack to the Yellow Rose. He'd been right to shoot the cowboy Mase.

He'd been wrong to kiss Rose Taggart and he damned well knew it. He'd done it anyway and he wasn't sorry but he wasn't interested in explanations.

The truth of the matter was, Rose just plain intrigued the hell out of him. There was an untouched lushness about her that drew him like a bear to honey, even while her tart tongue and frequently imperious manner stung him.

He'd like to be the man who made those innocent amber eyes glaze with desire. He could, he realized without conceit; even a kiss as quick and inadequate as the one they'd shared in the marshal's office had told him that much. Despite her local status as a somewhat elderly maiden lady—all right, call it old maid—she was ripe and ready for the picking.

He'd like to be the man who harvested her crop—but he wouldn't. By damn, he wouldn't! He made it a rule never to trifle with good women because the potential consequences were too many and too dire. No shotgun weddings or bastard children for him.

To Boone Smith, the opposite of good wasn't bad but "wiser"—wiser in the ways of men and the world. Libby fell in that last category, which did not make her a creature to be despised.

Still, he'd turned down her offer of sex, an offer even more attractive in retrospect and in consideration of his current state of excitement. Maybe he liked his women enthusiastic as well as willing, he rationalized. Maybe as the night grew older, his standards wouldn't be quite so high.

Too bad Rose wasn't a widow. Of course, if she married Jack Guthrie and he continued on as marshal the way he was headed, she would be and damned quick.

A shadow flitted near the door, and Boone sat up straighter. Damned kid probably thought that Indian blood made him invisible. Time to disabuse him of a dangerous notion.

Thus it was that when Tonio raised his head slowly and noiselessly through the hayloft opening, he found himself looking down the barrel of a Smith and Wesson forty-five. He gulped and held himself very, very still.

Boone spoke with soft menace. "Okay, kid, you been followin' me ever since I walked into the Yellow Rose. What the hell's going on?"

"Uh . . . I just wondered if there was anything I could do for you," Tonio mumbled.

Boone thought about that for a moment. "Yeah," he said then. "Yeah, there is. Come on up here and tell me everything you know."

The boy scrambled through the opening. "About Mase Williams?"

Boone's laughter was brief and self-deprecating. "Hell, I know all I need to know about him. Tell me about the Taggarts." And in a lower voice he added, "Tell me about Miss Rose."

Tonio was glad to comply. Rose was one of his favorite subjects, Boone soon discovered.

"Miss Rose is just about the finest woman in this town," the boy declared, hunkering down across from Boone in the moonlight. "She may be an old maid but it ain't because nobody's interested."

"No?"

Tonio nodded solemnly. "They'd be interested if she was homely as a mud fence—which you can plainly see, she ain't. Taggarts have been the big bulls in this pasture since before the war. Her daddy and brother run the biggest spread in these parts. Funny about that family, though . . ."

"What is?" Boone spoke with deceptive casualness.

"Don't none of 'em seem to care much what a man *is*— Mex, colored, Injun, it's all the same to them as long as he does a job of work. They are the most *color*-blind group of folks I ever run into."

"Sounds like you run into a few of the other kind." Boone slid down until his head rested on his bedroll. Carefully he positioned his hat over his face.

"Yeah, you could say that." The boy sounded bitter. "My pa was Irish and my ma half-Mex and half-Injun. What do *you* think?"

"I think you can waste a hell of a lot of time feelin' sorry for yourself if you've a mind to. Luck of the draw, kid. Maybe you got a hard row to hoe, but that ain't the saddest story I ever heard."

There was a moment's silence and Boone resisted the temptation to lift his hat to see how the kid was taking the rebuke. He didn't, and was gratified when Tonio let out a gusty sigh.

"Reckon you're right. At least I ain't no *woman*. Just look at Libby."

"I think you already have," Boone drawled.

The kid laughed. "Yeah, I have. I mean I did, but that's all over now that I know Sally Curtis loves me. Anyway, gettin' back to the Taggarts, they gave me a chance when nobody else would and I owe 'em for that. But Miss Rose... Miss Rose is just extra special."

"Because she helps you find ways to spend time with Sally?"

"You got her all wrong—she don't do that. In fact, she tried to talk us out of it but Sally and me, we know our own minds."

Spoken with the misguided certainty of the young. "Then why?"

"Because—" Tonio hesitated. "Ah, I can tell you. She's teachin' me to read. I guess that's kinda dumb at my age but—"

"It's not dumb." Boone felt himself softening toward the boy. "It could turn out to be one of the smartest things you ever did. Learning's important, all learning."

"There's something I'd like to learn from you," Tonio responded shyly.

"What's that?" *As if I didn't know.*

"How to handle a pistol the way you do." The hay rustled beneath the boy as he shifted eagerly. "I was watchin' when you shot ol' Mase—I've been watchin' ever since you rode into town. You're good, Mr. Edwards, damned good—maybe the best I ever seen. I don't know if what they're all sayin' about you is true—"

Boone let out a warning growl but the boy hurried on anyway.

"But I know what I've seen and if you could find your way clear to give me a few pointers ... Well, I'd be much obliged."

Boone lay there in the darkness, hat over his face, considering. He had no intention of teaching this boy a skill that would bring him nothing but grief, but on the other hand, the kid was a hell of a source of local information.

So what Boone said was, "I'll think about it. In the meantime, you were telling me about Rose. Sounds like she's just about perfect."

Tonio laughed. "Yep, she is. Except she's got a female tendency to worry too much." He laughed again. "And she might be just a tad stubborn from time to time, but that's all."

"Then why hasn't some lucky man snapped up this paragon of virtue?"

"One did. It was about five years ago when Miss Rose was sixteen or seventeen, just the right marryin' age. His name was Billy and he was Mr. Curtis's son—you know, from over to th' C and J? Billy fell off his horse and got drug to death right after him and Miss Rose decided to get married.

"Way I heard it, he got drunk over at th' Yellow Rose and fell off on the ride home, but Miss Rose don't know that. She thinks he was somethin' on a stick—swears she'll love him forever and never marry nobody else."

So that was why Marshal Jack hadn't got her roped and tied a long time ago, Boone thought with evil satisfaction. "Must be hard on the marshal," he suggested without the slightest compassion.

"Won't be much longer." Again hay rustled as the boy leaned closer, his voice dropping several tones. "The marshal talked to Miss Rose's daddy before he left on that trail drive to Kansas. I heard 'em. Old J.D. wants her married and yesterday wouldn't be soon enough."

"Why is that?"

"Because there's certain ungrateful folks in Jones who think she's a busybody." He sounded outraged on her behalf. "After all she's done for 'em—steppin' in when Crystal Springs hired away the schoolteacher, collecting food and things for poor folks, assistin' Doc Beatty and takin' over when he's too drunk to know what he's doin'—"

"Doc *Beatty,* you said?" Jesus, surely it couldn't be the same sawbones who'd dug a bullet out of him in Wichita. The world wasn't that small.

"That's right. You know 'im?" Tonio sounded pleased.

"Naw, man I knew was Doc *Beatton,*" Boone lied. But as Tonio rambled on, Boone lay there and thought about his current situation—and wasn't pleased.

He could ride out tomorrow. He wasn't a hundred percent recovered but he'd functioned adequately in far tougher circumstances.

He was loath to do that, however. He hadn't come to any conclusions about his future and he needed to make up his mind and stick to that decision—whatever it was.

If he couldn't outrun his reputation as Boone the gunfighter, maybe it was time to capitalize on it. That's what he'd been mulling over in a cantina in San Antonio—an offer of warrior's wages—when he took a knife in the ribs from a former compadre who'd already made his choice.

He'd filled that gentleman full of lead. "Why'd you do it?" he'd asked the dying man.

"Because if you're not with us, you're against us," the man wheezed.

"Hell, I might have gone your way if you'd given me a chance," Boone said, disgusted at yet another indication of the low value placed on human life. "You could at least have waited for me to make up my own mind."

"Don't make me laugh," the man said, and died.

The dead man, however, had a couple of friends who were very much alive—as dead men usually did. They were responsible for the lead Boone was packing when he rode into Jones all but done in.

Jesus, he was tired of running! Until he figured out what the hell he wanted out of life, he'd just as soon hang around this wide spot in a Texas road and watch the melodrama unfold.

There were a hell of a lot of questions yet to be answered.

Chapter Eight

Rose entered the C and J as Boone walked out, a box of cartridges in his hand. She felt the hated red tide rise up her throat and flood her cheeks at the sight of him. After what had happened yesterday—after what she had dreamed last night—after her disappointment upon awakening alone...

In short, Mr. Jeremy Edwards was the last person on earth she wanted to see. Squaring her shoulders, she prepared to sweep past him without the slightest acknowledgment.

As usual, the man failed to cooperate. He stepped directly into her path and lifted his Stetson. "Mornin', Miss Rose," he drawled, his slight smile deepening the creases in his cheeks. "You're lookin'... warm this morning."

Her jaw dropped in astonishment. How dare he make reference to the disgusting blush that shouted her mortification to the entire world? He stood there waiting expectantly for her reply, which would be a prelude to a conversation however reluctantly begun.

She'd show him! With a toss of her head that set her small feathered hat to bobbing precariously, she sidestepped and sailed around him, up to the counter where George Curtis watched the exchange with patent interest. Mr. Edwards's low, knowing laughter followed her, and then she heard the click of his bootheels as he left the store.

Almost sagging with relief, she leaned against the counter. "What did *he* want?" she couldn't help asking.

"Ammunition." George's eyes narrowed. "Gotta buy more when you go around shootin' folks."

A gross exaggeration, but Rose wouldn't allow herself to defend that—that gunman. "I was hoping he'd be buying supplies for the trail," she said, "since I'm sure he won't be living at the marshal's house after today."

"Oh, he ain't livin' there already," George announced cheerfully. "Slept in the loft at the livery last night. Don't know what his future plans might be but I don't think he'll be leavin' anytime soon."

Rose wanted to groan, even though she suspected George's opinion was more a case of wishful thinking than of solid deduction. "Actually, I have no interest whatsoever in the goings and comings of that...ruffian," she said in chilly tones. "I'm here to see if you've received those bolts of calico you mentioned to me a few weeks ago."

"I surely have. I'll ask Sally to show 'em to you." He half turned toward the curtain over the door leading to the back of the store. "Sally! Miss Rose wants to see them bolts of dry goods we just got in."

"Coming, Papa."

Sally popped through the curtain so quickly that Rose knew she'd been loitering behind it, listening. The girl looked lovely with her blond hair pulled back to reveal her dainty ears, a cluster of curls spilling over her forehead.

"This way, Miss Rose." Sally gestured toward shelves along the far wall running the height and breadth of the room. "We've got some real nice pieces to choose from," she added politely.

The girl's detached and businesslike air fell away when the two were out of earshot of the storekeeper. Sally cast a quick glance over her shoulder before grabbing Rose's arm.

"Is Tonio mad at me? It wasn't my fault, honest! Papa would have killed us both if—"

"Calm down, Sally." Rose disengaged the girl's clutching fingers. "What has Tonio to be angry about? After the way he practically attacked you in my kitchen, I should think you would be the one to be angry, or at least annoyed."

"Oh." Sally's furrowed brow cleared. "That's right, I should be." She laughed nervously. "But I'm not. I think Papa really believed me when I said Tonio forced himself on me on a whim."

Rose frowned. "Didn't he? If I thought the two of you were regularly engaging in...unseemly activities, I couldn't in good conscience be a party—"

"Oh, pish posh!" Sally said gaily. "If you see Tonio, will you tell him we'll...talk as soon as this blows over? And with all Papa's got on his mind, that should be soon."

Rose fingered a length of blue calico, checking the grain. "Something is worrying your father?"

Sally made a face. "That gunfighter. I swan, it's all he can think about—I guess it's all anybody in town can think about. Honestly, I don't understand it at all. Who cares if some drunk cowboy got shot?"

"Sally!" Rose stared at the girl, appalled by such an unfeeling attitude. "That's a terribly unchristian thing to say."

Sally's expression turned dreamy. "On the other hand, Mr. Edwards is so...*manly* looking that if it wasn't for Tonio—" She sighed and rolled her eyes. "Oh, well, one way or the other Mr. Edwards won't be with us long."

"I beg your pardon?" Rose frowned at the girl. "What on earth would you know about a man like that?"

"Well, Papa says—" Sally glanced past Rose, her lips suddenly pressing tightly together. "Now what do you suppose *she's* doing here?"

"Who?" Rose glanced around to see a veiled woman standing patiently at the counter, waiting for Mr. Curtis to acknowledge her. "Why, it's Libby Bowman."

"I don't know why Papa lets her kind come in here," Sally complained, "but you know him—says her money is as good as anybody else's."

Her money, Rose thought; *not her.* "I'll take this green cloth," she decided. "I believe my sister-in-law would like it."

"Don't go over there now," Sally hissed, "not while *she's* here."

"Don't be a goose, Sally. She doesn't have anything I can catch." Clutching the length of fabric, Rose walked directly to the counter and paused beside the other woman.

Mr. Curtis immediately glanced up from the stack of handkerchiefs he was counting. "Made up your mind, Miss Rose?"

Rose nodded. "But this lady was here first," she reminded him pointedly. "I don't mind waiting my turn."

"Oh, no, please go ahead." Libby kept her face averted as she spoke.

The storekeeper reached for the bolt of goods but Rose shook her head sharply. "Mrs. Bowman was here ahead of me. Kindly assist her first, Mr. Curtis."

"Goldarn it, Rose, you are the contrariest woman!" Curtis glared at her, then swung on Libby. "So what'll it be?" he demanded, all pretense of joviality gone.

"W-why—" Libby swallowed hard. "I'd like a bottle of Minard's Liniment, if it's not too much trouble."

When Mr. Curtis hesitated, Rose leaned forward over the counter and fixed him with a narrow gaze. "That's what he's in business for—to sell things. Of course it's no trouble, is it, Mr. Curtis?"

"I suppose not," he muttered ungraciously, giving Rose a glance that promised he'd have more to say to her on the matter at some future time. "If I got any. Wait here and I'll check in back."

"Please don't go to any trouble on my account," Libby pleaded, looking at the merchant. "I can come back another time—"

He didn't even acknowledge her offer, just spun around and disappeared through the curtained opening. Quickly Libby dropped her gaze again but it was too late; Rose had seen.

"Mrs. Bowman, what's happened to your face?" Rose caught the other woman's arm and tried to peer past the veil.

Libby touched her swollen cheek self-consciously. "That's why I need the liniment," she said incongruously, not answering Rose's question.

"Oh, dear." A new and horrible thought occurred to Rose and her lips tightened. "After the shooting last night, I saw you talking to Mr. Edwards. Could he be the one who—"

"No!" That single word was filled with horror. Libby whirled to grasp Rose's hands. "Marshal Guthrie and Mr. Edwards saved my life." She gave a bleak little laugh before adding, "Worthless though it may be."

Rose made no move to pull away. "Don't say that."

"Why not? It's true."

"Then you knew Mase Williams, I take it," Rose said slowly.

"I knew him, all right. He wasn't any worse than most of the rest of them until he started drinking. Then—" Libby shuddered. "This isn't the first time he's...hurt me. It's just the first time anybody ever tried to stop him. If Mr. Edwards hadn't shot him, he'd have killed me and the marshal both."

Rose was having a hard time taking all of this in. "But I understood—I mean, I thought his guns had already been taken from him. Didn't Mr. Edwards shoot an unarmed man?"

Libby made a scornful sound. "Mase carried a hideout gun in his boot and he was reaching for it. I only wish he'd been killed dead, because sure as a dog has fleas, he'll go right on abusing those weaker than—"

George hustled through the door with a bottle in his hand and she broke off her impassioned recitation instantly. He plunked the bottle down on the counter and glared at her.

"That'll be six bits," he said.

Libby began to untie the corner of her handkerchief to extract the coins but Rose stopped her with a hand on the other woman's arm. "It says twenty-five cents right here on the label," she objected, pointing.

Mr. Curtis gave her a murderous look. "That's a back-east price. I had to pay to get it here, didn't I?"

"I find it difficult to believe that you paid fifty cents in transportation charges on a twenty-five-cent item."

"Here, I have the money," Libby said quickly. She plunked down three quarters. "I don't mind."

"Well, I do!" Rose stood her ground, glaring at the shopkeeper. "How much would it cost *me* to buy a bottle of Minard's?"

"All right, all right!" Mr. Curtis threw up his hands in surrender. "Four bits, and not a red cent less." He slid two of the coins off the counter and into his palm, then turned his back on the women.

Libby looked at Rose, biting her lip. "You didn't have to do that," she said uneasily.

Rose smiled. "I think perhaps I did."

Sally rushed up as Libby left the store with her bottle of liniment. "Miss Rose, my papa is right—you'd take up with a heathen Chinaman!" the girl exclaimed. "No wonder everybody in town's so anxious to see you marry the marshal, 'cause you sure are headstrong."

Rose heaved a melancholy sigh. "There but for the grace of God . . ." She straightened and turned to the counter and the bolt of fabric. "I think I've changed my mind about this piece of yard goods," she said. "I hear Melville Jones has opened a new general store over in Crystal Springs. Perhaps I'll ask James and Diana to drive over there with me one day soon."

Walking away, she took great satisfaction in the certainty that George Curtis had been skulking behind the curtain and had heard every word. Her glow of satisfaction quickly dissipated in the harsh light of day, however.

There but for the grace of God go I was more than a handy platitude; in Rose's case, it was the truth. She had no idea what had caused Libby's fall from grace, but it might very well be something akin to Rose's own foray into sin—the difference being that Libby got caught and Rose didn't.

At least, she hadn't been found out yet. She still could be—doubtless would if she married. Unless . . .

Would a low-down no-account gunfighter insist on virginity? Even if Mr. Edwards *was* justified in shooting that cowboy—and Rose wasn't convinced on that score—it still didn't clean up his character a great deal. Would a man like that, a man with a few blots on his immortal soul, be more forgiving of a woman's trespass?

Probably not, she decided. She hadn't found men to be exactly understanding about such things. Look at Mary Lou Harris, for instance. The poor girl had been seduced by a man twice her age but when she turned up in a family way, who had been ostracized right out of town?

I've got to write to Great-Aunt Marie right away and finagle an invitation to New Orleans, Rose decided. Or maybe she shouldn't wait to be invited. Maybe she should just pack her bags and steal away like a thief in the night, before her father returned from Kansas. Maybe—

She walked right into Jeremy Edwards. So deep in thought that she didn't even see him standing outside the barber shop, she plowed into his chest. He caught her arms and held her upright and she had just a glimpse of his wicked smile before she whirled away.

He tipped his hat. "Didn't expect to run into you twice in one day," he said, settling the Stetson back on his dark head. He looked relaxed and easy, as if shooting men agreed with him. "Third time's a charm."

Jack came out of the barber shop and stopped short. He took in the scene at a glance, and his normally calm demeanor departed. "This man bothering you, Miss Rose?" he demanded. "Because if he is—"

Old Mrs. Dinwiddy, passing by, chose that moment to stop and stare. Three pairs of eyes swung to Rose.

"Yes—no—you're both bothering me," she declared, smoothing down the skirt of her simple summer gown. "If you don't mind—"

Out of the corner of her eye, she caught movement in the street. Glancing around, she saw a horse and buggy, which she recognized instantly. Doc was back! Lifting her skirts above her ankles, she skipped down the boardwalk steps to street level, calling out to him.

Doc Beatty pulled his spotted buggy horse to a stop, grinning down at his unofficial medical assistant from beneath his shaggy white mustache. Squinty eyes peered out of a puffy face marked by deep wrinkles. His shirt was untucked and his black string tie hung loose around his neck.

In short, Doc looked no different than when he'd left, which was to say, like an unmade bed.

Without waiting for an invitation, Rose scrambled up beside him on the buggy seat. "What kept you? I thought you'd never get back," she babbled. "I've had to take care of everything from snakebite to bullet wounds—"

Doc laughed and clucked to the horse, who continued his slow but steady progress home.

* * *

Rose poured two cups of coffee and carried them into Doc Beatty's examining room, where he was dusting off the tools of his trade. She set cups and saucers on a small wooden table and picked up a spoon to stir hers.

Doc looked up with a grin. "Sounds like I missed some excitement around here," he observed.

"You certainly did."

"Just as well. I had plenty of that kind of excitement before I ever came to Texas. Why, in Wichita's heyday as a cow town, I patched up more bullet holes than you could shake a stick at." He paused, a ghastly looking metal instrument in his hand. "Who you say done the shootin' over at the saloon?"

"A man who calls himself Jeremy Edwards."

"Calls himself, huh? I see. And that's the man you dug them bullets out of?"

"One and the same." She took a cautious sip of her coffee and burned her tongue.

"Was that the man on the boardwalk with you and Jack Guthrie and Matilda Dinwiddy when I drove in?"

Rose nodded, feeling a prickle of apprehension along her spine. "Do you know him? Have you seen him before?"

Doc shrugged. "Cain't be sure. Mebbe. I seen all kinds, that's for sure. You say there's some mystery about this fella?"

"Well, Mr. Curtis thinks he's some kind of famous gunfighter going under a false name. Clay Allison or Bill Hickok, somebody like that."

Doc shook his grizzled head. "Naw, ain't neither a'them."

Rose caught her breath. "Then you did recognize him!"

"Didn't say that. I just know who he *ain't.*" He sat down on a wooden rocking chair and reached for his coffee cup.

"How 'bout you, young lady? What have you been up to since I've been gone?"

"Well..." Rose considered her cup of coffee thoughtfully. "I'm thinking about taking a trip, actually."

"Oh? Maybe goin' to visit your friend over to Crystal Springs?"

"No. I was thinking of going a little farther than that."

"How far is farther?"

"Oh, maybe...to New Orleans to visit Great-Aunt Marie."

Doc's bushy white eyebrows soared. "The marshal know about this?"

"Why should he? It's none of his business. Besides, it's just an idea." Rose jumped up. "I've really got to get along home. It's wonderful to have you back, Doc." She hesitated with her hand on the door. "Uh...if you remember where you've seen Mr. Edwards before..."

"You'll be the first to know," he promised, raising one bushy eyebrow.

Feeling vaguely dissatisfied with the direction her reunion with Doc had taken, Rose turned toward home only to find the marshal waiting to waylay her. With a smile, he fell into step.

"Howdy, Miss Rose. Mind if I walk you home?"

"Would it matter if I did?" she inquired spitefully.

He gave her a puzzled glance. "Why, sure it would."

"In that case—" she sighed "—I guess I don't mind."

They walked for a few minutes in silence and then Jack said, "About the pie supper Saturday night—"

"I couldn't possibly consider it."

"Consider what?"

"Attending with you." She refused to look at him, just kept walking as quickly as she could. "That is what you were about to ask, was it not?"

"Well, yes, it was." He sounded disappointed.

They walked on, and after a while he tried again. "Uh, Miss Rose, I wonder if you'd care to join me for dinner tonight at the Blue Bonnet. I—"

They'd reached the picket fence surrounding her little house and he escorted her to the front door, where at last she turned to face him. "I'm sorry, Marshal Guthrie, but I have prior commitments."

"I see." He took off his hat and turned it between his hands, staring down at it unhappily. "Sounds like you're still out of sorts with me for my forward remarks of yesterday."

Oh, Lord, was he going to start that again? "Not at all," she declared. "I haven't given that a single thought."

He looked up quickly. "I'm not sorry, you know."

"Sorry?" She blinked in confusion.

"Not sorry I asked you to marry me. And I'm going to go on asking you and asking you until—until you get tired of saying no."

His impassioned tone embarrassed and alarmed her. She glanced quickly around, although no one was in sight. "Marshal Guthrie—Jack, please don't say any more. We cannot possibly have a future together. I'm sorry, but it's true. You don't know—"

"I know everything!" He snatched up her hands and peered into her eyes with such longing that she stared back, mesmerized. "I know that you are the finest, most beautiful, most tender-hearted lady it has ever been my privilege to know. I'll place you on a pedestal where you belong and worship at your feet!"

"Oh, my God!" She had never been worshiped before. This was too awful; she felt faint. If there was one condition to which she had never aspired, it was sainthood.

Snatching her hands free, she backed away from him until she stood pressed against the door. "Doc's back and I think you should go see him. Perhaps your eyesight has failed—you obviously have me mixed up with some other girl!''

Turning, she threw open the front door and darted inside. Breathless and left horrified by the scene in which she'd just been an unwilling participant, she banged the front door behind her and leaned back against it, eyes shut, breathing labored.

He didn't try to follow her, praise the Lord. After a few minutes she heard his bootheels on the step announcing his departure. Slowly her breathing returned to normal and she sighed. What a mess! Jack was a fine man, no doubt about it. Under different circumstances, maybe...

She sighed again and opened her eyes.

There in the middle of the parlor, grinning at her, stood Jeremy Edwards.

"What are you doing here?" she gasped, one hand rising to press against her breast. Her cheeks were bright with color and her lips looked red and ripe as cherries.

"Damned if I know," Boone said truthfully. "I was in the neighborhood and thought I'd drop in to see if you'd calmed down any since our last meeting."

"I—I don't believe you." She walked past him and into the kitchen; he followed. "You're obviously spying on me."

That didn't strike Boone as unlikely as he wanted her to believe. "Now why would I do a thing like that?" he wanted to know.

"How do I know why you do anything?" She whirled to face him, bracing her hands behind her on the table. "Maybe you're spying on the marshal."

"Now why would I do a thing like that?" Boone repeated gently. She was as nervous as a cat in a roomful of rocking chairs, and although she probably didn't know why, he did. He took a step forward, stalking her. She swayed back, but the table trapped her.

Her chin lifted proudly. "Maybe you want to shoot him, too!"

Boone's grin grew wider. "And maybe I don't. Maybe I don't enjoy shootin' people near as much as I like...other things."

Her angry brown eyes narrowed suspiciously. "What other things?"

"Oh, things like picking flowers...watching sunsets..."

She gave an incredulous if unladylike snort. Lifting both arms, she crossed her wrists between her breasts, shoulders tilting forward protectively. Nervous—she was very, very nervous.

He reached out slowly and gently and touched her cheek with his fingertips, not surprised when she jerked her head aside. But her gaze remained locked with his and she didn't try to run away.

"I can't believe...that flowers and sunsets are your favorite things," she burst out.

"They're not," he agreed. He stepped so close to her that he could feel the heat of her body and knew she could feel the heat of his. "My favorite thing is making love."

Before she could digest that, he swept her into his arms and crushed her mouth with his. Almost instantly her lips parted, and he thrust his tongue past the barrier of her teeth, aware on some level that something had changed here. When he'd kissed her last night in the marshal's office, he'd have sworn she didn't even know such things as deep, intimate kisses existed.

Either she was a hell of a fast learner or he'd totally misjudged her, he thought as she rose on tiptoe and slid her arms around his neck. Holding her by the waist, he lifted her more tightly against his throbbing groin and ravished her mouth, exploring and coaxing and demanding.

And she followed his lead, shyly perhaps, but without undue maidenly modesty. She was eager to learn what he could teach her, making no protest even when he slid one hand down to caress the curve of her buttock and press her harder against him.

He lifted his head and looked down at her. She stood with her face turned toward his, eyes closed and mouth moist and trembling. Her body was flattened against his from chest to knee, and that trembled, too—with wanting.

She was a compete enigma to him—a passionate virgin who'd reached the advanced age of twenty-two. And they called *him* mysterious!

She opened her eyes and they were glazed with desire, just the way he'd longed to see them. Damn! She smiled. "Why don't you kiss me again?" she whispered dreamily. "I wouldn't mind...."

That was pretty damned obvious. He started to answer and realized his voice was backed up somewhere in the pit of his stomach. He took a deep breath and made another start. "No need," he croaked. "I've proved my point."

She blinked and her body stiffened. "I don't understand. What have you proven?"

"That it's a damned good thing you're not going to marry Jack Guthrie." Boone reached around behind his neck and gently pried her arms away. "Because, sweetheart, he's not near man enough for you."

He turned and walked out the door, leaving her standing there drowning in shock and shame. She threw open the door and stared after him, hating him.

Wanting him ... to return and finish what he'd started in her dreams and continued in her kitchen.

Wondering if he meant to suggest that he *was* man enough for her.

Frightened, she scrubbed her wrist across her mouth, trying to erase the imprint of his kiss. The taste of him remained in her mouth. With despair, she suspected that it always would.

Chapter Nine

Boone opened the door to Doc Beatty's office and slipped inside. He'd given this visit considerable thought since he left Miss Rose Taggart slumped all weak and willing against her kitchen table. He might be making a hell of a mistake but he wasn't the kind of man to stand back and just let events take their course.

Doc looked up from a thick volume spread open before him on a rolltop desk. The light of the kerosene lamp deepened the already deep lines on his craggy face.

He nodded. "Howdy, Boone," he said. "I been about halfway expectin' you."

"Howdy, Doc." Uninvited, Boone draped his tall frame on the chair beside the desk. "Thought it was you."

"Ditto, my boy. Quite a surprise, I might add. Last I heard you were doin' some ranchin' in ... Colorado Territory, I believe it was."

Boone nodded. "Tried, but it didn't take."

"So here you are in our little backwater Texas town, recovering from various injuries and wearin' an assumed name." Doc's eyes narrowed and he lifted the cup situated in his right hand. "I have to wonder—"

"Don't." Boone shook his head wearily. "I'm not on the dodge and there's no paper out on me that I know of.

A'course, after that little fracas in San Antone..." He shrugged.

"So you're still on the right side of the law." Doc nodded without surprise. He sipped from his mug, then seemed to remember that he hadn't offered refreshment to his guest. "Would you join me?"

"I'll pass."

"But it's coffee, my boy." Doc's jowly face quivered with wry humor. "I, too, left Wichita for another start."

"Hope yours took better than mine did."

Doc sighed. "Most of the time I think it did. Other times—but that's my misfortune and none'a your own. So tell me, if you've a mind to, what brought you to Texas?"

Boone hesitated. "When I left Colorado I drifted to Dodge where I hired on with an outfit headquartered near San Antone. Come to find out it wasn't my way with cows they were interested in."

Doc nodded wisely. "Your reputation preceded you, I suppose."

"Yep. While I was still debatin', the outfit they were fixin' to go to war with tried to hire me—good money for a man who could live to collect it."

"But you didn't seriously consider hiring out your gun to either side," Doc predicted. "I've known a whole passel of lawmen who did, one time or another, but not you. I saw how you felt when you almost killed that kid in Wichita." He shook his grizzled head vigorously. "Nah, you wouldn't consider that."

"You're wrong, Doc." Boone's soft voice penetrated to every corner of the small office. "I did consider it—hell, I still am." He sprang to his feet and began to prowl the confines of the small room. "What the hell else am I supposed to do? They won't let me start over."

"But you've made a start right here," Doc pointed out. "You've changed your name—"

Boone shook his head. "Not really. My name's Jeremy Edward Boone Smith. Even using just the first two, I'm still suspect. That storekeeper Curtis is convinced I'm hidin' something, which I am. So what the hell's the use? If I'm always gonna be an outsider, I might as well get some return on it. Because apparently somebody hung a sign on my back when I wasn't lookin' that says gunfighter."

"You don't think ridin' in here, smack-dab down the middle of main street, passin' out in the marshal's office with assorted bullet holes and knife wounds in your hide, might've give local folks a clue?" Doc's eyes crinkled with amusement. "Shootin' that cowboy over at the saloon pretty much cinched it, from what Rose tells me."

Rose. "If I thought I could ever escape my reputation..." His voice trailed off, for even he was uncertain as to what that would mean.

"Why not?" Doc wanted to know. "Maybe not here, but there are other places. Eastern cities—"

"I came from the east." Boone shook his head sharply. "I'll never go back."

"Then head on west," Doc suggested, the soul of reason. "Territories of New Mexico or Arizona, even all the way to California if that's what it takes."

"People are people, Doc. The ones here in Jones don't even know who I am and they're still leery of me." Boone paused in his pacing. "If they knew—"

"They won't hear it from me." Doc stood up, offering his hand. "You're a good man, Jeremy Edward Boone Smith. I seen all kinds and I know—hell, I've patched up all kinds, some I probably shouldn't. In the end, you'll do what's right."

Accepting the proffered hand, Boone wished he could be equally sure.

* * *

Diana spread out the length of fabric on Rose's kitchen table, smoothing it with one hand. She smiled at her sister-in-law. "I saw this at the C and J and thought of you," she said.

It was the same fabric Rose had intended to buy, before Mr. Curtis irritated her so. "It's lovely," she said. "I can't thank you enough."

Rose gave Diana a hug. At five foot two, Diana was a couple of inches the shorter, and she was also a year younger. But because she and James had been married for almost six months, she often assumed the role of Rose's mentor and guide.

As she did now. "I wish we had time to make it up for you to wear to the pie supper Saturday night," she said.

"I really don't plan to go," Rose confessed, folding the cloth into a neat bundle, "so there's no rush."

"Not go?" Diana planted her hands on her hips. "You've *got* to go! The money's going toward the church building fund. Everyone in town will be there!"

"That's what I'm afraid of. Do you have time for a cup of coffee before James comes to pick you up?"

"Of course." Diana lifted her chin, speaking like the judge's daughter she was. "And if not, he can just wait!"

Rose loved that about her Eastern born and bred sister-in-law. She seemed so fragile and ladylike—which she was—but at the same time, she had a will of iron. Placing cups and saucers on the table, Rose wadded her apron around the handle of the coffeepot steaming at the back of the cookstove.

"So how is my big brother?" she inquired, pouring the coffee.

Diana laughed and sat down. "Fit to be tied. He heard about what happened at the marshal's office after the shooting."

Rose frowned. "What happened?"

"Rose Taggart, everybody in town knows that gunman grabbed you and kissed you silly! It's a good thing Marshal Guthrie is as civilized as he is—and also that he's held in such high regard in this town—or there'd have been even more trouble over it. And let me tell you, when James heard, it was all I could do to keep him from thrashing Mr. Edwards within an inch of his life!"

Rose felt a flare of alarm. "Thank heaven you stopped him!"

Diana gave her sister-in-law a pained glance. "Surely you don't believe that James would have trouble subduing— Oh!" Her blue eyes widened. "Do you think Mr. Edwards would have resorted to gunplay?"

"I don't know, but with James's arm just out of a cast, I don't think it would have been a good idea to find out." Privately, she thought that Mr. Edwards would make mincemeat out of James whether the weapon be guns, knives or fists; at the very least, it would be a confrontation between an amateur and a professional. She shivered at the thought.

"I hadn't thought of that." Diana sipped her coffee, then cocked her head and smiled. "Mr. Edwards really is an...*intriguing* individual. I find myself almost morbidly fascinated by his doings. So handsome and manly." She winked at Rose over the rim of her cup. "What a shame he's socially unacceptable."

"Yes." More of a shame than Diana realized. What would she think if Rose told her about Mr. Edwards's visit here last night? Right here in this kitchen, he had leaned her over the table and— Rose bit her lip. She longed to confide in her sister-in-law but couldn't bring herself to do so.

Besides, any tentative relationship she might have had with the gunfighter was now out of the question. There would be nothing more to tell.

But after James had called for Diana and Rose was once more alone, she wondered. Didn't gunfighters need love, too? Didn't they ever marry and have children?

She gasped and clapped one hand over her mouth at the very thought, but that didn't drive it away. Didn't gunfighters ever marry and *reform?* Jeremy Edwards wasn't tied to this town or even to this state. If he wanted to, he could take her away—to Great-Aunt Marie in New Orleans, for instance.

If he wanted to, he could probably take her . . . anywhere.

Boone Smith sat all alone in the Yellow Rose, drinking and brooding. With the exception of Tonio Ryan, Marshal Jack Guthrie had been the only man in town willing to associate with him, and now even that tenuous relationship was a thing of the past.

Boone hated the way other men steered clear of him, purely hated it. He was damned tired of being treated like a sidewinder always on the prod. When he'd worn a badge it'd been much the same, the only difference being that he was younger then and didn't mind quite so much.

Hell, he hadn't minded at all. He'd swaggered with the best of them, enjoying the admiration of the young bucks and the grudging respect of the old bucks. Now he'd give just about anything to be treated like a plain old cowboy.

Easy to say, since he had very little: the proceeds from the sale of his ranch in a bank in Dodge City, his horse and outfit. Not much to show for his years of hard living.

"Bourbon—leave the bottle," he instructed the bartender, banging his glass down on the polished mahogany. No wife, no children, no one who would care if he got his brains shot out tomorrow.

"Hello, Mr. Edwards."

The soft, feminine voice sent a shiver coursing up his spine and he turned slowly. Libby stood there, smiling uncertainly. Most of the redness and swelling had left her face, and in a soft gray dress with ivory lace at the sleeves and collar, she looked far different from the tawdry green-satin-clad woman he'd rescued just a few days ago.

"Mrs. Bowman." He dipped his chin in acknowledgment. "Would you care to join me for a drink?"

Libby glanced around quickly. At mid-afternoon on a Friday, the bar was nearly empty but it would begin to fill with rowdy cowboys soon. At a faro table in back, a gambler idly shuffled cards. Junius Cox snored off a drunk on the floor at the far end of the bar. Libby was the only woman in evidence, although a couple of others also worked the Rose.

"Why don't *you* join *me?*" she asked in that same soft voice. "We could go upstairs—"

Hell, he didn't want her feeling obliged. "You don't owe me a thing, Mrs. Bowman," he began. "It's not necess—"

"Perhaps not, Mr. Edwards, but it would please me a great deal if you would indulge me."

Why not? Boone wondered. He was tired of being alone, and here was an attractive woman practically begging for his company. He'd be an idiot not to accept.

She held out her hand with a smile. He took it and she led him toward the stairs.

Once in her room, she pulled out a bottle and two glasses and set them on the small table near the window.

"Very nice," he said, looking around. The room was small but neat and clean, and it was at the front of the establishment with a window overlooking the street. The bed covering was a deep green with heavy gold fringe, and neatly made up.

She handed him a glass of bourbon and lifted her own for a toast. "To a fine gentleman who just happens to be handy with a gun."

Boone dipped his head in acknowledgment and sipped. His throat was nicely anesthetized from the whiskey he'd had downstairs. "Thanks," he said, "but I didn't do that much. You should probably be thanking the marshal instead of me. He's the one helped you—I just gave him a hand."

"Perhaps." She waved toward a small straight-backed chair. "Please, have a seat."

He did as directed, although it went against the grain with the restlessness upon him this way. Sitting still took a major effort until she caught his glance, smiled again and set her glass on the table. Gazes locked, she reached for the lace collar of her dress and unbuttoned it.

"I came to Jones five years ago," she said in a conversational tone. Her fingers worked on the buttons while she talked. "I brought my five-year-old daughter with me, and for almost a year she stayed in a little room at the end of the hall. Then one night a drunk wandered in and—well, the next day I sent her back north to my people in Kansas City."

Boone watched the pale expanse of her breasts rise above the white cotton of her camisole as button after button fell open. How'd she do that, undress while carrying on a completely unrelated conversation?

"She couldn't have stayed with me much longer anyway. She was beginning to ask questions I couldn't answer." Libby lifted her wrists, one at a time, to unfasten the cuffs. "I miss her, though. Is there someone far away that you miss, Mr. Edwards?"

He took another drink before answering truthfully, "No." Not far away.

Libby pulled her arms from the sleeves and began to tug at the bodice. Rolling her shoulders and wiggling her hips, she managed to get the dress down around her waist, her plain white cotton camisole stretching taut across her generous breasts.

Boone watched the peeling away of layers of fabric with a feeling almost of detachment. Libby was an attractive and available woman, no doubt about that, but was he really interested in a quick coupling? He should be—it'd been a while for him and he was a man of strong appetites.

Take that kiss he'd shared last night with Rose Taggart. He might be worried about his masculinity if the very thought of her didn't bring with it a rush of desire. Too bad she was as pure as the driven snow. Too bad she wasn't the woman panting with the effort of getting her clothes off so she could bed him.

With a final shove, the gray dress landed in a pool of fabric at Libby's feet and she stood before him clad in camisole, petticoats, stockings, shoes and corset—hardly more exposed than when she was working down below. She looked at him with a triumphant smile on her face, a smile that died almost instantly.

"What is it?" she asked, still breathless from the tussle to disrobe. "Have I offended you?" She frowned at her body, as if surprised it had betrayed her. An expression of dismay touched her face. "Surely you're not one of those men who prefer—"

Boone choked on his whiskey. "No."

"Then it's just me, I guess." Stepping out of the circle of her dress, she walked to a wardrobe and extracted a dressing gown, which she pulled on. Whirling, she said in a low, passionate voice, "It isn't all gratitude, you know."

"Isn't it?"

She shook her head forcefully. "You've always treated me like a lady. I wanted to see how you'd treat me in bed."

"Maybe some other time," Boone said thickly. He was still thinking of Rose. He set his empty whiskey glass on the table, and Libby jumped to refill it.

"Then is there anything else I can do for you?" she asked plaintively. "I can't think what it might be."

Boone could. "You've been here five years, you say?"

She nodded.

"Then maybe you can tell me a little about the town ... and the people in it."

"Oh." With a sigh, she sat across from him in the only other chair in the room. "I see. You want to know about Miss Rose."

"Now how the hell—"

"I heard about the kiss. I guess everyone in town has."

"Well, hell, it was just a kiss." Disgusted, Boone glanced out the window. Marshal Guthrie stood on the boardwalk opposite, talking to Tonio Ryan. Damn kid, like a shadow, he was. He glanced toward the window behind which Boone sat, no doubt telling the marshal that the gunman was extracting his reward at that very moment. And the marshal would tell Rose—

Boone swung toward Libby. "Yeah, I'd like to know about Miss Rose. For one thing, she probably saved my life when I first hit town. For another ... God damn it, why hasn't she already married the marshal and had a houseful of kids?"

"Don't you know about Billy?"

"*Everybody* knows about Billy." Boone rolled his eyes. "At least, everyone knows he was her one true love. It surprises me—" He gave Libby a narrow glance. "May I speak frankly?"

"Please do."

"It surprises me to find such devotion on the part of a woman toward a man she never even slept with."

Libby gasped. Her lips parted as if she meant to say something but caught herself in time.

Boone's interest sparked. "Don't hold out on me, Miss Libby. What were you about to say?"

Her lips tightened. "I like Miss Rose," she said staunchly. "I'd never say anything to hurt her in any way."

Boone nodded. "I overheard what happened at the C and J yesterday," he told her. "I'm not interested in hurtin' Miss Rose, I'm interested in *understandin'* her. Did you know Billy Curtis?"

"I . . . knew him."

"Well, well, well. That's very interesting. What'd you think of him?"

She shrugged. "He was nice enough. A handsome boy, and he knew it. Once in a while he got likkered up and when he did, he could be . . . indiscreet."

"A common failing when a man's in bed with a beautiful woman," Boone murmured smoothly.

She flashed him a grateful smile, which quickly slipped away. "I just don't want to say anything that will hurt Miss Rose. You don't . . . I mean, you wouldn't . . . You won't tell her I told, will you?"

"No." He saw her struggling with her moral dilemma and knew he should put her mind at ease but he also knew he wouldn't. Whatever she knew about Rose Taggart, he intended to find out. Period.

Libby bit her lip. "You see, Billy and Miss Rose were more than friends—*much* more."

Boone felt his mouth fall open in astonishment, and he snapped it closed again. "Are you sure?" he asked dubiously. "Couldn't Billy have just been a braggart?"

"He could have but he wasn't. You see, he'd been working up his nerve to propose to her for weeks and he was coming to see me all . . . excited, if you know what I mean."

Boone swallowed hard. "I know."

"A few days later I heard they were engaged and then—nothing. I didn't see him for a couple of weeks. When I did, he couldn't wait to get up here." She gestured toward the bed. "When he gave me time to catch my breath, I asked him why and he said—well, he said that the day they got engaged she let him do it. They were back in Diablo Canyon and he apparently talked her into it. He was pretty proud of that, especially since she was a virgin. Because he planned to marry her, he didn't want to hurt her reputation by spreading it around, about his conquest. But after that once, she got scared and that's when he came back to me. And two days later, he was dead.''

''Do you think he told anyone else?''

''Oh, no! It was all right to tell *me* because who would I repeat it to? And if I did, who would believe me?''

''I would,'' Boone said softly. He was remembering: the way Rose slipped her arms around his neck, the way her soft lips parted beneath his, the way her hips pressed into his.

''You won't tell, will you?'' Libby leaned forward, wringing her hands together in her lap, which had the effect of deepening the cleavage between her breasts.

Nope. Telling was not how Boone intended to use the information.

''But I don't *want* to go to the pie supper!'' Rose wailed for the third or fourth time. ''I told Marshal Guthrie I *couldn't* go to the pie supper. Why are you doing this to me?''

Diana, seated on Rose's left on the buckboard seat, glanced at her husband in the driver's seat. ''Because I didn't slave over that hot stove all day making two box suppers to have one of them go to waste.''

''One of them's already wasted,'' James grumbled. ''Why I should have to bid on my own wife's cookin' is beyond me.''

''It's for the church building fund,'' Diana reminded him patiently. ''No one will bid against you, so think of it as a donation. But don't insult me by bidding less than a dollar, you hear? Why, back in San Antonio it would have cost you at least five dollars to eat with me!''

James smiled at his pretty blue-eyed wife. "And worth every penny of it, too."

Rose, seated between them, felt more than a little out of place. She'd made every excuse she could think of and they weren't having any of them, so here she was, on her way to the pie supper.

Would *he* be there? Don't be ridiculous, she scolded herself. A church pie supper was not the place you'd find a mangy gunfighter. He'd more likely be at the Yellow Rose.

James stuck his elbow in her ribs and she jumped, then glared at him in irritation. "What?"

"Did I tell you what I heard about that mangy gunfighter?" he inquired.

Rose's heart lurched and her pulse speeded up. "No, what?"

"Guess I don't have to worry about him botherin' you anymore."

Rose tossed her head. "You never did, but go on. Why not?"

"Because—" he leaned toward her, almost whispering "—he's spendin' most of his free time at the Yellow Rose."

Rose felt let down. "Goodness, James, a lot of men do that."

James grinned and raised one eyebrow. "Upstairs? In the company of Mrs. Libby Bowman?" He reined the horses toward the rigs parked near the little church on the hill just outside town. "I hear Mrs. Bowman is *very* grateful to him for shootin' that cowboy who was abusin' her. And I further hear Mrs. Bowman ain't backward about showin' her appreciation."

"James!" Diana, who had been leaning close to listen, bolted upright, her cheeks red. "That's no way to speak to your sister!"

"It certainly isn't," Rose agreed, disgusted with what James had just implied.

Mr. Edwards and Mrs. Bowman, doing what Rose had once done with Billy Curtis—offensive images floated in and out of her mind and she felt herself growing hot and flustered. When James pulled the team to a halt, she jumped up and nearly fell over Diana's feet in an attempt to exit first. Diana squeaked a protest and James made a grab for Rose's arm and missed.

"Hold your horses, Rose," he grumbled, jumping to the ground and hurrying around the buckboard to lend her a hand.

Which was no longer needed. As if waiting for them to arrive, Jeremy Edwards stepped up, put his hands on Rose's waist and swung her to the ground. Where had he been hiding, she wondered, to appear so precipitously?

Red-faced and embarrassed by what she'd just heard about him, Rose yanked away and smoothed her skirt of navy blue faille over her hips. She refused to look at him, instead turning toward her brother as he approached from the rear of the rig.

"Edwards, I'll thank you—"

"Yes, thank you," Rose cried, subverting James's intent. She turned abruptly and reached up to offer a hand to Diana.

Diana stared at the three of them with a guarded expression on her face. Rose supposed her sister-in-law was taking in the greatly improved appearance of the gunfighter, now clad in crisp white shirt and black string tie worn with a black broadcloth suit. Freshly shaved, black hair gleaming, he looked—Rose swallowed hard and refused to take further inventory.

Boone tipped his hat and a grin tugged at his lips. "Ladies, Taggart." He ambled away without another word.

Rose let out the breath she didn't know she'd been holding. "My goodness," she exclaimed, "I didn't think *he'd* be here."

"His money can build church pews right along with ours," Diana said tartly. She let her husband lift her to the ground and fastidiously arranged the train of her gown, a much more elaborate affair than Rose's.

Made of cream-colored faille with an overdress of cream and white striped India silk, the gown was trimmed with red bows and cream-colored lace. Diana had brought it with her when she came to the Rocking T as James's wife, and knew she looked lovely in it.

In fact, all the women were soon clustering around Diana to admire the creation, which was by far the most stylish in attendance. Most of the women, like Rose, wore simple gowns made by themselves or by the local seamstress. But that didn't mean they didn't hunger for the latest fashions.

While James joined the men out back and Diana explained each detail of her gown, Rose carried the two supper baskets to the long table arranged beneath the trees beside the church. Nothing more than a couple of long boards on sawhorses, still the table looked festive with the variety of baskets it held. Shortly the minister would call everyone together and, following a short prayer for high bids, would auction off the baskets, whose owners would then dine with the winning bidder.

Biting her lip, Rose looked around. Jack Guthrie hadn't arrived yet and she was glad, because she didn't want him buying her basket and forcing her to listen to a whole meal's worth of undying love.

Her glance met Mr. Edwards's, and she jerked away, swallowing hard. He wouldn't...would he? Surely he'd not humiliate her by bidding on her basket! Frantically her glance swung around and came to rest on Tonio Ryan.

He lifted his hat and nodded, grinning at her. Tonio wouldn't dare bid on Sally's basket—her father would kill him if he did—so why shouldn't he bid on Rose's? Quickly

Rose crossed the clearing to his side and stepped close to him.

Pulling a five-dollar bill from the pocket in the seam of her skirt, she dropped her arm to her side and thrust the money into his hand. He recoiled, giving her an incredulous glance.

"Buy the basket on the end—the one with the pink bow," she ordered beneath her breath.

He frowned. "But—"

"Don't argue with me—just do it." She took a step away, then swung to face him. "*Please.*"

He owed her. He'd have to do it, she thought with satisfaction as she joined the other women.

Chapter Ten

"*Sold,* to James Taggart for two bucks and two bits—one larrupin' good supper basket put up by—" Reverend Salt looked around innocently. "Now which one'a you lovely ladies claims the right to dine with this fine-lookin' feller?"

Diana came forward, feigning modesty, while her friends clapped and applauded. Accepting the basket offered by the preacher, she turned to James.

"I do declare, I had no idea *you* would buy my basket," she said in a mock-Southern accent. "Just don't think you've bought anything more than fried chicken and apple pie!"

James, in the spirit of the thing, offered an aside to his friends. "That's what *she* thinks! I'll get my money's worth, you can count on it." Amidst general laughter, he claimed his bride and his supper.

Lingering behind the cluster of men, Boone heard the comment and smiled to himself. He, too, planned to get his money's worth.

"Only a few baskets to go," Reverend Salt continued. He picked up the basket with the pink bow and looked inside. "Something mighty familiar about these eats," he said, a grin on his thin face. "Kinda remind me of what Miz Taggart brung, right down to the lace on the napkins, but I don't suppose that makes no never mind."

He winked at Rose, who groaned and rolled her eyes. Holding the basket aloft, he offered it to the highest bidder.

Boone saw Rose glance surreptitiously toward the knot of men and boys, locate Tonio and give the faintest of nods.

"One dollar!" the boy shouted, waving his hand to get the preacher's attention. The men around him hooted and slapped him on the back.

Reverend Salt beamed. "I got a dollar—who'll make it two?" He looked around, his smile changing to a frown. "Now where's that marshal of ours? I kinda thought he might be interested in this particular basket."

"Fight over to th' saloon," someone called. "He ain't back yet."

The preacher looked disappointed. "You gentlemen ain't gonna let that boy take this prize for a measly dollar!" he exclaimed. "Who'll gimme two?"

Rose was squirming but trying not to let it show. Boone, who'd overheard her instructions to Tonio, could see her embarrassment that it might go for as little as one dollar and only one bid. Tonio grinned and shrugged, no doubt pleased at the prospect of a four-dollar profit on the deal.

"Somebody fetch the marshal!" a male voice called from the pack, and laughter erupted.

"Guess that's it, then," Reverend Salt admitted sadly. "A dollar is bid by the young gentleman under the tree. Going once . . . going twice. . . ."

"Ten dollars."

Stupid gesture, Boone thought, when he could have had it for five-fifty. But the astonished buzz his bid created made it worth every penny of the inflated offer. He stepped forward into the clearing before the auctioneer, instantly the object of attention.

Boone's attention centered on Rose Taggart. At the sound of his voice she turned pale; then her cheeks blushed fire red.

He could see the progression, her first shocked reaction quickly giving way to a flash of pride at the high price her basket had brought; the pride fading in turn before the realization of what it meant—sharing a meal with the man who was the scandal of Jones, Texas.

Reverend Salt called for order, then turned twinkling eyes on Boone. "Mercy me, that's the high bid for the evenin'. Anyone want to stand between this gentleman and his fried chicken? Do I hear a higher bid? No? Didn't think so—sold! Come up here and collect your prize, sir. And you, Miss Rose Taggart, I'd say this gentleman has bought and paid for a whole lot of sparklin' conversation from you this evenin'."

Sally Curtis gave Rose a shove. "Lucky you," the girl exclaimed. "Now I don't know *who'll* be left to buy *my* box."

Nobody clapped as Rose moved reluctantly forward to meet the successful bidder; nobody seemed especially pleased except Reverend Salt. He held out the basket with a flourish and both Boone and Rose reached for it, their hands meeting over the handle. Rose hastily pulled away and Boone took the basket.

"Miss Rose," he murmured, "it is indeed an honor." Offering his arm, he led her to the edge of the crowd.

A flurry across the way announced a new arrival, and then Jack Guthrie's unhappy voice was heard. "What do you mean, her basket is gone? Goldarn it, I thought—"

Rose, one hand still resting uneasily on the curve of Boone's arm, half turned, her glance anxious.

Boone raised his brows in inquiry. "You want to speak to the marshal?" he guessed.

She shook her head quickly. "If you don't mind, I'd like to see who buys Sally's basket."

"Of course." He was in no hurry. The longer this dragged out, the more time he'd spend in her company. Why that

appealed to him he wasn't quite sure, but it did. Maybe he
just wanted to get her goat, or maybe he wanted to see how
far he could push her.

Or maybe...just maybe he enjoyed being around her. He
sure as hell hoped that wasn't it.

Reverend Salt picked up an offering tied with red ribbon. "Now here's a pretty box and I bet a pretty girl packed
it. What am I bid—"

"Five dollars!" Tonio Ryan stepped forward, waving
aloft the bill Rose had sneaked to him earlier. He glanced
defiantly around the circle of startled faces.

"No!" George Curtis lunged into the clearing, his face
beet red. "No daughter of mine will slave over a hot stove
for a—"

"George Curtis, you mind your manners!" Now it was
the preacher getting his dander up. "The boy's buyin' a
meal, not a wife! Remember, we are all God's creatures—
sold! To Tonio Ryan, one supper and nothin' more!"

Tonio sauntered forward, giving the storekeeper a challenging stare. Sally tugged at her father's sleeve.

"Papa, the preacher said it was all right. Papa, it's not my
fault! I didn't even know he had that kind of money!"

George shook her hand away. "You eat and you eat fast,
you hear me? And I want you right there, on those church
steps where everybody in town can keep an eye on the goin's
on!"

"Yes, Papa!" Sally almost skipped to take her place beside Tonio, who waited for her before the preacher. She gave
the boy a sidelong half smile filled with satisfaction.

Rose sighed. "All right, we may as well go and get this
over with," she announced grimly. "Do you see a place we
can sit?" Chin high, she gave Boone that imperious glance
that always made him want to laugh, but this time there was
a different edge to it.

Or did he simply think so because he knew her secret?

* * *

Rose sat on a tree stump at the edge of the church clearing, a lace-trimmed linen napkin spread across her lap. Mr. Edwards sat on the grass at her feet, his long legs sprawled out on one side and the picnic basket on the other.

Leaning over, she rummaged through the contents of the basket. He'd already eaten enough for two men. "Would you care for another piece of chicken, Mr. Edwards?" she asked sweetly.

"No, thank you, Miss Rose. But I could do with a slice of that apple pie."

"Of course." Drat—Diana had neglected to pack anything with which to serve the dessert. Forced to use her fingers, Rose managed to extract a wedge nearly intact. She leaned down to deposit it on the napkin laying beside him on the grass, pie filling clinging to her fingers.

Glancing up triumphantly, she found herself looking straight into his eyes—gray, clear as crystal and only inches away.

"Allow me to assist you," he murmured.

Before she could protest, he caught her hand and lifted it to his mouth. His tongue flicked out and proceeded to lick off the apple filling clinging to her fingers.

She gasped and her scalp tightened; for an instant, she thought she might faint from the pure, erotic pull of what he was doing to her. Her fingers had never been in a man's mouth before, and the way it made her feel seemed downright indecent. She wanted to pull away indignantly but found herself incapable of any movement whatsoever.

"There," he said with a satisfaction she could see in his face as well as hear in his voice. "Good as new." He placed her limp, damp hand on her lap and reached for the pie.

Rose almost choked on her own breath; no part of her seemed to be working correctly, including her mind. What was this man, a warlock? He kept her constantly off stride, and she wasn't much good at defense.

Maybe against him, there *was* no defense.

"Enjoying yourselves?"

She looked up, surprised to see Marshal Guthrie standing there looking glum. "I've had better times," she burst out.

"And will again," Mr. Edwards added smoothly, "maybe soon." His grin was cheeky. "Care to join us for a bite of chicken?" he asked Jack.

The marshal shook his head. "Way I look at it, that's my dinner you're eating, Edwards. Enjoy it, because it's the last one you'll ever eat with Miss Rose, if I have my way." He gave her a glance at once anxious and resolute.

Mr. Edwards shrugged. "When a lady puts herself on the block, she has to take what she gets." He popped the last bite of pie into his mouth, eating it with much gusto. "If you didn't drop by for food, what're you after, Marshal?"

"Oh, yeah." Remembering his mission, Jack turned to Rose. "Doc came up a few minutes ago. He's already had a nip or two and now he's out back there with a bunch of the boys and a jug. Thought you'd want to know."

Rose groaned. "Poor Doc. It's been ages since he went on a bender. I wonder what set him off?"

She glanced at her companion, not because she expected him to have an opinion on the matter but just to include him in the conversation as a point of etiquette. His face had grown set and hard, and he immediately stood up.

He looked down at Rose and he wasn't smiling. "Thank you for a most pleasant meal," he said, tipping his hat. "May I escort you back to your brother or—" He glanced pointedly at Jack.

"Why, I—" Confused, she, too, stood up. "Please don't trouble yourself further. I'll just pack up the basket—"

As she turned, she saw Doc Beatty and George Curtis approaching. Doc's craggy face looked flushed and excited, while George still seemed angry, no doubt at the preacher's interference.

The two new arrivals greeted Rose and she wondered why she felt such a sensation of impending doom. With uncertainty, she nodded toward Jeremy Edwards. "Doctor Beatty, I don't believe you've met Mr.—"

"Edwards." The gunman stuck out his hand. "Jeremy Edwards."

Doc looked down at the proffered hand, and Rose could almost feel the agonizing slowness with which his brain worked. He looked up at Jeremy Edwards and frowned.

"Why, sure," he mumbled. He shook the other man's hand heartily and announced in loud tones, "I just got back from *Wichita.* Nice place, *Wichita.*"

"So I hear." Jeremy Edwards stood absolutely still, so still that he seemed curiously detached from the rest of them. "I'm about to find myself some liquid refreshment, if you care to join me, Doc Beatty. You can tell me all about your trip."

"Good idea," Doc agreed readily. "Been a lot of changes since you had your trouble there, Boone. Yeah, lotta changes since the railhead moved on west. Dodge City's the place these days, so they tell me—"

The old man blinked and stopped talking, as if suddenly realizing he'd lost his audience.

"Boone, the Kansas gunfighter? Damnation!" George Curtis slapped his thigh triumphantly. "I knew you was one of the big ones." He grabbed the other man's hand and shook it heartily. "Glad to meet you, Mr. Boone. Glad you've decided to spend a spell in our little town."

Boone. Was that really his name? Rose stared at the man she knew as Jeremy Edwards, feeling an unexpected and unwarranted sense of betrayal. Couldn't he at least have told *her* the truth?

But almost immediately she saw the flaw in that, since he knew very well that she'd been bombarded by questions about him from the first day.

Doc raised one shaky hand to his mouth. "Oops." He looked guilty as sin. "Sorry, Boone, it just slipped out."

Boone gave a disgusted grunt. "What the hell?" he declared philosophically. "It was bound to happen. I'd have liked to tell some people myself—" he glanced at Rose "—but we don't always get what we want."

"Confound it!" Jack glowered at the newly revealed gunfighter. "Now I'll have to go through that stack of wanted posters again."

His disgusted glance settled on something over Rose's left shoulder and he lunged forward, shouting, "Hey, you men stop that! I told you there'd be no— Excuse me, folks."

"I gotta go, too," George said quickly. "Gotta see a man about a horse." He gave an unpleasant laugh and took off in the opposite direction, leaving Rose, Doc and the gunman alone.

Doc looked appropriately shamefaced. "I'm real sorry," he said, slurring his words. "I shouldn't'a had that last drink, only George Curtis always has the best liquor in the county."

"Forget it, Doc. The damage is done." Boone turned to Rose with a slight bow. "Care to dance, Miss Rose? That way everyone can get a good look at me all at once."

Rose started; she hadn't even realized the music had begun. Glancing around, she saw that the musicians were stationed at the edge of a clearing often used for community events. The feet of many dancers had worn away the grass, leaving a hard-packed surface.

She also saw George Curtis circulating through the crowd, whispering in one ear after another. It was almost funny, the way heads popped around to get a look at a real gunfighter.

Boone raised one brow sardonically. "Of course, if you'd rather not be associated with a bona fide badman—"

"Mr.—"

"Boone. Just Boone."

"Mr. Boone, I would be glad to dance with you."

Lifting her chin, she offered him her hand. He took it and led her to the exact center of the dancing area, where he turned to face her. "All right, Miss Rose," he said with a rakish grin, "let's give 'em something to talk about."

Placing his hand at her waist, he whirled her into a swooping turn around the floor.

He was a wonderful dancer, Rose quickly realized. He moved with a lightness that carried her along, aided by the guidance of his warm, strong fingers pressing into the curve of her waist. He held her with just the proper degree of closeness, but without undue familiarity.

Dancing had never been such fun! She was breathless and excited, and her feet flew faster and faster. She was a good dancer and knew it, but she'd never been this good before—or enjoyed it this much.

The music ended, and he spun her to a stop. Her bosom heaved with the force of her breathing, and she knew her face must be red and damp from exertion, but she didn't care; it had been wonderful!

He bowed over her hand. "Thank you," he said gravely, not even short of breath. "Perhaps you'll honor me with another dance later."

If she'd held a fan she would have fluttered it at him. "Perhaps." She smiled, realized everyone was watching her and tried to wipe it away.

Boone escorted her to the edge of the clearing, straight to her brother and sister-in-law. Tipping his hat, he left her.

James glowered. "That was some display you just made of yourself," he snapped. "Dancing with some two-bit gunfighter."

Diana stamped her foot, her normally placid expression angry. "Stop it, James. She was wonderful and so was he! I haven't seen such dancing since I came west. If Mr. Boone asks *me* to dance, I'm certainly going to jump at the chance."

Rose gave the other woman a grateful glance. "He is good, isn't he?" she said shyly.

"No better than you are. You looked as if you were having a wonderful time, Rose. When he swooped you around that far corner—"

"Women! You can find the doggondest things to get excited about." James turned away. "I want a word with Tonio. Back in a minute."

Diana watched him go, shaking her head. "I swan, James can be such—such an old man, sometimes. Before we were married he loved to dance and now I can hardly get him on a dance floor."

"Well, smile at Mr. Boone and maybe he'll ask you. That'll change James's tune quick enough!"

The two women laughed together. Before the sound had died away, Rose felt a light touch on her elbow. She turned in surprise to find a man she didn't know standing there.

Her first impression was that he needed a shave; her second, that a bath wouldn't be wasted. Although he was young—maybe no more than his late teens—she didn't like his eager expression.

"Miz Rose, how about a dance?" he demanded more than asked, his lips curling back over yellow teeth.

She frowned. "I don't believe we've met," she observed haughtily. "I don't care to dance with strangers."

"Name's Curly Anderson, from over Crystal Springs way. C'mon, now." He gave her arm a tug.

"Unhand her, you lout." Diana swept him with her scornful gaze. "Don't you understand English? She doesn't care to dance with you!"

Curly Anderson's brow lowered threateningly and his grip on Rose's forearm tightened. "Why not? Ain't I as good as some Kansas gunfighter?"

Rose tried to soothe his ruffled feelings. "That's not what she meant at all, Mr. Anderson." With her free hand, she tried to pry his fingers from her arm, without success.

"I certainly did," Diana corrected. She took a step after them, for he was slowly and inexorably pulling Rose toward the other dancers who had taken the floor. "Will you let her go or will I have to—" she stopped, apparently at a loss for an appropriate threat, then added triumphantly "—call my husband?"

"No need to bother Mr. Taggart." Boone appeared beside them, his expression solemn but not worried. "I suspect Mr. Anderson may be looking for me, anyway."

"No, he wants me to—" Confused, Rose looked from one man to the other and saw Boone was right. Curly Anderson's face held a crafty expression, and he grinned.

"I heard'a you," Anderson said, looking straight at Boone. "I used to run with an ol' boy knew you up Colorado way."

"That right? Turn the lady loose and we'll talk about it."

"Naw, I don't wanna talk about it. I wanna dance."

He yanked Rose into his arms, hard against his chest. It knocked the breath out of her momentarily, but most of all it made her mad—fighting mad. Without pausing to consider what she was doing, she stamped down hard on the booted toe of the man causing all the commotion.

Anderson grunted and turned her loose, just as Boone grabbed her arm and hauled her aside. His glance met hers as if to ask, *Are you all right?*

"Yes," she gasped, "but—"

"No buts." He turned her toward Diana and gave her a not so gentle push. "He wants me, not you. Go with your sister-in-law."

Turning quickly, Boone faced Anderson. "Don't suppose you're in any mood to listen to reason."

"You tryin' to insult me?" Anderson demanded.

Diana came up behind Rose and grabbed her by the arms, pulling her away. Rose watched the two men, mesmerized with dread. They were going to pull their pistols at any moment and start shooting—she saw it in both their faces. Watching the drama play out before her, she suddenly wondered if Boone, this man who had stared death in the face time and time again, might be the one man in a million who could overlook an indiscretion such as hers.

If only he could! With her emotions stripped away to fundamentals by fear, she realized that she was more attracted to this gunfighter than to any man she'd ever met . . . more impressed, more—

"You in that big'a hurry to die?" Boone said softly to the youngster. "I don't think so."

With the speed of a striking rattler, he reached out and slapped the kid across the face, right and left. The boy pawed for his gun but Boone grabbed the barrel as it cleared the holster. The weapon exploded, one shot striking the punch bowl. Glass shattered, spraying lemonade all over the area.

Women screamed and men came running. Boone didn't wait for reinforcements; he dropped the kid with a solid right to the jaw. When Jack arrived on the scene, Boone stood over his fallen foe, angry and breathing hard.

"What do you think you're doing," Jack shouted, "starting gunplay at a church social? That does it, I'm running you in."

Rose pulled away from Diana and darted forward. "Marshal—Jack, you've got it all wrong. Boone didn't—"

"Boone, is it?" Jack included her in his disapproval. "Hiding behind a woman's skirts, are you? Well, this time I've got you and I want to know—"

The man on the ground groaned and rolled over. Boone straightened, and his furious glance slashed at the marshal. "Ah, figure it out," he snarled, whirling to walk away. Tonio fell into step behind him, as if guarding his hero's back.

"Wait just a blasted minute. You can't—"

Rose touched his arm urgently. "Let him go, Jack. It wasn't his fault. Diana and I saw the whole thing."

And as she explained, she watched the gunfighter walk away, followed by the slender form of the boy with a bad case of hero worship.

James and Diana drove Rose home from the church social well after dark had fallen. At the walk leading to her door, they let her off, then hesitated for a few moments.

"Am I supposed to thank you two for a lovely evening?" Rose asked with deceptive lightness. "Considering all that happened . . ."

James grunted. "You wouldn't have wanted to miss the fun, would you? 'Course, it's nothing to what it's likely to be before this is over."

"Before what is over?" Diana inquired innocently.

"This business about the gunfighter. After that little set-to, I overhead a bunch of fellas from over Crystal Springs way makin' threats."

Diana made a soft, disparaging sound. "Oh, that's nothing! The young men from Jones are always feuding with those from Crystal Springs, and vice versa. Nothing will come of it, you wait and see." She yawned. "Sure you won't come on home with us, Rose? Your old room's right there waiting."

''No, thanks. I've got a busy day ahead of me tomorrow so I'll just say good-night.''

Rose stood in the shadows and watched them drive away, James's arm stealing around the shoulders of his bride. Rose sighed with envy. What would it feel like, to belong to the one you loved? It was a feeling she was never likely to know.

She let herself in to the unlocked house. Without lighting a lamp, she made her way to her bedroom and sat on the edge of the bed, thinking.

Worrying.

What if the men from Crystal Springs meant what they said? What if even now they were plotting against Boone?

Or worse, what if they were lying in wait for him somewhere? She'd heard by way of the Jones grapevine that Boone was still sleeping in Fred Loveless's livery stable. Perhaps she should warn him.

What was she thinking? She couldn't go creeping up streets and down alleys in the middle of the night! What did she think she'd do, sit there in the livery stable in the dark and wait for him to return?

But then a better idea occurred to her. She could leave a note. That's what she could do, leave a note pinned to his bedroll. If what James had intimated was true—if Boone was spending a good deal of time with Libby Bowman over at the saloon—he wouldn't see the note until morning anyway. But that would be all right.

She would have done her duty. If he got the note in time to take defensive action, fine. If he didn't, at least she had tried.

Lighting the kerosene lamp beside her bed, she carried it into the parlor where she kept paper and pen.

That's what she'd do, write him a note. Simple. Nothing whatsoever wrong with that.

Chapter Eleven

Rose pressed into the shadows against the side of the livery stable, her heart pounding. Straining all her faculties, she concentrated on the low voices coming from inside.

It was easy enough to identify the speakers as George Curtis and Fred Loveless. But she couldn't make out a word of what they were saying.

Still, she was pretty sure they weren't meeting in the dead of night to discuss the weather. They had to be talking about Jeremy Edw—Boone, she corrected herself. She had to start thinking of him by his proper name, assuming that was his proper name.

The low voices inside became suddenly louder, and Rose tried to melt into the side of the building. Thank heaven she'd changed clothing, for she was sure her drab brown dress and gray crocheted shawl would go a long way toward concealing her presence.

George Curtis and Fred Loveless paused in the livery doorway. "We can't lose," she heard Mr. Curtis say with satisfaction. "There's bound to be a showdown. He shoots them, they shoot him—who cares as long as it takes place right here in Jones."

"Right here in Jones," Mr. Loveless agreed. "Then we'll be famous, get the county seat and that railroad line sure, and our troubles will be over."

Mr. Curtis grunted. "Most of 'em, anyway. I still gotta take care of that damn Injun-Mex kid chasin' after my little girl."

"Best way's to marry her off," Mr. Loveless advised. "Let her husband worry about it."

"She's too young!" Mr. Curtis protested. "But that other 'un ain't. Nosy old maid just goin' around stirrin' up trouble." He scuffed a toe on the hard-packed earth, and Rose could imagine the scowl on his face. "The marshal's a good man but she's his blind spot—he wants her, damned if I know why. She ain't gonna get that many more chances. You see the way she's been actin' all skittish and flappin' her eyes at that gunfighter? I don't approve of that a'tall, but it might be somethin' we can use to keep him hangin' around."

"Hangin' around. Yep, long's he's hot for her—but I dunno, George. From what I hear he's already got somethin' goin' over to th' Yella Rose."

The two men moved toward the street. Mr. Curtis's voice drifted back. "Then that gives us two chances to keep him around long enough to shoot or get shot, don't it?"

Rose stood in the shadows for several minutes longer, her cheeks burning with mortification. Obviously it was true—eavesdroppers always heard ill of themselves. And of everyone else, apparently. Tonio and Boone and Jack hadn't exactly come in for praise.

Dark night sounds surrounded her: the creak of wood, the occasional snorts of horses and the stamping of hooves in the stalls inside, the whir of insects. Still she hesitated, wondering if she should go on inside or turn and hurry home.

Think logically, she scolded herself. She already had the note in her hand; all she had to do was climb up the ladder leading to the loft and leave it on his bedroll. The presence of the two men below in Mr. Loveless's "office" assured her that Boone hadn't returned here after the church social.

They wouldn't have been talking about him so freely otherwise.

He had to be at the Yellow Rose, she decided glumly. Libby Bowman was probably filled with gratitude toward her savior, and she doubtless knew many ways to express it.

I'll go home and forget all about warning him, Rose decided, taking a tentative step away from the wall—just as the moon sailed majestically from behind the clouds. Jumping back, she again pressed herself into the shadows, terrified at the prospect of being seen. Suddenly it seemed safer to go forward than to retreat. Resolutely she slipped through the open doors and plunged into the blackness inside.

It took only a few minutes of groping progress to find the ladder to the loft. Hampered by her long skirts and petticoats, she struggled up, the note clenched between her teeth. Cautiously she poked her head through the square opening of the floor above.

It was pitch-black up here, except for the silvery square of moonlight visible through the open hay doors. By its light she saw Boone's bedroll spread out and waiting, but nothing more. Holding her breath, she tiptoed up the remaining rungs of the ladder.

Without warning, hands clamped around her waist and swung her the rest of the way. She let out a squeak of frightened protest just as a hand fastened over her mouth. Had she walked into an ambush? Was someone up here waiting for Boone? Twisting, she kicked out blindly, clawing at the hand covering her mouth.

"Ouch—damn it, it's me! Settle down!"

She recognized Boone's voice and slumped with relief. "Thank heaven! I thought—" She choked her words off, trying to control her erratic breathing.

"I can't wait to hear this." He sounded cynical but also amused. "You must have a good excuse for crawling around in the hayloft of a livery stable in the middle of the night, but I sure as hell don't know what it could be."

"If you'll come out where I can see you, I'll be happy to explain," she said into the black void at the back of the loft.

"Anything for a lady." He stepped into the light.

She immediately wished he hadn't. He wore denim pants and his gun belt strapped around his hips and that was it. No shirt, no shoes, no hat—just man. She swallowed hard and tried to think of something to say. And failed.

"Well?" He cocked his head.

She stared at the corded muscles of his flat abdomen, shadowed by moonlight. "Well, what?"

He laughed. "Well, what are you doing here? Is this a social call or did you have something . . . else in mind?"

She felt her face flush and was grateful for the cover of darkness. "I . . . I was going to leave you a note."

"Ah, a note." He crossed his arms over his chest. "Where is it?"

She blinked and looked around, naturally seeing nothing that looked even remotely like the note. "I don't know," she admitted helplessly. "Lost in the hay somewhere. I had it in my mouth and then you scared me and I screamed—"

"A likely story." His voice sounded as if he was all but laughing out loud at her. He stepped closer.

She raised her chin and glared at him. "Why else would I come? I'm taking quite a chance, you know. I have my reputation to think about."

"But your reputation doesn't do you justice, does it?" His low, intimate voice wrapped around her like a velvet cloak. "You're more than the old-maid busybody everybody takes you for, aren't you, Rose?"

"I . . . I don't know what you're talking about," she said stiffly, turning her head away. She couldn't bear to look at him, all silver-gilded and strong and tempting.

"Sure you do." He caught her chin with his fingers and turned her face toward his. "I'm talking about this."

He was going to kiss her; he made his intentions quite clear. And she—she, heaven help her!—stood there stiff as a stump and let it happen. When his mouth at last touched hers, she closed her eyes with a sigh and let him transport her to another world.

A world of thrilling sensations, all centering in the touch of his lips on hers. His hand held her chin, his mouth caressed hers expertly, but nowhere else did they touch. She strained up on tiptoe, longing for a closer contact that was not forthcoming.

He lifted his head and she forced her languid eyes to open. Every part of her body tingled with a blazing sensuality completely new to her. Each time he kissed her, he seemed to instantly transport her to some new level of awareness—and there was no going back to those halcyon days when she'd had no idea what she was missing.

"You came for this," he said gently.

"No, I came to warn you." A feeble whisper that sounded false even to her ears.

"With a note."

"Yes. It—it's around here somewhere."

He curved his hand around the underslope of her left breast, his thumb stroking through layers of cloth across the sensitized tip. "A note. Shall we...look for it?"

Catching her breath, Rose arched her back to lift her breast more fully into his palm. His slightest touch did the strangest, most inexplicable things to her. His bare chest beckoned her touch and she lifted one trembling hand, thinking, *If he can touch me, perhaps it's all right if I touch him.*

She spread her palm over his chest; she had never imagined such strength and she reveled in the feel of his flesh beneath her hand. He caught his breath and she stared at him, her eyes wide.

His teeth were a flash of white against his dark face. "I know why you came," he said raggedly.

"Y-you do?" He knew about the men from Crystal Springs, about the plotting and scheming of Mr. Curtis and Mr. Loveless? "How—"

"Later. Later..."

Leaning down, he swept her into his arms—and she let it happen. Two strides brought him to the edge of his bedroll and he dropped to his knees to deposit her there. But he didn't straighten away from her, instead fumbling for the buttons on her bodice.

I must be mad, she thought dreamily while she allowed him to undress her. Even that one time with Billy, she hadn't taken off all her clothes—nor had he suggested it or tried to do it himself. It had been enough to simply tug up her skirts and loosen the drawstring of her pantaloons.

No, that was wrong; it hadn't been enough. Which must be why Boone's touch swept her away now; he was leading her into new and uncharted territory. Where, she did not for a moment doubt, she would once again be ultimately disappointed. But in the meantime... Oh, in the meantime!

He stripped her to her pantalets. She saw her breasts emerge from the ruffled cage of her camisole, larger and fuller than she expected, and then she couldn't see them at all because his hands covered the soft mounds and he began a massaging, kneading motion.

He kissed her again, and it was all the other kisses intensified a thousand times. His tongue thrust deeply, possessively into her mouth, and she wrapped her arms around his naked shoulders, urging him closer and deeper still.

Tormented by desire, she first resisted, then welcomed his probing hand between her legs. Bit by bit he encouraged her to spread her thighs to accommodate him. Through the thin lawn of her underdrawers, his hand burned her soft moist flesh. Pressing, rubbing, he soon had her groaning with a mixture of pleasure and frustration.

Then in a flash, he was gone. She cried out and opened her eyes to find him standing above her, throwing off his gun belt and pants. The first sight of his unrestrained flesh took her breath away, a cold dash of reality that brought her up on her elbows, wondering what in the world had brought her to this point.

But then he touched her again and she fell back on the blankets to receive him. He parted her thighs and knelt between them and she made no protest. Leaning over her, he sucked one nipple into his mouth and she arched up with a muffled wail of ecstasy.

Yes, yes, yes! Her breasts had been made for this; why had she never known? And that forbidden spot at the apex of her thighs—it, too, had uses unimagined, she realized, as his fingers brushed her slick, hot flesh, then eased inside.

Out of her head with excitement, she writhed beneath him, leaving herself completely open and vulnerable. He could have whatever he wanted from her: her mouth, her breasts, her widespread thighs and that which they guarded.

With his fingers he parted her flesh and positioned himself. She felt the pressure of him, huge and hot and intrusive, and then a flash of panic quickly gone when he filled his mouth with her aching breast.

She was unprepared for the erotic tremors radiating to every part of her from his suckling lips. He thrust his hips against hers steady and slow. She caught her breath, tensing—this wouldn't work! He was too big, he'd hurt her. No one could accommodate such an intrusion! But when she would have cried out, he left her breast and took her mouth, swallowing her cries.

And then he was inside her, to the hilt, and something strange and magical was happening. He began a long, even stroking that didn't hurt at all; in fact, she felt herself growing warmer and more liquid with every thrust. Spreading her thighs even wider, she sought to draw him closer and deeper. Her breasts still ached for his attention but something was happening down there that overshadowed everything else, something primitive and wild that drove away all other considerations.

A trembling started deep inside her, at that point where his stroke reached its apex, some growing tension and sensitivity that tingled and tightened all the way to the soles of her feet and the roots of her hair. She didn't know what it was but she couldn't have evaded or avoided it had she known.

She clutched him to her in a frenzy of passion, swept along by an inexplicable sensuality that brought her gasping to the pinnacle. He stoked the fires, driving faster and harder; she matched his pace effortlessly, as if she'd done this a hundred, a thousand times.

Only she hadn't, and when the convulsions took her she thought perhaps she was dying; her mind went blank and her body took over, sending wave after wave of rapture spiraling through her.

In her ecstasy, she flung her arms wide, and her right hand fell upon something cold and hard. Only when at last she drifted back to full awareness did she realize she held the barrel of his pistol in a death grip.

Tonio Ryan sat at the foot of the ladder leading up to the loft, hunched over up-drawn knees with his forehead resting on his arms. He had set himself the task of watching Boone's back trail, for he knew trouble was not far away. He had never imagined that Miss Rose Taggart would be the one to breach his security.

He knew very well what was going on above his head, not only from the soft groans and the light breathing that accelerated into gusty pants but also from an elemental knowledge of the appetites of men . . . and women.

But Miss Rose—now that surprised him. And she'd come to Boone, not the other way around. Did Tonio think less of her now, knowing what he knew?

He considered that for a minute before deciding that he didn't think less of her at all; he thought more of Boone. Tonio began to grin.

He also thought more of his chances with Sally. If it was all right for a maiden lady like Miss Rose to take a lover, he didn't see why Sally couldn't—especially one who loved her and wanted to marry her. Besides, if he took her virginity, her father would have to let them marry.

Wouldn't he?

Rose lay in the arms of her lover, enveloped by an incredible sense of well-being. Later she would probably be consumed with guilt and remorse—she knew she would, in fact—but for the moment she felt physically sated and gloriously content. It was a feeling unlike any she had never known before.

Boone kissed her temple and pulled her more snugly into the curve of his arms. His voice sounded softly teasing when he said, "So you came to warn me, huh? I can't imagine what of."

"Oh! You made me forget!" She sat bolt upright, realized she was naked and scooted over on her bottom until she was in shadow. "James heard some men from Crystal Springs talking and they're up to something. Then when I came here tonight to warn you of that, I heard Mr. Curtis and Mr. Loveless plotting to use you in their ridiculous quarrel with Crystal Springs. Who cares which town's the county seat or gets a silly old railroad spur?"

He just lay there looking up at her curiously, his face illuminated by moonlight. "So?" he said finally.

"So you have to do something—protect yourself."

"I always protect myself," he said gently. He reached out to stroke her naked breast with tender fingers. "I'm glad you came to me tonight, Virginia Rose Taggart."

"C-came to you?" Sitting with her legs curled under her, she instinctively leaned away from his touch, realized that she'd be locking the barn door after the horse was stolen, not to mention depriving herself of additional pleasure, and leaned back again. He fondled her breast and she sighed. "I . . . don't understand. You think I came here tonight specifically for . . . this?"

"Of course, but that's all right." He rolled over on his side, propping his head on one hand and using the other to caress the curve of her tensed thighs. "I don't think any the less of you because of it. In fact, I respect a woman who knows what she wants and goes after it."

Sitting there in the shadows, naked as a jaybird and edgy as a rattlesnake, Rose pondered his meaning. Only one explanation occurred to her. *He knew.*

He knew about Billy. Maybe not by name, but he knew somebody else had been first. Billy had told her the truth; men *did* sense these things.

"I—I can explain," she said miserably. "It was only that once and because you're a man who . . . well, maybe you've made mistakes, too, and can forgive . . ."

His hand stilled on her leg. "What are you talking about?"

"Why, about Billy." She wrung her hands together. "He told me that if I ever let another man get . . . close to me, he'd know I wasn't—" she swallowed hard and forced herself to say the word "—pure. I didn't think it would matter because we were getting married but then he died and—oh, God, I'm so ashamed!"

"Wait a minute." Boone's strong hand closed around her knee. "You're ashamed because you weren't a virgin?"

She winced at the use of that word; she'd never heard it said right out before except in church. "Well, of course. What other reason could I possibly have to remain unmarried when I want a husband and children more than anything in the world? I'm supposed to be an old maid, only I'm not—I'm such a liar!" Trembling, she covered her face with her hands.

"Rose, don't do this to yourself." She felt the soft warmth of his lips against her knees. "I didn't want a virgin. I knew you *weren't* a virgin—otherwise I'd never have touched you, no matter how much I wanted you. I don't go around defiling innocent young maidens."

Waves of humiliation washed over her. "Then that's why you made love to me—because you knew all along that I'm a loose woman?"

"A loose woman? That's laughable in the extreme." He sat up and reached for her but she pulled back. "What's the matter with you, Rose? I didn't want a virgin and you're *not* a virgin, so we're both happy."

His words struck her like blows. "You don't . . . love me even a little?"

He went very still, and in the moonlight his face looked completely expressionless. "Not likely," he said with soft finality, "but I'm willing to give it one more try just to be sure."

He caught her in his arms, toppling them both over backward in the hay. His mouth found hers, and his hands covered her breasts insistently. His knees thrust between hers and he gathered her in, their bare bodies twisting and pressing, sliding together and parting as he entered her with an enthusiasm that demanded an equal response.

Then they were joined, moving as one with an urgency that wiped away all caution and restraint. Wilder and faster, higher and higher, until she felt almost crazed with the pleasure he gave her—and then that fierce hot excitement grabbed her again and hurled her over some invisible line, stunning her with its elemental force.

This time there was no tender aftermath spent in each other's arms. As soon as he pulled out of her and rolled over, she did the same, moving away from him. Grabbing her clothing, she pulled garments on willy-nilly.

"Hey," he demanded, still breathless. "What is it? What's the matter?"

"If you don't know—" she hooked her petticoat at the waist and stood up "—I'm not going to tell you!"

"Aw, Rose, come back to bed." He patted the blanket upon which he lay. "I'm sorry if I've said the wrong things, but you wouldn't want me to lie to you, would you?"

For a moment she thought, *Yes! Lie to me! Tell me I mean more to you than just a fast tumble in a hayloft!* But she didn't really want him to lie, even if her heart was breaking. She glared at him, at that warm and wonderful body, which she now knew even better than she knew her own.

She knew how it fit with hers, how hard and strong and supple it was, how capable of giving the most intense pleasure. She swallowed hard and straightened her sagging shoulders. "I hope they shoot you!" she cried, whirling toward the ladder. "If you're a gentleman, you'll forget this ever happened!"

"If I was a gentleman, it never *would* have happened," he called after her in a low, laughing voice. "But neither one of us will ever forget it."

Tonio barely had time to roll away from the base of the ladder to avoid Miss Rose's foot in the middle of his back. He was sure she never even saw him as she ran out of the livery stable, clutching her shawl around her shoulders.

He was glad she was gone; the soft sounds of pleasure, the gasps and little cries he'd been hearing from the loft were about to drive him crazy.

He wanted to hear those same exclamations of satisfaction from Sally—and he would. If it was all right for a gunfighter like Boone to tumble a fine woman like Miss Rose in a hayloft, then it was all right for Tonio to plan the seduction of Sally Curtis.

After all, he loved Sally—loved her with all his heart. He was determined to marry her and spend the rest of his life with her. Boone sure as hell couldn't say the same thing about Miss Rose.

Rose threw herself inside her little house and pressed against the front door, her heart beating like a drum. She'd run all the way home, sticking to shadows but still terrified she'd be seen and recognized.

Now what was she going to do? Undressing in the dark, she slipped into her virginal white cotton nightgown and crawled into bed. And lay there thinking... remembering.

After an hour or so of torment, she jumped out of bed and scurried into the kitchen for a dipper of water. It tasted stale and warm on her tongue and she spit it out in the basin. Standing there in the dark, head hanging dejectedly, she tried to come to grips with her situation.

She was enamored of an opportunist! He didn't care a fig for her; he'd wanted only one thing and he had got it—to her everlasting shame. But with her body still replete with satisfaction, with the memory of his hands and lips on her breasts and his hips thrusting against hers, would she be able to resist him now that she knew what she'd been missing?

Everything in her cried out for him! Was it ever this way between husbands and wives? she wondered as she crept miserably into her lonely bed. What would it be like to spend every night in the arms of someone who could lift you to such heights of delight? She shivered with delicious anticipation.

Was it this way between James and Diana? she wondered with fresh insight. She remembered some of the intimate looks she'd intercepted between the two of them, marveling at her own stupidity at not understanding before.

Yet how could she have known, have guessed? She had lost her virtue to Billy without gaining knowledge; Boone had given her the key to understanding, if nothing else.

She might as well face it: she wasn't strong enough to resist him by herself. She must have help. And there was only one place she might get it.

Jack.

What if she took one last, desperate gamble and told him the truth—that she was used goods? Did he love her enough to forgive her? Would he want her anyway?

Dare she take that chance?

Chapter Twelve

The entire population of Jones, Texas, buzzed with gossip and speculation about the gunfighter, Boone. Rose heard his named bandied about everywhere she went.

"Papa says this gunfighter's the biggest thing to hit town since the news of General Lee's surrender," Sally confided when Rose stopped at the C and J to pick up a tin of coffee. "Papa says that soon as word gets out he's here, there's bound to be somebody come lookin' for him."

Rose frowned. "Gunfighting and gunfighters are not a proper topic of conversation for a young girl, Sally Curtis."

Sally made a face. "Don't be an old stick-in-the-mud, Miss Rose. Just because he bought your basket at the church social doesn't make him respectable. Folks are talkin' about *you*, too, in case you didn't know."

Rose lifted her chin a notch higher. "There's nothing whatsoever to talk about," she said sharply.

Sally shrugged. "Maybe." She didn't sound convinced. "Anyway, Papa says a showdown's comin' sure. He says if Mr. Boone wins, Jones will be famous. If he loses, Papa says we'll bury him in the graveyard behind the church and folks will come from miles around to see where the famous gunfighter went to his final reward."

"Your papa talks entirely too much," Rose said tartly. "It looks to me like he'd have more important matters to attend to."

Sally's expression changed, grew secretive. "Which reminds me—have you seen Tonio lately?"

"Not since the church social. You ate with him, didn't you?"

"Yes, but with everybody watchin' us like hawks, it wasn't much fun. I've not seen him since. He did send me a message by Emmett Cox but—"

"Sally, it's wrong to get Emmett involved. He's just a little boy." The vivid memory of Sally's and Tonio's guilty expressions when surprised in her kitchen brought a frown to Rose's face. "What are you and Tonio up to? Honestly, if I thought the two of you were going to create such a ruckus and upset your father so terribly—"

"Oh, pish posh, Miss Rose—don't worry. Can I get you anything besides the coffee?"

In Rose's experience, anytime anyone said don't worry it was time to worry plenty. Still thinking about Sally and Tonio, she nearly bumped into the marshal on her way out of the store.

Jack stepped aside for her, lifting his hat politely. "Morning, Miss Rose. You're looking lovely this fine summer's day."

"Thank you, Marshal Guthrie." She bit her lip, feeling awkward and ill at ease with him. Could he tell just by looking at her that she'd been with the gunfighter—"been with" a polite euphemism for what they'd actually done. She looked away, unable to meet Jack's openly admiring gaze.

"That was quite a revelation Doc made at the church social," he continued. "About Jeremy Edwards, I mean."

"Yes." She didn't know what else to say.

He looked at her closely. "You didn't know, did you?"

"His real name? No, of course not." Surely he didn't think she'd keep such knowledge a secret from him!

He nodded, looking satisfied. "I knew that but some folks have suggested... Well, you know, after the man bought your basket and all, and you nursing him when he first came to town—"

"You mean there's been gossip," she said tightly. "Well, that's just fine!"

"Now, Miss Rose, no need to get riled. You know how people like to talk." Jack shifted from one foot to other anxiously. "Pay it no heed—I don't. I know you to be the finest, most honest, most forthright woman—"

Each word added to her load of guilt, since she knew for a fact she was none of those things. Fortunately the arrival of Mrs. Dinwiddy interrupted his flow of compliments. The little woman took one look at Rose, pointed her nose into the air and sailed past as if to avoid contamination.

Rose all but groaned aloud. Her reputation was suffering because of her association with Boone, and nobody even knew the *half* of it.

Jack didn't seem to notice anything amiss. "Anyway," he went on, "now that I know his real name I'll have to go through the wanted posters one more time."

Rose caught her breath in alarm. "Do you expect to find anything?"

Jack shrugged. "I don't know. I almost hope I won't."

She nodded understandingly. "If he's as dangerous as they say he is, I wouldn't like to see you trying to arrest him."

Jack's eyes widened. "Oh, it's not that. It's..." Shame-faced, he glanced away. "It's just that I sorta like him." He gave her a charmingly helpless smile and shrugged.

That she could understand. She sorta liked the gunman, too, despite her best efforts not to.

Stopping at Doc's on the way home, she found him suffering from the effects of the previous evening's indulgence, complete with bloodshot eyes and trembling hands. In fact, he looked as dour and dejected as she felt.

"I tracked Boone down at the Yellow Rose this morning to apologize," he said over a cup of strong black coffee. "He all but threw me out. He's actin' mad enough to kick his own dog."

Rose kept her attention focused on the contents of her cup, unwilling to deal with the information that Boone had apparently gone straight from her arms to Libby's. "It's not like you did it on purpose, Doc," she said, trying to console him. "If he hadn't lied about his name—"

"He didn't exactly lie," Doc said tiredly, "and even if he did, he had good reason. His whole name's Jeremy Edward Boone Smith. He's fightin' a reputation he sure don't deserve."

"You knew him back in Kansas?" Rose prodded, trying not to appear as interested as she was.

Doc nodded. "He was a lawman, and a danged good one. He got into a few showy gunfights that weren't his fault and they wouldn't let him live 'em down. Lost his girl—"

"His girl?" Her head jerked up and she frowned.

"Nice girl, not much gumption, though. Don't really know what he saw in her besides a pretty face, which in the long haul ain't near enough. Told him so, one of the many times I patched him up. He told me to mind my own business." He laughed grimly. "Which was good advice. You'd think at my age, I'd a'learned how to take it."

Rose left Doc hunched unhappily over his coffee cup. What a mess, she thought, turning up the little walkway to her house. The gunfighter had thrown the entire town into a tizzy, but most of all, he'd changed Rose in ways she'd never get past.

She was pleased to find Diana waiting inside.

"James was coming to town to talk to Tonio," Diana explained. "For some reason, the boy didn't come back to the ranch last night and James wanted to find out what if anything he'd learned about that gunfighter."

"Wonderful," Rose grumbled. "My own brother—doesn't anybody have anything else to talk about besides that man?"

Diana's eyes widened. "Goodness gracious, we are testy this morning. Get up on the wrong side of the bed, dear?"

No, got up from the wrong bed, Rose thought unhappily. "I'm sorry, it's just that... I was downtown and everybody's talking about *that man* and they're all looking at me in that funny way and it just—it just..." She gave her sister-in-law a helpless glance.

"You poor little thing, you're a nervous wreck. Here, sit down and I'll fix us a fresh pot of coffee and we can talk." Diana guided Rose into a kitchen chair and proceeded to stoke up the fire in the cookstove and measure coffee and water into the tin pot.

After setting it on the stove, she took a seat opposite Rose and leaned forward. "Don't let them upset you," she advised. "You must face them all down. You've done nothing to be ashamed of and—"

"But I have!" The confession burst out, unplanned and unbidden. "I have done something to be ashamed of, Di."

"W-why—" Diana looked startled but she recovered quickly. "Eating a box supper with that man hardly constitutes a shame. My word, that was for the church building fund. You should be praised instead of censured."

Rose nodded miserably. "Yes, but that isn't the half of ." She took one look at Diana's stricken expression and buried her face in her hands, afraid to go on.

She felt a supportive hand on her arm, and then heard Diana's hesitant voice. "I don't wish to pry, but if there's something you'd care to tell me, dear... I'll be happy to listen, and help if I can.''

Rose looked up sharply, eyes burning with unshed tears. "Promise you won't tell James?"

Diana looked almost frightened of what was to come. "Of course, if that's what you want," she declared staunchly, visibly bracing herself.

Rose licked her lips. "I've done... something unforgivable. Since he moved out of the marshal's house, Boone sleeps in the hayloft over the livery stable and last night I went there and—"

Diana gasped, her eyes wide and horrified. "You didn't!"

Rose nodded miserably. "I did. I only meant to warn him about what James said—remember? About the men from Crystal Springs? But one thing led to another and he...we... Oh, I could just die!" She squeezed her eyes closed in mortification.

"My God," Diana breathed. "He forced himself on you!"

"I...I wish I could say that. But no, he didn't force me. I...consented."

Diana leaned across the table and grasped both Rose's hands in hers. "How awful!"

Rose groaned and shook her head, not knowing how to say the words that would describe how she'd felt. "I didn't know...I couldn't dream—"

Diana squeezed the hands in hers. "Of course not. How could you, a maiden lady such as yourself?"

Rose shook her head slowly. Now that the truth was coming out, she intended to share it all, even if it shocked Diana so profoundly that her sister-in-law lost all respect for her. "You don't understand, Diana. It wasn't awful, it was wonderful. We did it...twice...and I thought about it all night long and wished we could do it again!"

"Oh, my *God!*" Diana looked on the verge of fainting. She pulled herself together with an effort. "Well, is he going to marry you?" she demanded indignantly. "Surely even a low-down gunfighter knows he can't go around defiling innocent women and get away with it! James and Jack will see that he does the right thing by you, whether he wants to or—why are you shaking your head at me, Virginia Rose Taggart? You know you'll have to marry him!"

"He didn't defile an innocent woman." Rose bit her lip and sucked in a quick breath. "He...wasn't the first."

Diana's blue eyes were enormous in her pale face; she looked about to faint. "Who—"

"Billy Curtis, the boy I was engaged to and who died before you married James and came here. Why do you think I've refused to consider marriage all this time? It's not because of my undying love for Billy, it's because I've been keeping that terrible secret. Now I've made things worse by... by..." She swallowed hard and blinked away tears of relief, relief that at last she'd shared her awful burden.

The truth seemed to dawn slowly on Diana. "Then that's why you've been so resolute in your refusals to the marshal," she deduced.

"Yes. I want a home and children more than anything in the world but I could never marry without first confessing my sin—well, up until last night it was sin in the singular but now it's plural. And you know what, Diana?"

"Please don't tell me there's more," Diana pleaded. "This is all too much to take in!"

"I'm afraid so," Rose admitted sadly. "Because the truth is, I never dreamed it could be that way between a man and a woman—I mean, the way it was with Boone." She shivered. "I...don't think I'm strong enough to resist him. I don't suppose that makes any sense to you but he somehow makes me feel...complete."

"Oh, dear," Diana breathed. "Rose, this is worse than I imagined."

"I know. I'm truly sorry."

"You *don't* know. Rose, you're in love with this man!"

"No—I can't be!"

"You are. Well," Diana added briskly, "you'll just have to get over it." She leaned forward again, all business. "You'll have to tell Jack the truth. I know you'll be taking a chance but you've got to do it. If he cares for you half as much as I think he does, he'll not only forgive you, he'll marry you anyway."

Rose felt a tiny spark of hope flicker somewhere deep inside. "Do you really think there's a chance? Because I'm just about at the end of my rope. I mean, what if I'm . . . in the family way?"

Diana's cheeks turned bright red. "It doesn't always happen the first time," she said.

"I know that. You and James have been married for almost six months and you're not—" Something in Diana's expression stopped the flow of words. "Are you? Diana, are you and James having a baby?"

The two women met at the end of the table and fell into each other's arms, laughing and crying at the same time.

"When?" Rose asked.

"December, I think." Diana wiped damp eyes with her hands. "It's still a while and I didn't want to say anything to you until I was sure. We're very happy."

"You and James love each other very much." Rose heard the wistfulness in her tone.

Diana nodded shyly. "Yes. But I didn't take to him at all at first. I thought he was too forward and much too sure of himself. He just wore me down—" she laughed softly "—and I've never regretted it. Rose, you said it was...wonderful with that gunman. Are you sure there's no chance that he might make an honest woman of you?"

Rose shook her head. "Not the slightest."

"Then Jack's your only chance," Diana said. "But first...exactly what did you mean when you said it was wonderful?"

Rose wore her yellow muslin dress, the one that was only two years old, and spent an inordinate amount of time on her hair before it satisfied her. Standing before the mirror over the dresser in her bedroom, she perched a small feathered hat atop her curls and pinned her mother's cameo brooch at her throat, then gazed at herself critically.

She wasn't entirely satisfied, but this was the best she could do. Nothing could disguise that determined expression; Jack could take her or leave her.

The walk to the marshal's office downtown, one she had made many times, seemed today to take forever. Somehow Rose felt as if every house and store she passed shielded knowing eyes that followed her progress with disdain.

The closer she got, the more nervous she became. If she could just reach her destination without running into Boone, that was all she asked. And she was almost there. Just another few steps—

Boone walked out of the barber shop and directly into her path. It wasn't an accident, either; he stopped, deliberately forcing her to do likewise. He lifted his hat and gave her a smile that was almost a challenge.

"Afternoon, Miss Rose."

His warm, low voice made her want to groan. She fought to keep her gaze pinned to his face; last time she'd seen him he'd been stark naked. How could she be expected to think straight with such memories churning around in her head?

She tilted her chin to a haughty angle, gave him a withering glance and took two steps to one side. "Please spare me your further attentions, sir," she said coldly. "I do not wish to continue our brief acquaintance."

His stormy gray eyes narrowed. "And what if I do wish to continue it, Miss Rose?"

"Your wishes are of no consequence to me," she said grandly. Without another word, she marched past him and through the open doorway of the marshal's office. Boone's low, taunting laughter followed her.

At her entry, Jack looked up from his worktable. "Miss Rose!" He jumped to his feet and came toward her, beaming. "This is an unexpected pleasure."

"Yes, well—" Aware of bootheels on the boardwalk outside, she wondered if Boone would follow her here. Her scalp tightened with tension and she drew in a shaky breath.

"Have a chair," Jack invited. "I was just catching up on my record keeping but it'll hold. Was there something you wanted or is this a social call?"

"Well…" She hesitated, wondering how he'd react if she simply announced that she'd decided to marry him.

He gave her a tentative smile. "At the risk of seeming bold, would you care to continue our conversation over dinner at the Blue Bonnet Café? I know you've turned down all my other invitations to dine but hope springs eternal, as the poet says."

"Actually, I—"

"Please, Miss Rose, give me a chance to make amends for my impetuosity of the other day. It's preyed on my mind ever since. I promise I won't embarrass you with further protestations of my affections."

What a good man he is, she thought, looking into his handsome and sincere face. *I would be so lucky if he'd have me once he knows the truth.* She gave him a tentative smile. "Thank you, Marshal Guthrie. I accept your kind invitation with pleasure."

He looked completely astonished, then he bowed with a flourish and presented his arm.

She had made Marshal Jack Guthrie a happy man and she felt just awful about it.

The Blue Bonnet Café boasted one large room filled with tables, plus a kitchen catering to a clientele leaning heavily toward beef, beans and fried potatoes. Because no liquor was served or even allowed on the premises except for that previously consumed by tipsy diners, the Blue Bonnet was considered respectable enough for ladies.

With a flourish, Jack seated Rose at a table near the window in the half-filled dining room. Grinning proudly, he took his place across from her.

The waiter—none other than Junius Cox, looking uncharacteristically sober—galloped up, two tin cups in one hand and a battered coffeepot in the other. Slapping the cups down, he sloshed a dark and pungent brew over the rims.

"Special of the day is beef and beans," he intoned, adding, "howdy Miz Rose, howdy, Marshal."

Rose regarded him with some surprise. "Junius! I had no idea you were employed here."

The skinny little man shifted uncomfortably. "Don't spread it around," he muttered. "I was swampin' over to the Yella Rose till that damned gunfighter—" He glanced around anxiously. "Well, never mind that. You want two specials?"

"What's the alternative?" Rose asked, strictly out of curiosity.

"Well, we not only got beef and beans, we got beans and beef. Or if you're real finicky, the cook'll fry you up a couple of eggs to go on top, or you can save the eggs for dessert—it don't make me no never mind." He cackled with laughter.

Jack gave Rose a questioning glance and she nodded. "The lady will have beef and beans and I'll have beans and beef,'' he said. "And Junius, take your time. We're in no hurry." He turned to her with a smile. "We've got lots to talk about, I think."

Rose tried to return his smile but her face felt frozen. It was going to happen, just as she wanted it to. He was going to propose to her again before the night was over. And when he did, she had to somehow summon the strength to tell him the truth.

Sitting there in the Blue Bonnet Café, she prayed for the courage to do what she must.

Walking home through the early dusk, Rose felt herself growing more and more tense with every step they took. Once back at her little cottage she would invite him in and warm up the coffee while she tried to figure out some way to tell him what he must know.

Maybe she should simply say to him, "Jack, I've been meaning to mention that I'm not actually the old maid everyone in town assumes I am...."

"Howdy, Marshal... Evenin', Miss Rose, Marshal Guthrie... How yawl?"

Everyone they passed on their leisurely stroll called out some kind of greeting. Beside her, Jack's sigh signified contentment.

"Everyone in Jones has the greatest of admiration for the job you've done as marshal," Rose remarked. It was certainly the truth, yet she felt curiously uneasy, as if she was merely buttering him up.

"That's kind of you to say, Miss Rose." He smiled at her with much satisfaction. "I came west to prove to myself and to certain others that I could make my own way without family money or connections. I'm grateful to Jones for that opportunity."

"You're from Philadelphia, if I remember correctly?"

He took her arm to assist her down the steps leading to street level between blocks. "That's right."

"Do you ever think of going back there?"

He was silent for a moment while they crossed the street and ascended again to the boardwalk. They were passing the C and J now.

"Would that...make a difference to you? I have family there, and a law practice waiting for me to take up the reins should I care to return. If I thought for a minute that would influence you—"

They heard it at the same time: a muted, muffled gasp and then the rasp of gravel beneath thrashing feet. Some kind of scuffle? Their puzzled glances met.

"Stay here," Jack commanded at once, stepping toward the narrow alley between the general store and its neighbor, a milliner's shop. He peered into the shadows, then walked boldly forward.

Rose let him get a few feet ahead, then plunged after him. Not for a moment did she hesitate, for some instinct told her that her intervention would be as timely as the marshal's.

Thus it was that when Jack stepped out of the alley at the opposite end, Rose was right at his heels. And she saw as clearly as did he the origin of the sounds that had alarmed them.

Tonio Ryan held Sally Curtis locked in his arms, his mouth devouring hers. So intense was his lovemaking that he obviously had no idea they'd been discovered, just as he seemed to have no idea that Sally was not cooperating.

Her small feet scrabbled at the gravel beneath them and her elbows bent as she tried to break the boy's hold. Forced backward at a precarious angle, she fought him and he didn't even seem to know it.

Jack grabbed a handful of the boy's shirt collar and jerked him upright. Torn from Tonio's arms, Sally gasped and fell against the wall for support. The bodice of her dress was askew, several open buttons allowing the lace on her camisole to show. Her blond hair hung in a tangle around a face that was deathly pale.

"What the hell!" Tonio came around crouched and ready to fight, his hands clenched. His sensuous mouth curled in a snarl.

Then he saw who faced him and his young face twisted in confusion.

Rose ran to Sally, taking the girl in her arms. "It's all right," she promised, patting the trembling shoulders. "We're here."

"He's crazy," Sally wailed. "I don't know what could have got into him!"

Jack scowled at the boy. "Tonio Ryan, I can hardly believe what I just saw. Don't you know better than to treat a lady like that?"

"Now just a damned minute!" Tonio swallowed hard and licked his lips, his glance skittering from one of them to the next. "What'd I do that was so all-fired wrong?"

Jack glanced uneasily at Rose, then at the belligerent boy. "You know very well what you did," he said grimly, "and if we hadn't shown up just now you'd have done plenty more, from the looks of things. See how you've frightened the poor girl—she's trembling."

Tonio's strong jaw shot out. "If the poor girl was gonna get so damned scared, why'd she meet me out here in the first place, then sashay around like she wanted it? What's a man to think?" He bent over and grabbed his hat off the ground, straightened and clapped it on his head. "I love her, but I'm only human!"

Jack's face hardened. "If Sally led you on—and I say *if*— then it was obviously done in all innocence. There is never any excuse for a gentleman to take advantage of a lady, regardless of the situation. If you misunderstood, that's your mistake, not hers."

Sally, sobbing noisily in Rose's arms, lifted her head enough to peer at Tonio, then wailed louder still. Pressing her forehead into Rose's shoulder, the girl closed her eyes and covered her ears with her hands, as if she couldn't bear to deal with the situation a minute longer.

Rose glared at the boy. "You should be ashamed of yourself!" she exclaimed, hugging the weeping Sally. "I thought better of you, Tonio!"

Tonio rocked back on his heels, his young face curiously vulnerable despite his anger. "Just a damned minute," he blazed. "No matter what a woman does, she's not asking for it?"

Jack darted an apologetic glance at Rose. "That's correct. Occasionally a lady may inadvertently do something that—" he gulped hard "—that a gentleman could misconstrue, but it is his responsibility to remember that woman is the weaker sex. As such, she is to be cherished and revered, not mauled in some alleyway."

Slowly the confusion disappeared from Tonio's face and he rocked back on his heels again, his smile cynical. "That's all you know about it," he sneered. "How about Boone and Miss Rose in the hayloft? If you think you know so much about ladies and gentlemen, explain that!"

Chapter Thirteen

Rose's blood ran cold; she felt as if she'd just taken a mortal blow. Caught completely by surprise, all she could do was stare at Tonio in horror. Could he know? *How* could he know?

"Hayloft?" Jack looked completely taken aback. "How'd a hayloft get into this?"

"Ask Miss Rose," Tonio suggested uneasily.

"I'm asking you!"

The boy's bravado all but disappeared. "Miss Rose paid a little visit to the gunman in the hayloft over to the livery stable last night." He couldn't meet Jack's incredulous gaze but added defensively, "Does that mean she ain't no lady?"

"Why, you lying little—" Jack backhanded the boy, sending him staggering. The marshal's face twisted. "After all Miss Rose has done for you, you ungrateful pup! Apologize and do it fast."

An ugly red stain marked the left side of Tonio's dark face. The boy crouched, one hand hovering above the butt of the revolver holstered at his hip. "I don't apologize for the truth," he spat. "Ask her. She'll tell you."

Rose turned to Jack, aghast. *I'll lie,* she thought wildly. *I can't tell him the truth, not now—not after Tonio's blurted it out in the most brutal fashion imaginable.* But even as she watched Jack turn his head to look at her with eyes filled with pain and confusion, she knew she couldn't do that.

In her arms, Sally stirred. "Oh, Miss Rose," the girl whimpered. "I never knew what Tonio was like—how awful he could be. If I had, I'd never have let him—I mean, given him a chance to—"

Jack whipped his head around to glare at Tonio again. "You lyin' piece of—I won't insult Miss Rose by asking her to dignify that with an answer." He took a step forward, his hands clenching. "But I am going to teach you a lesson you won't soon forget."

Tonio's revolver leaped into his hand so fast Rose gave a little scream of shock and fear.

"I wouldn't try that, Marshal," the boy said, voice soft and dangerous.

"Stop, both of you!" Rose released Sally and gave the girl a little shove. "Go, Sally. This is no longer your concern."

Sally sniffled and began to button her bodice, which was still awry. "But—"

"Sally, *go!*"

She did, shuffling down the alley with many a backward glance. Rose watched the girl round the corner, then drew a deep breath, which didn't steady her at all. Slowly she turned toward the two men poised on the brink of disaster.

"Put your gun away, Tonio," she said, her voice trembling with strain. "Jack, we must talk. Please."

Jack shook his head. "Not until he apologizes. He can't go around spreading lies—"

"Jack, *they're not lies!*"

She saw his shock and disbelief and closed her eyes against his disillusionment.

"Rose . . . surely you don't mean . . ."

And Tonio, miserably adding, "Ah, Miss Rose, I'm sorry."

"I know you are, Tonio." She opened her eyes and faced them. The boy had holstered his weapon and stood staring down at his booted feet as if ashamed to face her. But it wasn't his fault, she realized, it was her own. Or perhaps Boone's, if he'd confided in the boy, which didn't seem possible. "Please go now, Tonio, and let me talk to Jack."

"You sure?" Tonio gave the other man an unfriendly glance.

Rose nodded, also watching the marshal. Arms hanging stiff at his sides, he stood there as if in a state of complete shock. "Will you let me explain?" she pleaded. "I won't blame you if you refuse but I'd like to tell you..." She licked her lips, unable to go on.

He blinked and gave his head a slight shake, as if trying to wake up from a bad dream. "Yes, of course," he said, but it sounded automatic. "Here?" He looked around the alley as if surprised to realize where they stood.

"Let's go to my house where we won't be disturbed."

"All right. Your house."

But the stunned, uncomprehending expression had not left his face.

She told him everything, sparing herself nothing. She began with Billy and their one encounter in Diablo Canyon and ended with Boone and their one encounter in the hayloft of the livery stable.

"I never meant to deceive you," she whispered at last, willing him to believe her. "That's why I couldn't encourage your interest or seriously consider your proposal of marriage, even before that gunfighter came to town. I knew after Billy died that I could never marry—"

"Why not?" Some of Jack's shock seemed to be fading, and he looked more confused than anything else.

"Well..." She gestured helplessly. "Because I wasn't what you thought I was—what the whole town thinks I am. I'm no better than...than Libby Bowman."

Jack ran his hands through his hair, a gesture indicative of his confusion. "Is Mrs. Bowman then beneath your contempt?"

Rose recoiled. "Of course not. How could I cast the first stone—or any stone, for that matter? I don't know what set her on the path she follows."

He nodded. "Exactly. Oh, Rose—" He took her hands in his and stared into her eyes. "Had I but known what set you on the path you followed—about Billy Curtis, I mean—it would have had no bearing on my feelings for you."

"You say that, but I can't believe..."

"Believe. I have a younger sister. She, too... transgressed...and was left to face the consequences alone."

"I'm so sorry." Rose squeezed his hands, offering comfort.

"The man she loved didn't die, he simply abandoned her when he discovered she was...in the family way."

"W-what became of her?"

"Today she is happily married, the mother of three. She met a man who loved her for all her fine qualities without dwelling on her past."

Rose swallowed hard. "I'm glad. My case, of course, is different."

"Yes," he agreed. "Billy—at the risk of sounding hardhearted, he's no longer of any consequence because you were young and he is dead and gone."

She nodded, thinking that if they'd had this talk just twenty-four hours earlier, everything would be different. "I feel so guilty because I hardly even remember him," she confessed. "It seems so very long ago."

She looked up at him suddenly. "But Boone was only yesterday. I wish I could explain what happened but I can't.

I don't expect you to forgive me for that, Jack, and I won't ask you to try—or even to understand, because I don't.''

"No, I see you don't. Nevertheless—'' He took a deep breath and faced her with determination. ''I still want you to be my wife.''

Rose stared at him, eyes wide and lips parted. ''Are you joking?'' she finally managed to ask, her voice ever so faint. ''Because if you are—''

He gave her hands a peremptory shake. ''I mean every word I've said—with one condition.''

So she'd seen her salvation only to have it snatched away by a condition. What condition would he impose? That she prove her commitment to him in her usual way? She gave a weary laugh and tried to pull her hands from his.

"No, Rose, listen to me. I want to marry you only if you are one-hundred-percent sure you're finished with Boone forever. That's my only condition. I know you are not the kind of woman who would take your wedding vows lightly, and strangely enough, I don't think Boone would, either.''

"How can you speak kindly of him under the circumstances?'' she blurted. ''Or me, either, for that matter.''

"Because anger shouldn't blind us to extenuating circumstances,'' he said gently. ''I guess it's the lawyer in me.'' He hesitated. ''Rose, do you want him or me? That's what it comes down to.''

She didn't hesitate for a single instant. ''You!'' she cried in her gratitude. ''I could never have a future with him. He's a rolling stone who'll never have room in his life for a wife and children. I'd settle for nothing before I'll settle for less, whatever mistakes I may have made in the past.''

"Then I'm satisfied. I love you, Rose Taggart, and I'm ready to spend the rest of my life trying my level best to make you happy, if you will consent to be my wife.''

She couldn't believe this was really happening, that any man could be so understanding and generous and noble. She

smiled at him through a haze of tears, and all she could do
was nod.

He stood and lifted her to her feet, sliding his arms
around her waist. "Then we'll be married as quickly as we
can arrange it," he said, "because I know that once we've
said our vows, the gunman Boone will pose no further threat
to us."

His lips touched hers in their first kiss, firm and warm and
offering a wealth of comfort...but none of the passion she'd
so recently discovered. That wasn't important, she assured
herself with conviction born of desperation. Jack Guthrie
was a good man, and she would be a good wife to him.

If only Boone would stay away from her long enough for
them to be married.

Outside the kitchen window, Boone stood in the shadow
of the cottonwood trees and watched the marshal draw Rose
into his embrace. With a ragged oath, he turned away.

Damn Tonio for blurting out the truth about the encounter in the hayloft, but at least the kid'd had the guts to come
over to the saloon to confess what he'd done. Boone had
expected to find Rose in a swoon and the marshal in a killing rage, but instead he'd found...this.

Whatever this was. Could any man overlook a transgres-
sion as fresh and raw as that between the beautiful Miss
Taggart and the loathsome gunfighter? Twenty-four hours
ago she'd come creeping up the ladder into the loft, and no
matter how she might rationalize, it had been for purposes
other than conversation.

But then, perhaps she'd convinced Jack that nothing had
really happened. Or maybe she'd told him she'd been
forced. Or maybe—

Hell, she'd told him the truth, Boone thought with disgust, watching the pair through the lighted window. One
kiss and they separated chastely and sedately; the marshal

now held her hands and stared into her eyes, saying who knew what while she listened raptly.

Jack Guthrie was a good man. Boone tried to shake away that certainty and failed. He'd be a good husband to Rose, better than a two-bit gunman with a reputation could ever hope to—dammit, that wasn't the issue, he reminded himself. No matter how much he might long for a normal life that included wife and children, he'd never be able to have it until he escaped the notoriety trailing him like an evil shadow.

By the time that happened—if it ever did—Rose would be long married with a houseful of kids. Boone tried to imagine her doing with Jack the things she'd done with *him* last night and failed—maybe because the very thought infuriated him so.

Whirling in the darkness, he walked a few steps away from the house and stopped short, breathing hard. He had to know what the hell was going on in there. Had she told Jack everything, or some truncated version that portrayed her as the helpless victim? Had Jack renewed his marriage suit—and had she accepted?

And then Boone asked himself the most important question of all. *If it comes to it, can I really stand by and watch her marry someone else?*

At the front door, Jack lifted her hands in his and pressed them against the sides of his face. Sighing, he released her. "You've made me a very happy man," he said.

The lamp in the parlor behind them threw enough light on his face so that she could be sure he meant what he said. She gave him a trembling smile. "Jack Guthrie, you must be the finest man in creation. You do me great honor."

He smiled. "I love you, Rose. I won't ask you to say the same—not yet. When you finally say those words to me I want to know that you mean them with all your heart."

"I . . . I hope that day will come soon."

"It will," he said with quiet confidence. "Will you tell James and Diana tomorrow?"

She nodded. "They'll be very happy for us."

"Good. The support and approval of friends and family are important." He released her hands with reluctance and took a step down from the porch. "It's hard to say good-night, but soon we won't have to. Pleasant dreams . . . dearest."

The endearment startled her but she managed to smile. "And to you, too." She blew him a little kiss, stepped inside and closed the door.

Oh, dear God, had she done the right thing? It was the only thing, but was it also the right thing?

She carried the lamp into her bedroom and set it on the chest of drawers against the wall. Completely drained, she sank onto the side of the bed and let her head fall forward as all the doubts rushed over her.

Outside her window, Boone stared at the patch of light behind her curtain while his curiosity—no, his *need to know*—grew. He could follow Jack and ask the other man point-blank, but that would in all likelihood lead to some kind of altercation. No good.

Or he could ask Rose herself. Hell, he had to know what was going on. If the marshal intended to come looking for the low-down sidewinder who'd made love to his woman, the low-down sidewinder should be prepared.

The back door was unlocked, as Boone knew it would be. Moving with silent care, he crossed the kitchen and parlor, remembering where the pitfalls were without any particular effort; details often meant the difference between life and death in his line of work. Light spilled from beneath her door and he halted, steeling himself for the confrontation he knew was coming.

Then he reached out, threw open the door and stepped inside. She whirled, her face as white as the cotton gown she clutched to her breasts. Her shoulders, bare and pale as ivory, trembled as if with cold...only the atmosphere in this room wasn't cold, it was warm.

Hot.

"You!" She said the single word with contempt. "Get out of here! You have no right—"

"Don't I?" Boone looked at the bed, then at the woman. "Last night you came to me uninvited. Maybe tonight I'm returning the favor."

She caught her breath and her eyelids fluttered, as if she was too embarrassed to even look at him. "Things have...changed since last night," she managed.

"Changed how?" He stepped to the bed and rested one hand on the bedpost.

She lifted her chin and met his gaze without flinching. "I'm engaged. Marshal Guthrie proposed and I accepted. We'll be married as soon as arrangements can be made."

Boone's hand clenched around the tall wooden bedpost but he kept his voice cool. "Does the good marshal have any idea what he's getting?"

She swayed slightly, as if he'd landed a heavy blow. "What is he getting, in your opinion?"

"A woman who doesn't love him and never will."

She looked relieved, as if she'd expected him to call her names. "How could you possibly know that? Jack's a fine man, a wonderful man, a man any woman would be proud to...to..." She stumbled to a halt and looked at Boone with wide, frightened eyes.

"To marry. We can't pick who we're going to love all that easily, can we?" He walked around the foot of the bed and she shrank against the wall, clutching the froth of cotton cloth before her like a shield. She wore petticoats and black high-button shoes, but above the waist she was naked.

And painfully, painfully aware of it, he realized, crowding her. "You're taking advantage of a fine man you don't love and never will," he said flatly. "What's worse, you know it."

He'd made her angry now, he saw; her chin lifted in that royal manner he secretly found so appealing. "You have little room to talk," she flung at him, "after the way you corrupted Tonio Ryan. At least Jack is an adult, but Tonio—Tonio is just a boy!"

That stopped Boone in his tracks, less than an arm's length from her. He frowned. "What the hell are you talking about? Tonio didn't mean to tell Jack about your little visit to me, it just slipped out. The kid's sorry as hell—"

"For all the good that does."

She tossed her head, her dark hair settling around her creamy shoulders. One strand curled down between the enticing globes of her breasts, drawing his attention to the deep cleavage.

He swallowed hard and spoke from between clenched jaws. "Tonio's not responsible for this mess."

"No, *you* are. Tonio worships you—he thinks you can do no wrong. If you have so little respect for women, why should he? Why do you think he was attacking poor Sally—"

"Poor Sally is a tease and a flirt."

Rose threw back her shoulders, which had the effect of revealing another inch or so of her luscious breasts. "Leave Sally out of it! You're the one who corrupted him, not that poor child."

Boone gave her a slow, knowing smile. "But I didn't corrupt *you*, did I?"

He took the one step that separated them, and before she could resist, he hurled her shield aside. She gasped and he had just a glimpse of perfect uptilted breasts crowned with ruby before he swept her into his arms. He took her mouth with fury, his lips crushing hers and forcing them to part so he could rush inside.

He felt her hands thrust through his hair, her fingers clenching in an attempt to push him away, but he would not be denied. Her nipples tightened into points of fire against his chest and finally he left her mouth to kiss his way down her throat and over her collarbone.

At last his yearning mouth encountered the softness of her breast. Concentrating upon first one and then the other, he drew her nipples into his mouth, rough in his eagerness to possess.

She slumped against the wall, panting, making no protest other than her agonized breathing. He slid one possessive hand up her leg beneath her petticoat, his seeking fingers sliding over first her stocking, then the bare flesh of her thigh. Lifting his head, he looked at her in his triumph, one hand massaging her breast while the other slipped into the damp moist heat between her thighs...plunging deep.

Her eyes closed and her breath came in short, painful gasps. Her hands rested on his shoulders but she no longer sought to push him away. He moved faster, his fingers plunging deeper. She quivered like a wild thing and he felt her release building—

"The marshal won't ever be able to do for you what I can. Will he...make you feel like *this?*" Boone leaned into her, his hands working on her and in her to bring her to the climax he knew was almost upon her.

She moaned deep in her throat and from somewhere summoned the final vestige of strength. Whimpering, she caught his wrist and tightened her thighs, stilling the rhythmic plunging of his hand.

Opening her eyes, she shuddered. "No," she admitted in a raw voice, "but he'll...marry me. Can you say the same?"

Almost in slow motion—for letting her go was perhaps the hardest thing he'd ever done—Boone straightened, releasing her. He felt as if she'd thrown a bucket of cold water in his face.

"That's what I thought." Her lips trembled, as did the arms she crossed over her breasts.

He felt as if he'd wandered into a bad dream. "You know what I am. I can't marry anyone and you damned well know why." Could that be his voice, so naked and vulnerable? "I'm a marked man, Rose, the target of every would-be gunman who crosses my trail. I've tried to outrun my reputation, but it's always right behind me. I couldn't marry you if I wanted to—I couldn't marry any woman. It wouldn't be fair."

"Fair!" She choked out a scornful little laugh. "If you loved me..." She half turned, her chin against her chest. "I hate you, Boone Smith," she whispered. "I'll hate you until the day I die for what you've done to me—and what you're trying to do."

Out at the Rocking T, Diana Taggart ministered to her husband, James, who just that day had reinjured his arm in an altercation with a stubborn horse.

"You must go see Doc Beatty tomorrow," she scolded, carefully pulling his shirt sleeve down over the swollen limb. "Really, James, you should be more careful."

"I'm careful enough," he said shortly.

"And I'll go along to town with you and have a nice visit with Rose," she continued, dropping the shirt on the bedroom rug.

James frowned. "But you saw her today."

Diana gave him a disdainful look. "So? I like her."

"But you said it makes you queasy, ridin' in the buckboard now that you're—" He raised his eyebrows, giving her a cocky grin.

"It does, but—" She bit her lip, wondering how much she could safely tell him about Boone, and deciding not much, with his temper. Mentioning Marshal Guthrie seemed safe enough. "I have a feeling," she admitted, "well, it's more than a feeling, it's a definite hope."

"Now you've got me curious." James swung around on the bed and pulled her onto his lap, careful to spare his injured right arm.

Diana leaned forward to kiss him lightly on the lips, enjoying the silky stroke of his mustache. "I think Rose may have reconsidered about accepting the marshal's proposal," she said with satisfaction. "That is, if he asks her again."

"Do you mean it?" In his enthusiasm, James hugged her so tightly that she gasped. "Of course he'll ask her again. He's besotted with her!"

Diana slipped her arms around his neck. "Maybe so, but he may decide he doesn't like—" She stopped short.

James frowned. "Doesn't like what?"

"Well—" she hedged "—you know. Competition."

"Jack doesn't have any competition." His eyes narrowed. "Unless you're talking about that—"

He jumped off the bed so unexpectedly that he nearly spilled his wife onto the floor. "Dammit, Diana, are you talkin' about that low-down mangy gunfighter?"

She'd said too much and tried to cover her tracks. "Mr. Boone did buy her basket at the church social," she pointed out breathlessly, untangling herself from the voluminous folds of her nightdress. "And everybody knows he kissed her that time in the marshal's office. He's been an annoyance, th-that's all."

"Isn't that enough?" James glowered. "You know, I've been remiss in my duty as head of the family in J.D.'s absence, not calling that blackguard's bluff. He can't get away with making *my* sister unhappy."

Diana clutched at his bare shoulders, pressing herself against his chest. "Please, James, forget I mentioned it. Rose isn't unhappy. In fact, unless I've completely misjudged Marshal Guthrie, she's probably an *extremely* happy woman right this minute—maybe even an engaged one. Promise me you won't interfere unless she asks for your help."

James slid his good arm around her waist and pulled her slender form tight against him. He grinned; he kissed her; but he didn't promise.

The next day along about mid-afternoon, he rode into town alone, stopping first at the doctor's office. Doc Beatty applied a light splint to the injured arm and sent James on his way with a warning to show a little more respect for the healing process. James grunted noncommittally and went in search of Boone.

He was gratified shortly thereafter to see the gunman walking down the street toward the Yellow Rose. James stepped off his horse and tossed the reins over the hitching rail. He was waiting for Boone when he reached the saloon.

Boone saw Rose's brother and stopped short. He knew the man's reputation as a hothead—that trait seemed to run in the Taggart family. Boone felt fairly confident, however, that Rose had not confided to her brother about personal encounters with any man, himself included.

Still, James Taggart's face was grim and he held himself with wary stiffness. He was, as usual, wearing a gun belt with a Colt .45 in the holster.

"Taggart." Boone approached the other man warily, uncertain what was coming but prepared for anything—he hoped. "You lookin' for me?"

James stepped onto the boardwalk, his jaw thrust out belligerently. "I hear you've been annoyin' my sister."

"You hear that from her or you been listenin' to idle gossip?"

"Gossip?" James's lips thinned, as if he hadn't considered that aspect of the situation. "I won't have her name dragged through the mud by you or any other man. I'm tellin' you to stay away from her."

Boone's grin turned downright wintry. "And if I don't choose to follow your good advice?" he inquired softly.

"Then it'll be up to me to see that you do. You've had your fun. Biddin' on her basket at the church social was one thing, but forcing yourself on her later—"

"*Forcing* myself on her?" Boone's lips curled back over his teeth, and he started to turn away. "You don't know what the hell you're talkin' about. I suggest that before you say anymore you have a little talk with your sister. You just might find out she's not the innocent victim you seem to—"

Deliberately James blocked Boone's path, his face a mask of rage. "You mangy polecat!"

Boone sidestepped the fist whistling awkwardly toward his jaw and, without breaking stride, backhanded James Taggart. Although almost negligently delivered, it was nonetheless a powerful, full-swinging blow. It caught the smaller man solidly on the side of the head.

James stumbled to the edge of the boardwalk, struggling for balance. Pitching off backward, he hit the hitch rail and flipped over to land facedown in the dust.

Horses snorted and danced out of the way, and a sorrel yanked free and trotted away. Boone glanced coldly at the still form of James Taggart, shrugged and pushed on through the swinging doors into the Yellow Rose.

Chapter Fourteen

Doc Beatty peered at Rose, his eyes mere slits in a puffy face. "Too bad you're a woman," he said. "You'd a'made a mighty fine doctor."

She paused in her recitation of the health trials and tribulations suffered by the residents of Jones during Doc's absence. He hadn't been gone all that long, but it seemed like forever while she was struggling to fill a gap for which she felt considerably short of qualified.

She gave him an incredulous glance. "If that's a compliment, thanks. I did what I thought I had to do."

He sighed. "So do we all—most of the time, anyway." His face seemed to sag. "Rose, never take to the bottle. Drinking not only numbs your mind, it numbs your conscience and your good sense."

So does love. The thought flashed across her mind and she felt her scalp prickle with apprehension. So did...other things, whatever name could be put to the things Boone had made her feel. He touched her, and out the window flew her mind, her conscience and her good sense.

But that, of course, wasn't love. That was some kind of horrible power he exerted over her, with no apparent effort on his part. She hated him for flaunting it, really hated him.

But Doc she loved. Most of the time he treated her like an equal, not like some helpless and flighty female—and never like an old maid to be pitied and protected. At the moment, she supposed Doc was still feeling bad about showing up drunk at the church social and blurting out the real name of the man they'd known as Jeremy Edwards.

Well, she didn't consider what Doc had done a mistake, only the drinking that led up to it. She knew he'd had trouble with the bottle off and on for a long time, but in the four years he'd been in Jones he'd rarely slipped—at least, to her knowledge.

One more person whose life had been disrupted by Boone's arrival in town, she thought darkly.

Doc cleared his throat, as if embarrassed to be talking so much. "Did you see the Johnson kids while I was gone?" he asked, all business again.

She nodded. "There's no improvement there at all, that I can see. What is it, Doc?" Rose paused in rolling a bandage, holding the wad of cloth in her lap. "The oldest boy is just skin and bones and the baby—" She shook her head hopelessly.

"Malnutrition, plain and simple." He put down his cup and picked up the pipe resting in a large metal ashtray, a stream of fragrant smoke curling from the bowl. "I appreciate you checkin' on 'em for me, Rose. Miz Johnson won't let me inside the door anymore, since I told her to quit wastin' her money on patent medicines and buy those children some decent food."

"I took over some things from my garden," Rose offered, "beans, a few tomatoes."

"They won't eat 'em," Doc predicted. "That whole family seems to think they can't eat anything that didn't moo or oink while it was alive." He shook his head mournfully. "Well, we gotta keep tryin'."

That, unfortunately, was true. Rose nodded and bent to her task. No matter what the odds, they had to keep trying.

It was nearing midday and she was already behind in her self-appointed schedule. She had a number of things still to do—clothing to deliver to a family on the north side of town, several books she wanted to lend to little Emmett Cox.

Then she intended to have a long talk with Tonio Ryan, even if she had to ride all the way to the Rocking T to do it. With all that ahead of her, she'd intended to arrive earlier in the day to speak to Doc Beatty, but after her various ordeals of the previous evening...

Ordeals and narrow escapes. She'd come within an inch of succumbing to Boone only minutes after accepting Jack's marriage proposal, and that self-knowledge terrified her. She had pledged herself to the marshal and she would keep her promise.

But if last night was any indication, it wasn't going to be easy. She had finally decided that the more people who knew and supported her decision to marry the marshal, the better. And everyone in town would support it, she was sure, since Jack was universally regarded as the best catch in the county.

Steeling herself, she said quickly so as not to lose her nerve, "Doc, Marshal Guthrie has asked me to marry him. We're engaged."

Doc looked startled but he smiled. "That's good news long overdue." He slumped in his chair. "Jack's a fine man, but I gotta say, I'm surprised."

"Why is that?" Frowning, she hefted another pile of fabric onto her lap.

"I figured if anything was gonna happen in that quarter, it would'a been a long time ago. Then after seein' you and Boone together at the church social I kinda wondered if there might be something brewin' there."

"Have you heard gossip?" She tightened her lips with displeasure. "He bought my basket, but that's all."

"Well, yeah, but then he danced with you and come close to killin' that boy from Crystal Springs that bothered you."

She stared at the doctor in dismay. "He didn't come close to killing anybody! He didn't even draw his gun. He could have—he certainly had provocation. It was Curly Anderson's bullet that hit the punch bowl, not Boone's—"

She caught her breath, realizing she was actually *defending* the man. She drew herself up straight. "I admit I tended to him when he first came to town, but only because Jack asked me to," she said stiffly. "I barely even know him and that's the way I want to keep it." She set the bandage on the small worktable and reached for another end of cloth. "Jack loves me," she said staunchly.

There; that should exhaust the topic, since everybody in town, including Doc, knew how persistently Jack had pursued her.

"And you've finally decided you love him back, I take it."

She lifted her chin and tried to meet his eyes. "Yes, that's exactly it. My goodness, Doc, I had no idea you were such an expert on love!"

He gave her a crooked grin. "Why d'ya think I took to drink? I was married for thirty-seven years and fourteen days and then she up and died on me. Wasn't a damned thing I could do about it, either, doctor be damned. I loved that woman every single one'a them thirty-seven years and fourteen days, which was a damn good thing because there were times— Well, I just wouldn't want you gettin' into anything for the wrong reasons."

Rose's fingers felt cold and clammy, despite the heat of the day, and she rubbed her hands together. "Believe me, it's for the right reasons." Eager to change the subject, she added,

"I have more good news."

"Eh?" Doc raised shaggy eyebrows.

"Diana is expecting."

"James's wife? You don't say." He beamed.

"Yes. Imagine... a baby." Rose sighed with a combination of pleasure at the thought of becoming an aunt and jealousy that she, although a year older than Diana, was not yet a mother. She concentrated on the pleasure. "Diana's thrilled. I haven't heard from James yet but I know he's just as happy."

"He didn't mention it when he came by this morning," Doc said. "Guess he had other things on his mind."

Rose frowned. "James was here?"

"Yep. Hurt his arm yesterday and come by for me to splint it. Boy seems to think he's indestructible." Doc shook his head and reached for the ledger on one corner of his cluttered desk. "I expect his missus will be comin' in to see me when she gets a little further along. When's the blessed event?"

"Not till—"

The office door banged open and George Curtis stuck his head through the opening. His eyes glowed with excitement and his face was red and damp with perspiration. "Got an injured man here, Doc." He glanced expectantly at Rose.

Doc stood up. "Well, bring 'im in." He gestured toward the examining table at the other end of the room. "What happened?"

"Fight downtown. That gunfighter Boone is cuttin' quite a swath, let me tell you. Knocked this fella over a hitchin' rail and didn't even wait to see him light."

Doc grinned. "Doesn't sound like too much potential for damage there, but bring 'im on in anyway." He turned to Rose. "If you could put the kettle on—"

"Of course." She started for the door leading to the kitchen with one final glance over her shoulder. That quick look was enough to bring her to an abrupt halt.

Three men hauled an unconscious fourth through the door and deposited him on the padded examining table at the far end of the room. Rose gasped.

The injured man was James.

"Steady—keep that arm steady, Rose."

Rose nodded, concentrating on holding James's injured arm perfectly still. On the table, James groaned and turned his head aside. His complexion was waxy white, and lines of strain stood out around his mouth.

Fortunately he hadn't regained consciousness until after the broken bones in his forearm had been realigned. Rose didn't have to be told that this break was far worse than the original one. Despite her experience assisting the doctor, she'd grown queasy watching the manipulation necessary to prepare the arm for splinting.

Now she glanced up at George Curtis, the only one of the men who'd stayed after James was carried inside. "What happened, Mr. Curtis? You say that man Boone did this?"

"That's right—I saw the whole thing." The storekeeper sounded eager to talk about it. "James had just ridden into town and was minding his own business when Boone came along. Words were exchanged—don't know about what."

The quick and shifty way he cleared his throat told her he knew exactly what the two men had talked about. She tightened her lips in disapproval, and after a moment's hesitation, he continued.

"Anyway, something was said and then for no reason I could see, that Boone just hauled off and knocked your brother a'flyin'. James sailed off the boardwalk and lit on his bad arm on the hitching rail in front of the Yellow Rose before he hit the ground. That man killer didn't even wait to see what damage he done—just laughed and went on into the saloon and started drinkin'."

Rose bit her lip, and her hands trembled so badly that Doc gave her another warning glance. Still, a sense of fairness made her question the story she'd been told. "Surely Boone didn't do such a thing completely unprovoked. James must have said something, done something, however unintentionally. He does have a temper. Perhaps—"

"You defendin' that desperado?" George stared at her as if she was some kind of turncoat. "Think, Rose—he's like a sidewinder layin' in wait. Everybody who's crossed him has ended up with the short end of the stick. Mase, Curly Anderson, now James. Who's next, do you reckon—Marshal Guthrie?"

"There." Doc finished strapping the wooden splint in place and laid James's arm gingerly beside the injured man, who was breathing more easily. The remnants of his shirt lay bunched around the arm, left where they fell when Rose cut the sleeve away. The lighter splint Doc had applied earlier in the day had been shattered in the fall.

The injured man sighed and his lashes trembled.

"James?" Rose whispered. "James, it's all over. C-can you tell us what happened?"

James licked his lips and opened eyes cloudy with pain and shock. "I told Boone to leave you alone, Rose," he said in a gravelly voice. "He... declined to be reasonable."

Rose felt as if all the blood were rushing from her body in a single tide of disappointment. A deep resentment curled in the pit of her stomach, and she drew a quick painful breath. "But why would he do this?" she cried. "I told him very plainly that I want nothing further to do with him. Why won't he leave me alone?"

"'Cause he's a no-good rattlesnake?" George Curtis suggested hopefully.

"Nah," Doc Beatty countered, "unless he's changed drastically in the last four years. Boone must'a thought he had reason to disbelieve you, Rose."

All three men looked at her, waiting for a response.

"No!" she exclaimed. "He couldn't possibly have misunderstood. My God, I got engaged to—I mean, I *am* engaged and Boone knows it!"

George gave her a broad grin. "Heard that good news this mornin' from Marshal Guthrie," he said heartily. "Everybody in town's tickled pink, let me tell you. A'course, you ain't married yet, and if today's happenings are any indication of what to expect—"

Rose glared at him. "What's that supposed to mean?" She was beginning to feel trapped; everything was happening too fast.

George shrugged. "Think about it. That gunman's sweet on you, Rose. If he's willin' to beat up a man with a busted wing just for warnin' him off, what'a you think he'll be willin' to do to a man with the brass to marry you?" He shook his head. "I know *I* wouldn't want to be in Jack Guthrie's boots. Until the two of you have said your I do's, I don't think anybody in this town's gonna be safe."

"Hogwash." Doc looked from George to Rose, then at his patient. "George, you're disturbin' this boy. You wanna gossip like an old lady, take it outside."

"Sure, Doc." George looked at Rose, his expression sly. "Guess this is just one more thing that Boone'll get away with. James tried—I suppose Jack will, too, when he hears." He crossed to the open door. "Guess it's my duty to go tell 'im."

"No!" Rose started after George, then stopped to give her brother a distracted pat on the shoulder. She couldn't let Jack go after Boone. If Boone was pushed far enough, there was no telling what he might do—because he was capable of doing just about anything he wanted to. "James," she said, "rest here. I'll be back in a few minutes."

James struggled to rise onto his good elbow but he didn't have the strength and fell back. "Where you goin', Rose? You can't—"

"You're wrong. I'm the only one who can."

And she would. She'd make it crystal clear to that bullying gunman and to the entire town that she wanted nothing whatsoever to do with him, no matter what it took. This time no doubt concerning her feelings would remain in anybody's mind.

Her fury and outrage grew with every step she took. George Curtis fell in behind her, but she ignored him. His comments had been self-serving; she knew that. He still had the crazy idea that he could use the presence of the gunfighter to increase the town's prestige.

But what he'd said hadn't been crazy. Boone must be every bit as bad as George thought or he'd never have savagely attacked a man with a broken arm. *And my brother to boot,* she reminded herself. *If Boone had ever cared even the tiniest bit for me, he'd never have hurt my brother.*

So there it was. She had given herself to a man who was no more than an unfeeling villain. And last night, minutes after pledging herself to another man, she'd come near to making the same mistake again.

It was too awful. She must make a public display so convincing that even Boone would accept it, and she must do it before Jack got wind of what had happened and went in search of the gunman. Surely then Boone would leave town. Surely...

Dimly she realized George had been joined by Fred Loveless, then by several other townspeople. No one spoke to her or approached her in any way as she marched down the boardwalk toward the Yellow Rose Saloon, but she knew they followed in an ever-growing knot of interested and curious onlookers.

What she would do once she reached the saloon she deliberately refused to ponder. She'd never been inside such a place, or even considered it. But since she was sure that's where she'd find him, that's where she headed now.

She'd think of something when she got there.

Boone leaned against the bar inside the Yellow Rose, feeling like a damned dog. He held his third shot of bourbon in his hand and glared at it as if it were somehow at fault.

He wasn't proud of himself for the way he'd dealt with James Taggart, but he'd been on the ragged edge ever since Rose's announcement of her engagement last night.

Engaged to Jack Guthrie—didn't that just take the cake? *Had to be Jack,* Boone thought sourly; *anybody else I could shoot.*

The few drinkers inside the saloon were giving him a wide berth. Libby showed no such restraint, however. Entering through the swinging doors, she saw him at once and walked right up to him. Her pretty face looked worried, but he was in no mood to concern himself with anybody else's troubles.

"I heard the news," she said. "I'm sorry."

"Don't be." Boone spoke roughly. "He got what he deserved." He tossed down the bourbon and glared at her. "People in this town need to learn how to mind their own business."

Libby blinked, ignoring his implied criticism. "Who got what he deserved? I was talking about Rose's engagement to the marshal. What're *you* talking about?"

Hearing it said out loud made Boone's stomach lurch— *Rose's engagement.* As if the marriage was a foregone conclusion. Well, it wasn't. She hadn't married Jack Guthrie yet.

"I had a run-in with James Taggart a little while ago," Boone said. "He took a swing at me and I backhanded him over the hitch rail. No more'n he deserved, but the way folks come runnin', you'd have thought he was made out of glass."

"Oh, Boone!" Libby looked alarmed.

"You, too?" Boone gestured for Max, the bartender, who'd been watching with guarded attention. "Leave the damned bottle this time." He added to Libby, "I could'a shot him, you know. I thought I was doin' him a favor just slappin' him around a little."

"By your lights, I suppose you were." She watched Max pour the shot of liquor and set down the bottle before moving away. "You ever wonder why James didn't go on the Rocking T trail drive this spring with his pa?"

"Nope. Didn't wonder, didn't care."

"You should have. Because the reason he stayed home was a broken arm—his right. I heard it still hasn't healed properly. That means..." She let her voice trail off, letting him draw his own conclusions, looking at him through her lashes as if ashamed on his behalf.

"Jesus." He'd almost managed to rationalize his bad temper toward James until this new bit of information. Now he'd been gently informed that he'd just beat up a man with a bad arm.

He oughta feel real proud of himself. The way his luck was running, Marshal Guthrie would walk in here any minute and draw down on him, which would be tantamount to committing suicide. Then Rose really would despise him.

Why the hell am I still here? Boone wondered. *I could have ridden out of here days ago.*

Why the hell didn't I?

And at that very moment, the reason he'd stayed in Jones came storming through the doors and paused just beyond the threshold, all but breathing fire.

* * *

Rose didn't dare give herself time to think. Egged on by her growing audience, she felt she had no choice but to burst through the doors and confront the man who'd brought her and those she loved to grief.

Boone stood at the bar at the end nearest the door, Libby Bowman beside him. He held a shot glass in his hand and he barely looked up at Rose's entry.

This was not the Boone who had held her in his arms and made love to her. This was some hard-faced stranger, she realized. He looked rumpled and mean and he needed a shave. She swallowed her trepidation and marched right up to him.

Her entourage halted just inside the doors and she felt the weight of their expectations, along with those of everyone else in the room. Libby stared with a kind of horrified disbelief, then took a step away from Boone as if fearing guilt by association.

Rose glared into his unrepentant eyes, her fury increased tenfold by the lack of remorse she saw there. "Coward," she cried in ringing tones, "beating up on a man with a broken arm! I hate you—I wish I'd let you die!"

"No, you don't."

He put down his glass and turned deliberately to face her; it took all her strength of character not to recoil a step. His eyes blazed and he leaned forward, to all appearances as angry as she was.

He spoke in a low, harsh voice. "Your brother came looking for trouble, and I gave it to him. I didn't know he had a broken arm—"

"Would it have mattered?" She curled her lip.

"Probably not, once he threw the first punch."

"Liar!" She heaped scorn on him. "It was an unprovoked attack!"

"Says who?"

She tossed her head. "You think I'm going to tell you that? Why, so you'll have somebody else to abuse? I don't think so!"

"Look," he said, his lips curling derisively over even white teeth, "I don't know what you're here for but—"

"This," she said, and slapped him as hard as she could.

The sound of her hand across his lean cheek echoed through the room. Without missing a beat, Boone grabbed her by the shoulders, hauled her up against his chest so hard it knocked all the air from her lungs and kissed her.

She had never imagined a kiss could be so angry; all she felt was humiliation, she told herself.

Humiliation and a burning need to surrender. She was so tired of denying what she felt for this man! She could sense his hurt along with his anger, which further sapped her determination.

But any continued relationship between them was impossible. She couldn't weaken now.

He set her away from him in the complete and utter silence that had fallen over the barroom, then released her.

"How dare you." She reached up to wipe the back of her hand across her lips scornfully. "I'm an engaged woman!"

"Maybe so," he conceded, "but you're not married yet."

His challenging glance included everyone in the room. Then he turned . . . slowly, arrogantly . . . back to the bar.

Chapter Fifteen

The town of Jones, Texas, closed ranks around Rose Taggart following her public confrontation with the Kansas gunman. This did not indicate a lack of speculation on the part of local citizens, however.

Just what had the man meant when he reminded Rose that she wasn't married yet? Some thought that meant Boone would kill Jack Guthrie before letting him marry her; others believed that once Rose and Jack were safely married, Boone would leave them alone.

These and other interpretations were endlessly debated in the days immediately following what came to be known as "the incident in the Yellow Rose." Even old Mrs. Dinwiddy had a theory—that Boone was just the first arrival in a conspiracy of Kansas outlaws to take over the entire state of Texas.

Only George Curtis and his cronies seemed able to spot the silver lining in this particular black cloud. "*Somethin's* gonna happen," George told Fred during one of their morning meetings on the boardwalk. "Them three are buildin' up to a showdown."

Fred nodded agreement. "Showdown. What'a you figger?"

George shrugged. "Who knows? The marshal's been awful patient so far but he's got his limits just like the rest

of us. Boone's spendin' most of his time drinkin' and gam-
blin', lookin' like he could chew up nails and spit out tacks.
Then there's Rose, with that Taggart temper simmerin'
away. If somebody don't do something, she may just take
it in her mind to shoot Boone herself.''

"Shoot Boone herself," Fred echoed. "Boy, howdy!"

"Boy, howdy," George agreed. "Now the question is,
what can we do to take advantage of this situation—for the
good of our fair city, of course?"

"Of course," Fred agreed. "Sh—here he comes!"

Boone stepped onto the boardwalk where he paused to
look around. He'd spent the night at the Yellow Rose,
drinking too much and winning an inordinate amount of
money at the gaming tables. At present he was on his way to
the livery stable with every intention of riding out of town—
maybe for good, he hadn't quite decided.

Rumpled, in need of a shave and a good night's sleep, he
felt so ornery a sheepdog couldn't get along with him. His
hostile gaze slammed into the two merchants loitering on the
boardwalk; they shuffled their feet and looked away with
sick smiles.

Too bad. Boone was ready to take on a sack of wildcats
if they looked sideways at him. In a dangerous and deadly
mood, he strode straight for the front door of the C and J.

But before he could reach his destination, little Mrs.
Dinwiddy came sailing out. She saw Boone advancing and
stopped short, clutching a brown-paper-wrapped parcel beneath one arm and her small parasol between tiny lace-
mitted hands.

"You!" she exclaimed. "What are *you* still doing in
Jones?"

"Ma'am." Out of habit, Boone lifted his hat politely, then
almost snarled at her, "It was a free country, last I heard."

She blinked watery blue eyes behind little Ben Franklin glasses. "Not for the likes of you, it ain't! Botherin' our young ladies, shootin' our men—"

"Only them that need it," Boone cut in, giving her an evil grin he hoped would scare her off. Hands resting on his gun belt, he took an ominous step toward the open door—which was, of course, a step toward her as well.

Mrs. Dinwiddy shrieked and raised her parasol. "Help! This man's attacking me!" She brought the parasol down on Boone's head with surprising strength—not once but several times in rapid succession.

Discretion being the better part of valor, Boone covered his battered hat with his arms and backed off the boardwalk, vanquished by a five-foot termagant. Reaching street level, he spun and headed for the livery.

"And don't come back!" she shouted after him. He could just imagine her shaking her parasol threateningly while exchanging satisfied glances with Curtis and Loveless. "We don't need *your kind* in our town!"

Maybe not, but *his kind* sure as hell wasn't going to be driven away by somebody's granny.

The ride cleared his head and did the buckskin a lot of good, too. Boone's entry into this country was a blur to him; he'd been in bad shape then, looking for a place to hole up and lick his wounds.

Now he savored the place he'd found, a land of lush, green valleys and oak- and cedar-studded hills. Boone squinted up to watch a red-tailed hawk soar overhead, circling effortlessly as it scanned the endless emerald hills for prey.

Wild and free. Where was the kinship he usually felt with such creatures? He watched the hawk disappear into the vast blueness of the sky... alone. And he felt more affinity for it in that bleak moment than he had before, when it had seemed king of all it surveyed.

Turning the buckskin toward town, he rode in sullen silence, wanting to figure out what the hell he was trying to prove at Rose Taggart's expense.

That he could take her away from Jack Guthrie? That issue was never in doubt. Boone knew as well as he knew his own name that she'd become engaged out of desperation. She didn't love Jack but she needed a defense against Boone. He also knew she was sincere when she said she'd be a good wife and do her best to learn to love Jack in time.

It was not news to Boone that women had a hard row to hoe. So many things were forbidden to them, and those who trespassed paid the penalty of public disgrace. Rose Taggart was a hot-blooded woman trying like hell to live her life according to the tenets of respectable society. Although Boone knew he'd shown her a physical fulfillment she couldn't even have imagined, he also realized in his more rational moments—such as now—that he'd done her a grave disservice.

He couldn't offer her marriage because he couldn't offer her any kind of life that didn't involve constant danger and the possibility, even probability, of sudden death at the end of the most innocent-appearing trail. A real home, children—these were not in the cards for a man with his reputation.

If he convinced Rose to throw in her lot with him—and he was supremely confident that he could, if he chose to try—he'd be sentencing her to a life for which she was unfitted and unprepared. And if he was killed, she could even end up like Libby.

Boone knew more about Libby now than made him comfortable, for there was little he could do for her. Daughter of a Nebraska dirt farmer, she, too, had followed a man unwilling or unable to offer her marriage or respectability. He'd abandoned her a few years later in Chicago with a month-old baby daughter, a raft of debts and not a cent to pay them.

Libby had found a way to survive, but it was not a way he'd have Rose thrown into. Libby had managed to keep her child with her at first, but now the little girl lived with relatives. Libby sent money when she could; she wasn't even sure if her daughter knew her mother was still alive.

That's what happened to women who fell for fast-talking, footloose men, and he'd not see it happen to Rose—not even if the man was himself. The marshal was a good person, Boone reminded himself over and over again. He would make Rose happy.

If Boone could keep his mind and his hands off her.

Make that just *hands* because there was no way in hell he was going to be able to keep his thoughts off the woman he was beginning to suspect he loved.

Boone sat alone at a table at the Blue Bonnet, drinking strong black coffee while he waited for his steak and beans. Although there were many other diners, they all gave him a wide berth.

Which irritated the hell out of him, as usual. What did they think he was going to do, stand up and start shooting?

The tinkling of the bell over the door announced a new arrival. Boone glanced around without much interest, saw the marshal and felt the hairs at the nape of his neck prickle aggressively. He hadn't seen the law since his encounter yesterday with Rose in the saloon. He'd overheard somebody say Jack had been in Crystal Springs on business, but he'd thought maybe the man simply had the good sense to avoid him.

Which obviously wasn't the case, he saw as Jack tossed his hat onto the rack provided for that purpose by the door and walked directly to Boone's table.

"Howdy," the marshal said. "Mind if I join you?" Without waiting for an answer, he pulled out a chair and sat down.

Boone waited until the other man got settled before offering wryly, "Sure, grab a chair."

Jack grinned, melting some of the ice between them. "Thanks, believe I will."

Junius Cox scurried up. "We don't want no trouble here, Marshal," he said as if reciting a message entrusted to him by someone else. His expression, however, remained expectant—even hopeful.

Jack gave the waiter a bland smile. "No trouble, Junius. I'm just having a cup of coffee with my good friend."

Junius looked disappointed. "Oh," he said, frowning.

Jack leaned his elbows on the table. "That is, if I can *get* a cup of coffee. Any chance of that?"

The waiter snapped out of his trance. "Sure thing, Marshal. Comin' right up." He scampered away with many a backward glance.

Jack returned his attention to Boone. "Thought it might be time for us to have a little talk," he said mildly.

"How so?" Boone kept his face expressionless. The last time he'd seen the marshal, Jack had been in such a rage that if there'd been a gun handy, dollars to doughnuts he'd have used it. Now he sat there, despite additional and far more serious provocation, as calm as the eye of a hurricane.

Suddenly Jack grinned, an open expression of delight. "Maybe you've heard that Miss Rose is engaged to marry me."

"I heard," Boone said around the sour taste in his mouth.

Junius approached and the conversation broke off. The waiter plunked a platter of food down in front of Boone and a cup of java before Jack. "Anything else?" the waiter asked, ever hopeful.

Jack shook his head. Looking disappointed, Junius departed and Jack picked up the conversation again.

"Yeah, there's something else." He fiddled with the handle of his cup but didn't drink. "I know what happened in the Yellow Rose, of course. Must have been forty different people eager to tell me all about it."

Boone picked up his knife and fork. "Kinda thought I'd hear from you—about that and the little altercation with James Taggart." He speared the slab of beef on his platter. "Not that I expect you or anyone else to believe me, but I didn't know he was tryin' to pick a fight one-armed."

"Oh, I believe you." Jack finally lifted his cup and drank.

Boone raised his brows in surprise.

"James told me." Jack met Boone's surprised glance. "That's the way the Taggarts are. There's not a liar in the bunch."

"That right?" Boone couldn't stop the corners of his mouth from turning down at this bit of news. He didn't exactly consider Rose a liar, but she hadn't rushed to tell the truth about her personal affairs, either. Not that he blamed her, but Jack Guthrie had blinders on!

"Including Rose," Jack continued in the same carefully mild voice. "That's why I'm here."

"Care to be a bit more specific?" Boone hesitated, a forkful of tough beef halfway to his mouth.

Jack sighed. "I know," he said softly.

"You know." Boone began to eat. *Sure you do,* he thought.

"Everything."

"Uh-huh."

Jack made an exasperated sound. "Gonna make me spell it out, are you?"

Boone's appetite mysteriously fled. "This was your idea, remember?"

Jack's voice, already low, dropped another notch. "I know about Billy Curtis—I know he's the reason Rose has put me off all these months while I was trying to court her. And I know about you."

Boone put down his knife and fork, very slowly and very carefully. "Say what's on your mind, Marshal."

Jack licked his lips. "This'll sound crazy, I expect, but in a way, if you hadn't come to town, I don't think she'd ever have agreed to marry me. Because she wouldn't marry me until I knew the truth, and she was afraid to tell me the truth until it was forced on her. Does that make sense?"

Too much sense to Boone. "Then it's Tonio you should be talkin' to since he's the one who told you." His face felt stiff enough to crack. He couldn't help adding, "He thought at the time you were mad enough to kill him."

Jack nodded. "I was. It was very painful to hear that the woman I love . . ." He stopped and swallowed hard.

"No need to go on," Boone said brusquely. He shoved away his almost untouched platter of food.

"Yes, there is," Jack insisted doggedly. "We need to get it out in the open. It was painful to hear that the woman I love had . . . been intimate—" he heaved a great sigh as if the worst were past now "—with a man I like and respect." He mopped one hand across his forehead. "Jesus," he said, sighing, "I'm glad that's over."

Boone was still hung up on a detail. "What does that mean, we need to get it out in the open?" He half rose from his chair to lean across the table. "What the hell—*did you think I'd use what we did against her?*"

"No, no of course not."

Boone dropped into his seat, peripherally aware that half the men in the café had risen when he did as if expecting him to launch an attack across the table at the marshal. "Then what the hell did you mean?"

Jack looked and sounded almost giddy with relief. "Just that I realize Rose does not love me . . . now. But I'm sure someday she will. Until that day comes, she'll be a faithful wife."

"Rose Taggart is a fine woman," Boone agreed. *You don't know how fine, you son of a bitch, but I do.* "If that's all you wanted—"

"Almost. I have two . . . favors to ask you."

"All right." Boone slumped in his chair, but there was no relaxation in him.

"First, I'd appreciate it if you'd avoid further personal overtures and treat her like the engaged woman she is. It's not that I'm worried about her . . . ability to resist temptation, it's just that I don't see why you should make it any harder on her than it already is."

The man had the nerve of a bank robber. "I'll think about it," Boone snapped, eager to get away. "What else?"

Jack grinned. "We're going to officially announce our engagement tomorrow night at a party at the Taggart ranch. The whole town's invited, and both Rose and I would be most grateful if you'd come and help us put an end to this unfortunate gossip."

Diana stared at her sister-in-law with an expression of horror and fascination. "He didn't! What did Boone say?"

Rose shivered. "He said, 'Don't try to put me on my honor.' And Jack said that was exactly what he was trying to do."

"Oh, Rose." Diana sat down on the foot of the bed in Rose's old room at the Rocking T Ranch and clasped her hands together before her breasts. "This is the most romantic thing I've ever heard!"

"Romantic?" Rose wanted to weep, she was so exhausted from worry and lack of sleep. "How can it be romantic when I'm so *confused?* Di, am I doing the right thing? Is it fair to Jack, for me to marry him now?''

"Jack loves you—he adores you! He'll give you a wonderful life with a home, children. I know you want children.''

Rose nodded miserably.

"Rose, dear, you've held nothing back ... have you?''

"Nothing,'' she whispered, "except ... the depth of my feelings for Boone.''

Diana reached up and took Rose's cold hands to draw her down on the edge of the bed. The guests would begin arriving for the engagement party within the hour, and many last-minute tasks remained undone. But Diana seemed to sense the severity of Rose's malaise.

"Has Boone sought any greater commitment from you than ... that which he has apparently found with Mrs. Bowman?''

"N-no.''

"Has he ever said he loved you? Offered you anything beyond the shame and degradation of life as his mistress?''

Rose laughed shakily. "Actually, he hasn't even offered me that. He just seems to expect me to be available when and where he wants me.''

"That's not enough,'' Diana declared stoutly, "not nearly enough!''

"I know, but ... Boone needs me, Di.'' Rose felt her eyes mist over and blinked to keep the moisture at bay. "He doesn't know it but he needs me. He needs me to see that he eats properly and that his clothes are in good repair, that he gets the proper amount of sleep each night and that he has someone for whom to strive.''

Rose twisted around to stare into her sister-in-law's eyes, so that Diana could share her torment. "Jack will marry me hoping love will come. Sometimes I wonder—if I love

Boone perhaps marriage will come. Or if it doesn't, is it really that important?''

"Yes, dear, it is." Diana spoke with total conviction. "Where would civilization be if women did not insist on the commitment of marriage? Where would our children be?" She rested one hand lightly over her abdomen. "Some day, after you've been married for years and years and you have a devoted husband, children and grandchildren around you, you'll look back on all this and know that I was right. You'll remember the adventure and romance, not the heartbreak that might have been."

Rose laughed shakily. "Do you promise?"

"I promise!" Diana jumped up. "Quick, splash some cool water on your eyes and cheeks and hurry downstairs. It's going to be a wonderful party."

"Let us pray," Rose muttered.

Diana waved one hand airily. "Don't worry, Boone will be gentleman enough to stay away."

Rose wasn't so sure.

Boone rode into the ranch yard near dusk, one of the last to arrive. Watching his arrival, Rose clutched the edge of a trestle table groaning with food. Nearby, musicians tuned up at the edge of a wooden dance platform hastily erected for the festivities.

Almost the entire respectable population of Jones had been invited, and it looked as if they'd all shown up—along with a few individuals not quite so respectable. Rose looked around quickly for Jack and saw him, smiling at her as he came down the steps from the house.

He must have sensed her concern for he met her halfway across the yard.

"Boone's here," she whispered.

He nodded. "I told you I invited him."

"Yes." She licked her lips.

"You ready?"

"Yes."

Drawing a deep breath, she turned and took his arm and together they went to meet the man who seemed to be changing the course of so many lives.

James beat them to it, however, stepping forward to offer his left hand to Boone. "Glad you could make it," he said, narrow-eyed.

Boone stuck out his own left hand without hesitation. "Wouldn't miss it for the world," he said, his mouth tilting ironically. "How's the arm?"

"Healing." James drew Diana forward. "You know my wife?"

"Not officially." Boone made a slight bow over her hand. "Thank you for allowing me to visit your home, Mrs. Taggart."

"You're too kind," Diana murmured. She looked slightly overwhelmed by the situation—or the man.

And then, at long last, Boone turned to Rose and Jack. "Marshal. Miss Rose." He touched the brim of his hat with two fingers in a kind of salute.

Why did he have to look so good? Rose wondered without real hope of finding an answer. Freshly shaved, boots polished, shirt and pants pressed—by whom? She did not offer her hand.

"Good evening, sir." Oh, she sounded so stiff and insincere! But she hadn't seen him since that horrible day James had been hurt and she had stormed into the saloon.

Jack, standing slightly behind her, leaned forward to offer his hand, and in so doing, brushed against her shoulder. "Glad you could make it, Boone. Can we offer you some refreshment after your ride? We have coffee and lemonade, or perhaps you'd favor something stronger?"

Boone's teeth flashed against his dark skin in a smile that didn't get near his eyes. "Much stronger," he said gently, "but first I want to offer my congratulations and best wishes to you and your lovely bride-to-be."

Rose caught her breath but Jack's broad grin revealed nothing but pleasure.

"I'm a lucky man," Jack said happily, sliding his hand beneath Rose's elbow.

For the longest moment, Boone stood there looking at Rose. Then he said, "That you are, Marshal. That you are."

Feeling numb, Rose watched the three men walk toward the corral and one of the bottles stashed there. They disappeared from sight, and Diana turned to Rose with a wide-eyed and helpless expression.

"Oh, dear," she said faintly. "I see what you mean. He really is something, isn't he?"

"Yes, but what?" Rose wondered out loud. "God in heaven, what?"

Boone drank sparingly, well aware that he needed to keep his wits about him tonight. He felt as if he were walking a tightrope between his true feelings and those he'd put on special for this occasion.

The music began, provided by two fiddles and a guitar. Smiling dancers began to take the floor. He turned to Jack.

"Mind if I ask your intended to dance? There are a couple of things I want to say to her that I think she needs to hear."

Jack's hesitation was brief but pointed. "Sure, go ahead."

Boone nodded. Deliberately and without haste, he pushed away from the corral and walked toward the knot of women clustered around the punch bowl.

She saw him coming. He watched her stiffen, a look almost of panic touching her face, then quickly disappearing. He saw her whisper to Diana and thought she might try to find a way to avoid him, but she surprised him by instead stepping forward to meet him.

She spoke first. "I owe you an apology," she said in a determined voice. She didn't seem to care who heard her.

"Not at all," he inserted politely before she could go on. "I'm the one who—"

She tightened her lips, which took nothing away from their lush shape. She looked beautiful tonight, with her dark hair carefully arranged in curls and swirls, and a sky-blue satin gown accenting her many attributes. He did not, however, think she looked especially happy.

"Will you let me at least *pretend* to be gracious?" she hissed at him. "James told me what happened and I now realize his injury was not entirely your fault. Certainly you did nothing to provoke a physical attack such as the one I launched against your person in the—"

He laughed. He hadn't meant to but he couldn't help it and wasn't sorry, even when he saw heads turning their way. "An attack against my person? You slapped my face, Miss Rose. I richly deserved it and *I* am the one who must apologize. I'll do so now if you'll give me a chance."

She closed her eyes as if seeking strength and apparently finding it, for when she looked at him again she seemed calmer. "Pray proceed, Mr. Boone."

He gave her a slight bow. "I apologize, Miss Rose. I apologize for publicly humiliating you at the Yellow Rose and for... any other things I might have done that displeased you."

Eyelids half lowered, he watched her. She knew exactly what he was talking about. Like him, she had not forgotten his visit to her bedroom where she had flung her engagement in his teeth.

And he had met it with proof of the mastery he held over her body. Even now, if he let his glance stray to her mouth, then slowly down the pale smooth throat to the swell of her breasts above the blue satin—*dammit, no!* He wasn't going to play those games with her anymore. He kept his attention strictly on her face, and therefore didn't miss the hot sweep of color into her cheeks.

"I accept your apology," she said stiffly. "Let us say no more about it."

"Excellent. In that case—and of course, with the permission of your fiancé—" He glanced toward the men still loitering near the corrals; Jack smiled and nodded. "May I have the honor of the next dance?"

"Oh, God!" She looked at him, panic-stricken, then glanced hastily around to see if anyone had overheard. No one had, with the possible exception of Diana, who kept her face turned carefully away.

Boone couldn't help smiling at her. "I promise I'll behave with the utmost decorum," he promised. "Come, Rose, it will go a long way toward putting these rumors to rest."

He held out his hand and she looked at it, then into his eyes. He nodded encouragement. Slowly, as if she lacked the will to resist, she lifted her hand and slipped her cold fingers into his.

Taut as a bowstring, he led her onto the dance floor and took her in his arms.

Chapter Sixteen

The music began. Boone held Rose in his arms with just the proper degree of respect. As they began to move, other couples cleared a space around them until they danced nearly alone.

Rose loved to dance, and Boone was as wonderful a dancer as she remembered, leading with grace and confidence. Still her tension and dismay grew with every sweeping step. She dared not abandon herself to the joy of the music or the magnetic appeal of her partner. Holding herself stiff and erect, she followed him with decorous precision.

Yet her hand in his grew warm, and she felt her cheeks glow with the rush of exhilaration she could not completely tamp down. Boone excited her as no other man ever had, or, she suspected, ever could or would. Because of that, he was a greater danger to her than a diamondback rattler.

The music ended and he whirled her to a breathless halt.

"Thank you for the dance," he murmured, bowing slightly. "I won't trouble you again."

"Wait." Without thinking, she reached out to pluck at his sleeve with nervous fingers. "Is it over, Boone?"

He looked into her eyes and his were unfathomable. "Is what over, Rose—Miss Rose?"

"Us." She barely breathed the word because she didn't want anyone else to hear. "I am going to marry Jack, and very soon."

He lifted his gaze to some point beyond her right shoulder. "Then I suppose it must be over, assuming nothing untoward happens to the groom." He gave her a quick, lopsided smile that suggested he might be joking.

"Boone—"

"Leave well enough alone, Rose." He took a step toward the edge of the platform. "Will you excuse me? I have a very strong hunch that all hell is about to break loose."

He leaped to the ground and hurried across the clearing, weaving his way between the party guests. Feeling unaccountably let down, Rose frowned after him.

And saw Tonio and Sally, half-hidden behind an oak tree. They appeared to be arguing; Tonio grabbed Sally's elbows and yanked her up on her toes while he said something to her that didn't look very friendly.

So engrossed were they that neither was aware of her father and Boone, converging upon them from opposite directions. Anticipating the worst, Rose looked around anxiously for Jack.

George reached the young couple first. He grabbed the collar of Tonio's shirt and hauled him back. With a curse, Tonio clawed for the revolver on his hip. Sally screamed and threw herself on her father's arm, even as he raised it to deliver a blow.

Boone's hand streaked out just as the gun cleared the holster, clamping down over the barrel and swinging it to one side. Tonio was effectively sandwiched between the two older men.

"Dammit, Boone, whose side you on anyway?"

"Yours, you young jackass." Boone wrested the gun away and turned to confront Sally's furious father. "Let him go, Curtis."

"The hell you say!" Curtis glared at Boone, tightening his grip on the boy's shirt until he was practically strangling the kid. "I warned this half-breed to stay away from my girl and you see how he listens." He shook Tonio as a cat shakes a kitten.

"Get your hand off him *now* or I'll break it off." Boone said the words with such chilling certainty that Curtis blanched and stepped back, his hand falling away.

Which gave Tonio the opportunity he needed. Whirling, he threw himself at his tormentor.

"You got no right to be givin' me orders," he snarled. "I've had about all I—"

Boone brought the boy up short with an arm clamped around his waist, so suddenly and so tightly that Tonio grunted and doubled over. Boone spared a quick glance toward the rapidly growing circle of observers.

"Show's over," he snapped. "Go on back to your party while I have a word with this young hellion."

Tightening his grip on the boy, Boone half dragged, half carried Tonio away from the party. Once behind the farthest corral, he dumped the boy on the ground with a disgusted grunt.

Tonio lay there for a moment in the shadows, gasping like a beached trout. When he'd regained his breath, he staggered to his feet. "What the hell's the matter with you?" he raged, going up on the balls of his feet to confront Boone eye to eye. "I wasn't doing anything wrong!"

"Making up to Sally Curtis right under her pa's nose when you know he'd just as soon shoot you as look at you? You don't call that anything wrong?" Boone stepped aside to give the boy room to roar. Leaning against the corral, he crossed his arms over his chest and waited stoically.

Tonio obliged. With pantherish steps, he paced about raging and swearing and flinging his arms around. He cursed George Curtis back several generations and questioned his fitness to be called a man.

Finally the boy subsided to stand there breathing heavily, glaring at Boone. "That *storekeeper's* gonna push me too far one of these days," he predicted angrily. "Well, to hell with that! No matter what he does, he's not gonna keep me and Sally apart!"

"You say storekeeper as if it's a dirty word," Boone observed.

The boy's lip curled. "Isn't it? That's no way for a man to live, sellin' gewgaws to ladies!"

"No?" Boone's eyebrows soared. "And how should a *man* live?"

"Why..." Tonio frowned. "Free to do what he wants to do with nobody to tell him he can't."

Boone nodded, face impassive. "What about Sally?"

"What about her?" Tonio cocked his head and his eyes narrowed suspiciously.

"While you're bein' free, what'll she be doin'?"

"Why, she—" Tonio frowned. "How would I know?"

"You love her, don't you? Isn't that what this is all about?"

"Well, yeah..."

Boone put it bluntly. "So do you want to marry her or just sleep with her?"

Tonio thought about it for a moment. "I wanted to marry her before, but now..."

"Now what?" Boone shoved away from the corral to crowd the boy a step. "You think you can just bed her and walk away? She's a decent girl—"

Tonio frowned. "I didn't think you liked her."

"I don't. What difference does that make? I think she's shallow and selfish, but so are most people. She's also a decent girl from a decent family. What happens if you get her pregnant?"

"I . . . I don't know," Tonio admitted. "I hadn't thought about that much lately."

"Well, *start* thinking about it!" Boone shoved his forefinger into the boy's chest. "What if her father catches the two of you together once too often?"

"I told you I'm not taking any more off George Curtis!"

"Meaning you'll shoot him?"

Tonio looked cornered. "If I have to."

"Good. That's real good." Boone shook his head in disgust. "Sally'll really love that, you shootin' her pa."

"It probably won't come to that," Tonio said sullenly. "But what if it does?"

"You ever shoot a man?" Boone's cold, unemotional voice lashed at the boy.

"N-no, but I'm good enough with a gun. There's gotta be a first time for everything." The boy's chin came up defensively.

Boone shook his head slowly. "Not for everything. You ever make love to a lady?"

"Dammit, Boone, why you askin' me all these questions?"

"Jesus!" Boone glared at the boy. "I'm only asking the questions you should be asking yourself. You're feelin' your oats, boy—don't you think I understand that? But you don't know what the hell it is you really want. And while you're trying to find out, you're about to get yourself in a whole peck of trouble."

"I do know what I want," the boy muttered under his breath.

But Boone heard. "Out with it, then." He gestured impatiently with the fingers of one hand.

Tonio stared at Boone. "I want what you've got," he burst out. "You had your lady and I want mine. After I have her—'' He shrugged and his young face wore an expression of callous disregard, which suddenly changed to eagerness. "I want to be just like you, Boone—just like you!"

Boone stared at the boy in stark disbelief. His stomach clenched; he felt sick. Had it come to this, then? What was it Rose had accused him of—corrupting the boy? He'd denied it then, but he couldn't deny it now.

"Like me?" Moving with the lightning speed that branded him a warrior, Boone grabbed the boy by the front of the shirt and dragged him close. "You don't know what the hell you're saying."

Tonio caught at the hand imprisoning him but didn't try to break away. "I do," he exclaimed. He sounded breathless with excitement. "Let me go with you when you leave. You won't be sorry—I can watch your back trail, cook, clean up, take care of your horse and your weapons, anything you want. I can learn from you. You can teach me—"

"I think I've already taught you too much and all of it the wrong things." Boone shoved the boy away and flexed his hand. "What in the hell do you think my life is like, that you're so eager to share it?"

"You get respect!"

"That's not respect, it's fear." How could the boy mistake one for the other? Or perhaps one was as good as the other to a kid growing up a half-breed in a town like Jones, Texas.

Tonio refused to back down. "Nobody messes with you. Men step off the boardwalk when they see you comin'. You get all the women you want—"

Boone groaned.

"You do! Libby and Miss Rose both—"

"Don't bring Rose into this." Boone surged forward, fists rising in an unconscious threat. "You could cause her a lot of trouble."

Tonio's dark head drooped. "I reckon I already done that when I said what I did to the marshal." He looked up defiantly. "But they've worked all that out or they wouldn't be fixin' to get married. Ain't that right?"

"Maybe so, but there's others who don't know and whose opinion she values."

"Yeah, you're right about that." Tonio looked thoroughly ashamed. "Miss Rose is just about the finest woman ever to walk the earth, but truth is truth—she went to you." The boy said it with wonder. "After all the men she's turned down, she went to you."

"Shut up." Boone didn't need to be reminded, and rage threatened to break the bounds of his control; yet why he was so angry he couldn't have said. "She's going to marry another man. Show a little respect."

"She picked you," the boy insisted stubbornly. "You had her first."

Boone winced. "And couldn't keep her. I had nothing to give her."

Tonio's eyes went wide. "Did you want to keep her?"

Did he? Boone had refused to let himself consider that question because it was pointless. A lot of questions in his life were pointless—his whole damned life seemed suddenly pointless, but there was still time for this boy to make wiser choices.

He began to speak in a low, intense voice that grew in volume as the words spilled out. "Why the hell you think I came to Jones in the first place?"

The boy looked startled. "You were shot."

"I was shot," Boone agreed sarcastically. "I was sitting in a two-bit cantina in San Antone tryin' to decide whether to hire out my gun to the highest bidder. A man I thought was my friend got tired of waitin' for me to make up my mind and stuck a knife between my ribs."

Tonio's eyes flared. "You shoot 'im?"

"Hell, yes!" Boone glowered. "And then his friends sho
me. Next time we run into each other, more lead will fly."
He stared out into the blackness beyond the circle of ligh
that was the engagement party. "You know why I came to
Texas in the first place?" he demanded suddenly.

Tonio laughed. "It's the land of opportunity," he sug
gested.

Boone nodded. "That's what I thought when I left Colo
rado Territory. I was wrong."

"I hear Colorado's real pretty country," Tonio re
marked.

"Yes. Good range up there on the high plains. I had me
a nice spread, ran a few head of cattle and did a little pan
nin' for gold."

"But you didn't stay," Tonio said smugly, as if tha
proved something.

"That's right. I left—after a few badmen from Kansa
recognized me and decided to try their luck. The point is
I've just about run out of places to hide. Ever since Wich
ita—"

"I know about that," Tonio inserted eagerly. "One of the
hands here at the Rockin' T was there when it happened. He
said there never was anybody faster with a gun than you. He
said—"

"He's wrong. There's always somebody faster. Or luck
ier, or some other damn thing. I've been shot, I've been
knifed, I've been beat to a nubbin'. I've toted a star on some
occasions and I've been on the receivin' end of the atten
tions of the law on others. But I never hired out my gun to
the highest bidder. That to a man is like whorin' to a
woman—the end of the line."

"You're thinkin' of tryin' it now, though," Tonio pre
dicted softly.

Boone shrugged, embarrassed at being so easily read by
a mere boy. "I told you, my choices have about dried up

I'm a lot of miles and years from Wichita but I can't seem to run away from my reputation.''

"I'll be famous some day, too," Tonio said in an awed tone.

Boone resisted the urge to grab the kid by the throat and shake some sense into him. "If you are, let it be for something more than the way you handle a gun."

Tonio's glance grew sharp and eager. "How old were you when you killed your first man?"

He'd been sixteen, a soldier for a cause already lost. It had happened so quickly and so unexpectedly that when it was over and he realized what he'd done, Boone had staggered off into the brush and— He didn't want to remember that day, the day he lost his innocence. Damn Tonio. "Back off," he said harshly. "You're about to cross a fine line here."

"Younger than me, I bet." Tonio patted his gun belt, seemingly oblivious to the older man's deep feelings. "But I got time. I'm learnin'. I watch you—"

"And see the wrong things. Don't you hear what I'm saying, boy?"

Boone realized he wasn't getting through to the kid, so he spoke with brutal honesty. "I've been betrayed by men I thought were my friends, abandoned by women I thought loved me. I'm thirty years old, an age where a man should have a wife and a family and a stake in life, and what do I have? A horse, a gun, a bad reputation and no future. That's why I couldn't keep Miss Rose, even if I wanted to. I'm a man to be pitied, not held up as an example."

Tonio shook his head and his dark eyes glowed clear and untroubled. "No," he said, "I don't believe you. It's me— you don't think I'm tough enough, smart enough, I don't know what. But you're wrong, dead wrong. You're wrong about something else, too."

"And what might that be?" Boone felt drained by wha
he'd just revealed to this ungrateful little pup. He'd neve
taken a more honest look at what his life had become an
he didn't like what he'd seen.

"I'm no kid. If I want Sally I'll have her, and anybod
who gets in the way better be ready to get hurt."

Boone watched Tonio stalk away into the darkness be
yond the corrals. The boy had the bit between his teeth, n
doubt about it. He was at a crossroads and he could go ei
ther way.

Like me.

George Curtis was waiting when Boone walked into th
circle of torchlight illuminating the engagement party. "Yo
manage to talk some sense into that half-breed?" he asked
but not belligerently. George apparently knew who h
wanted on his side.

Boone shrugged and kept walking toward the punch bov
on the refreshment table. People saw him coming an
stepped aside to let him pass. None of them spoke to him
This was what Tonio wanted?

George fell into step beside him. "Nice party," he said.

Boone kept walking.

"A few folks came all the way from Crystal Springs fo
the festivities. The Taggarts got friends everywhere."

Boone reached his destination and picked up a punch cuµ
He didn't know what Curtis was getting at but he figure
it'd be something he wouldn't like.

"They say Curly Anderson's over there talkin' big."

"Curly Anderson?" Boone frowned over the rim of hi
cup.

"The boy you tangled with at the church social."

"That right." Boone turned his back on Curtis, ostens
bly to survey the crowd. His glance settled instantly on th
two people he least wanted to see.

Rose and Jack held smiling court near the door of the two-story frame ranch house, Diana and James Taggart beside them. Rose smiled at Jack and said something that made him chuckle; Boone saw the marshal's arm sneak around her waist and squeeze.

Turning away quickly, Boone realized George Curtis still hovered at his elbow. He gave the man an unfriendly glance.

George swallowed hard and his fleshy face quivered. "Uh, you plannin' on stayin' around for the wedding? Fred says he don't mind you sleepin' in his stable, makes him feel safer, in fact. Ain't nobody gonna mess with no horses guarded by a man with your reputation. Heh, heh!"

Boone could almost understand Tonio's desire to take this man's scalp. "I'll be out of there tomorrow," he said, making his voice cold and flat. He didn't know where he was going but anything that made Curtis and Loveless happy couldn't be good. "As for the wedding..."

Boone hesitated, his glance moving once again to the happy couple. He saw Jack take Rose's hand and raise it to his lips; he saw the worshipful expression in the other man's eyes and felt the gorge rise in the back of his throat.

He turned to George Curtis and said in a soft, malevolent voice, "As for the wedding...it hasn't happened yet, has it? Who knows what any of us will be doing on that fateful day?"

For the first time in years, Rose felt like the belle of the ball. Surrounded by so much public approval, she'd almost managed to shove aside her reservations about this marriage.

At least she had while Boone was out of sight. Now that he'd returned, her sense of euphoria evaporated.

Jack didn't seem to notice as he raised her hand to drop a light kiss on her knuckles. "Having a good time?" he asked indulgently.

"Oh, yes!" She said it dutifully, putting a little extra certainty into her tone. "Everyone's been very kind."

"It's a happy occasion." His expression turned serious. "Rose, there's something I'd like to talk to you about."

Her heart leaped with apprehension. "Now? Is something wrong?"

He chuckled. "Far from it. It's just that . . . I don't want to wait."

She blinked. "Wait for what?"

"For you." He squeezed her hands. "Rose, let's get married right away."

No! she wanted to scream at him. *I'm not ready!* Despite her best efforts to resist temptation, her glance flew across the clearing to settle on the dark countenance of the gunman Boone, standing beside George Curtis. She shivered; he looked cold and distant, like a complete stranger. If only she could think of him that way!

Marry Jack, the sooner the better, the little voice of her conscience scolded her. Why wait? Even now she could be pregnant. If she was, did she really want to know the baby was Boone's? Wouldn't it be better not to be sure, both for her sake and for Jack's?

She met the marshal's hopeful gaze. "A-all right, if you're sure."

He looked startled, and then a broad, pleased grin creased his face. "God, yes, I'm sure! Would two weeks be too soon?"

Two weeks! She licked her lips and forced herself to nod. "I think I can be ready that quickly, if that's what you really want."

"I do," he said sincerely. "More than anything. Once you are my wife, I can spoil you and pamper you as you deserve."

She hated it when he talked that way. Adulation made her uncomfortable. She wasn't some plaster saint to be worshiped, as he very well knew. She'd much prefer it if he'd treat her as an equal, but it seemed unlikely that would ever happen.

"There's one other thing."

She tried not to stiffen too noticeably. "What?"

"After we're married, Rose, I wonder..."

"Yes, Jack?"

"Perhaps I'm misjudging your feelings, but it doesn't seem to me you've been real happy living in Jones lately. I remember you mentioning a desire to visit your relatives in New Orleans."

"Oh, Jack!" She turned to him with a delighted smile. "Are we going to New Orleans on our honeymoon?" Saying the last word made her blush, but the prospect of the trip excited her beyond measure. She hadn't even thought about a honeymoon but realized she should have, since Jack had the means to afford such a trip.

How much easier to begin her married life away from Boone's watchful eye. She resisted the urge to glance at him again. It was going to be hard enough to allow Jack the...intimacies...that were a husband's right. To do it with Boone in the vicinity—the same state, even!—might be more than she could endure.

"We'll go anywhere you choose for our honeymoon," he vowed. "New Orleans, Paris, London—where ever you'd like."

"How exciting!"

"Then I'd like to take you to meet my family in Philadelphia. They'll love you, Rose."

She was less sure of that than he seemed to be but agreed dutifully. "Of course, Jack."

"And if you like it there—"

She waited, a fixed smile on her face.

"—we don't ever have to come back to Texas. I could re-sume my position in my family's law firm and we could set-tle there if you would—"

The rest of his words were lost when she threw her arms around his neck, hurled herself up on tiptoe and planted a big, grateful kiss on his cheek.

Rose and Jack stood hand in hand on the edge of the platform erected for dancing, facing their guests as the party drew to a close. Boone lingered on the fringes, wondering at her dazzling smile.

He'd seen her throw her arms around her intended and had speculated on what occasioned such an unseemly show of emotion. Being a woman, she was probably reacting to a gift—a gem, perhaps, or some other valuable bauble. His mouth curved down in disapproval.

Jack held up his hands for attention while Rose stood smiling at his side—or maybe simpering was a better word for it, Boone thought darkly.

"Friends, neighbors," Jack began, "my fiancée and I thank you for coming here tonight to share our happi-ness."

Shouts and hoots of approval greeted this announce-ment, until once again Jack held up his hands. When si-lence was restored, he continued, "We want to invite you all to the wedding, which will be two weeks from today at—"

Jesus! Boone spun away, plunging deeper into the shad-ows. *Two friggin' weeks?*

"But that's not all." Rose's lilting voice seemed to go straight as an arrow to Boone's heart. "Tell them the rest of our exciting news, dear."

"Gladly." He squeezed her hand. "Mr. and Mrs. Jack Guthrie will, in all likelihood, be setting up housekeeping in Philadelphia." Into the shocked silence that followed, he spoke almost gently. "Guess you'd better start looking for a new marshal, because two weeks from today, the job'll be open. I've been lucky so far, but I'm a lawyer, not a fighter. There are many men better suited to wear this badge.''

He looked over the heads of the stunned guests as if seeking out someone in particular. ''Think about it.''

Chapter Seventeen

Rose sucked in her abdomen and tried to will her waist two inches smaller than it would ever be. Diana, holding the corset strings like the reins to a team of horses, braced herself and pulled with all her might.

Rose's head spun as the scant supply of air still in her body whooshed out. Gasping, she grabbed hold of the foot post of James's and Diana's bed and hung on with grim determination.

"Stop!" she pleaded. "This is impossible—no matter what you do, I *still* won't fit into your wedding gown!"

"Oh, yes you will," Diana promised. "Just a tiny bit tighter—"

Rose shook her head vigorously, her dark unbound hair spilling over her shoulders. "Have mercy, Diana! I'm two inches taller than you and at least two inches bigger around the waist. You couldn't melt me and *pour* me in your dress. The more you pull me in here—" she jabbed at her waist "—the more I stick out...other places."

It was true; the strangulation of her waist by the whalebone corset had at the same time pushed her breasts up and her hips out. She looked like some denizen of a dance hall, she thought as she caught her reflection in the mirror.

Diana was loath to give up so easily. Flushed and perspiring from exertion, she wrapped the corset strings around her sister-in-law's waist and tied them in a slip knot.

"Give it one more try," she insisted, turning toward the enormous pile of white ruffles and flounces on the bed. "We don't have *time* to make you a proper gown of your own. So you're a little bit uncomfortable—it's only for a few hours. You'll be astonished how little time it takes to change your life completely!"

She tossed a petticoat through the air and Rose caught it on the fly. "Here, put this on while I find the front of the dress."

Rose did as directed, knowing it was hopeless. Bending over, she ducked her head to let the heavy wedding gown settle over her, then straightened and worked her arms into the long sleeves.

Her head emerged from the froth of lace. Gasping with effort, she held out her arms to let Diana settle the gown around her.

It was an exquisite creation, she admitted readily. Diana's mother had kept three seamstresses busy for weeks while she oversaw every stitch. Now Diana wanted to lend it with love.

But the darn thing just didn't fit!

"I can't," Rose gasped, trying to suck in even more so the bodice would meet in back. "I'm just bigger than you are, Di—admit it. Even if you could lace me into this thing, I'd pass out before I was halfway up the aisle."

Pulling down the bodice, she tried to wiggle her shoulders out of the sleeves. "Besides," she said, her voice muffled and breathless from her efforts, "I don't really feel comfortable in white."

There—she had it around her waist. Wiggling her hips, she worked the gown down until it lay in a satin puddle at her feet. She stepped out triumphantly. "Believe me, I appreciate your generosity, but it's impossible. Besides, I don't need anything all that elaborate. Something simple will do—maybe I'll just wear my yellow cotton. It's almost new."

Diana blinked hard and tears sprang to her eyes. She'd been teary all morning, and Rose wondered fleetingly if something had happened last night at the engagement party that she knew nothing about.

Diana scooped the gown up in a big armful, looked down at the crushed satin and began to cry.

Not even waiting to untie the corset knot, Rose guided Diana to the bed and sat her down. "What is it, hon?" she begged, hugging the sobbing woman. "What's wrong? You're feeling all right, aren't you? Doc says a woman in your condition—"

"Oh, bother my condition!" Diana dabbed at her eyes with a wad of satin. "Under no circumstances will you wear yellow! It would be a scandal."

Rose sighed. "I suppose you're right. But there's no time to make something new. Where would I find enough white yard goods for a proper gown?"

Diana thrust out her trembling lower lip. "I *want* you to wear my dress, Rose."

Rose laughed helplessly. "What can I do, Diana? I'm too big! You should have married a man with a smaller sister."

Diana apparently saw no humor in that statement, for she let out a frustrated howl and the tears fell faster. "Don't joke," she sobbed. "I already feel bad enough about this. I almost f-forced you into this engagement and now everything's m-moving so fast. And you're not even going to have a proper w-wedding gown!"

Rose stared at her best friend in dismay. "Diana Taggart, don't tell me you have doubts at this late date!" She sat down hard on the floor at Diana's feet. "You *told* me not to settle for anything less than marriage. You *told* me I was upholding centuries of tradition and the honor of my sex.

You *told* me what a fine man Jack is, and how lucky I am that he loves me enough to forgive—''

"Don't go on!" Diana looked around wildly. "I said all those things before I saw that gunfighter Boone at the engagement party, so tortured and so...romantic. Rose, I was watching him when Jack announced your wedding plans. I don't think he's going to let you do it."

"Get married? He can't stop me!" Rose scrambled to her feet. "What am I saying? He doesn't want to stop me. He got what he wanted from me—no, don't look at me like that, you know it's true!"

Diana drew a quick, hiccupy breath. "You're right, I do. I'm being silly, I suppose. Will you f-forgive me?"

Instantly contrite, Rose sat down on the bed beside her weepy sister-in-law, putting one hand lightly on Diana's knee. "There's nothing to forgive. I've seen enough expectant mothers to know they're not always responsible for their actions."

Diana tried to smile. "That's very generous of you, dear. In that case, will you allow me to say one more thing?"

"Of course."

"*Wear my dress!* It will bring you luck as it did James and me. We're happier than I ever dreamed possible." Diana twisted on the bed. "I have this awful feeling that you and Jack are going to need all the luck you can beg, borrow or steal to even get to the altar."

But in the end, even Diana was forced to bow to the inevitable, and her beautiful gown was once more packed away in the attic at the Rocking T.

"Someday," she sighed as she smoothed the folds of satin and lace. "Surely someday another Taggart bride will wear my beautiful wedding gown on the happiest day of her life."

"Perhaps your daughter," Rose offered, eager to avoid more histrionics. "I do have another idea to solve our immediate problem."

"Oh, dear," Diana said faintly.

Rose smiled and spoke coaxingly. "Desperate times call for desperate measures. I have a white summer silk with green trim that I've only worn a couple of times. Perhaps we could do something with that—take off the pink rosettes and green ribbons and replace them with whatever we can find at the C and J."

Diana groaned. "Not an old dress! That's bad luck, Rose. A bride deserves something special."

"We can make it special. It's really a very nice dress, and it fits me perfectly. Please, Di, at least come look at it. I really don't think we have much choice in the matter."

"I suppose you're right." Diana sighed, then brightened. "I have a box of trims and notions my mother sent and there may be something there we can use. Let's do go look! How's the dress made?"

"It's a princess sheath with a train, draped and decorated in all kinds of complicated ways."

"It has a bustle, of course."

"A small one." Rose followed Diana out of the bedroom, thinking wryly that perhaps she should just talk to Jack about an elopement.

Rose ran her fingers down the length of silk braid, judging the quality and finding it wanting. "Diana, do you think this might be useful?" she asked doubtfully.

At the opposite end of the counter at the C and J, Diana looked up distractedly. She held the end of a bolt of ruching in her hand, its color so faint a blue that it looked almost icy.

"If it's white, buy it," she ordered bluntly. "We need yards and yards and yards of *something* to replace all that green ribbon.'' She glanced around at the fabrics and trims littering the counter. ''Surely this isn't all Mr. Curtis has in stock.'' She glared toward the back of the store. ''Mr. Curtis! Mr. Curtis, where's the rest of it?''

Watching her sister-in-law's determined stride as she went in search of the elusive storekeeper, Rose laughed softly under her breath. If George Curtis was holding out, he'd find himself in more trouble than he could handle.

She didn't think he was, though. She was surprised he had as much stock as he did. These ribbons, now—she picked up the white satin lengths and fluttered them between her fingertips.

Hearing footsteps, she turned, expecting to find Diana returning. Instead, Libby Bowman stood there.

''Good afternoon, Miss Rose.''

''Good afternoon, Mrs. Bowman.'' Rose held up the ribbons for display, treating the newcomer no differently than she would any other woman. ''Which do you like best, these ribbons—'' she indicated the ruching ''—or this?''

Libby smiled, the stiff set of her shoulders relaxing a trifle. She herself wore an olive green gown with a wealth of bright blue trim, a bit garish but neat and modest. ''That depends on what you plan to do with it.''

''Of course.'' Rose felt herself blushing. ''It's for my wedding dress. Perhaps you've heard that Marshal Guthrie and I plan to be married a week from Saturday?''

Libby's mouth tightened the tiniest trifle. ''Yes, I've heard. I believe everyone in town has.''

''Oh.'' Rose hardly knew how to respond to that so she hurried on. ''Because I have so little time, I'm restyling a dress I already have.'' She smiled. ''You won't tell anyone, will you? I'm sure once we've finished with it, no one will know. Diana insists it's bad luck to get married in an old dress but what can I do?''

"Maybe you..." Libby twisted her fingers together unhappily and licked her lips.

She looked almost sick with anxiety, Rose realized, or some other strong emotion—trepidation or fear of some sort. But what could Mrs. Bowman's concerns have to do with Rose? "Do *you* think wearing an old dress will bring me bad luck?" she asked curiously.

"No, but something else might." Libby drew a deep breath. "I know I have no right to speak to you about this but I feel I must—"

A commotion at the back of the room interrupted her, and Libby glanced around distractedly. Diana and Mr. Curtis were approaching, talking animatedly.

Libby took a step back, as if she'd lost her nerve. Impulsively Rose reached out and touched the other woman's hand lightly.

"Please, don't go until you've explained your meaning. Is there something you believe I should know?"

Libby snatched her hand away and her cheeks seemed even paler than usual. "No, nothing. I have to go—please excuse me."

Diana, frowning, halted beside Rose. "Was that Libby Bowman?" she demanded, watching the woman hurry through the doorway. "What on earth was she saying to you?"

Rose shrugged, wondering herself what that had been all about. She felt a vague uneasiness she couldn't explain, a suspicion that she should follow Libby and demand an answer. Or better yet, forget the entire incident.

"Well?" Diana demanded.

"Nothing," Rose murmured, shaking free of disquieting thoughts. "Just polite chitchat." She turned on Mr. Curtis with a bright smile. "So have you something else for us to look at?"

* * *

Marshal Guthrie escorted Rose and Diana from the C and J, every scrap of white ribbon and braid and trim in the entire establishment in a neatly wrapped parcel beneath his arm. He'd come in just as they concluded their business and had offered to escort them to Rose's cottage.

On the boardwalk, he stopped abruptly, a frown wiping away his pleasant expression.

Rose followed the direction of his gaze and saw Boone riding down the middle of the street on the buckskin. For one crazy instant she was transported back in time to that day weeks ago when the gunfighter had first arrived in Jones.

That day he'd been all done in and his horse hadn't looked a lot better. Today the same horse was fat and sleek and the rider rode tall and confident.

Still, there'd been that same aura of danger then, which was even more pronounced now. Rose shivered and glanced at Jack for reassurance.

The marshal looked almost sad. At that moment Boone turned his head and saw the three of them. Rose waited for the cool nod of acknowledgment—which didn't come. Instead his glance flicked over her in a manner that was downright insulting. Then he looked away, dismissing all three of them.

"Of all the rude—" Diana's tone conveyed outraged astonishment.

Rose glanced at Jack, understanding the sadness she saw on his face. "What's happened to him?" she whispered, glancing after the straight figure on horseback. "He never acted like that before."

Jack sighed. "He moved into the Yellow Rose the day after our engagement party. He's drinking, gambling—he'll walk clear across the street to avoid meeting me. Man's acting downright surly."

"Perhaps that's the way he really is," Rose speculated aloud. *The Yellow Rose*—that meant Libby Bowman, of course. She shivered. Libby must have been trying to say something about Boone earlier inside the C and J. What could Boone have told her? What might she have guessed?

"You're absolutely right," Diana agreed with certainty. She caught Rose's arm with steely fingers. "Come, Rose, we must hurry home and get to work. We haven't a moment to spare if we're to get you ready in time."

That, Rose knew, was gospel truth.

Boone sat alone at a table at the rear of the Yellow Rose Saloon, idly shuffling a deck of cards. The game had folded more than an hour ago with him the big winner for the evening. His luck had been running high ever since he hit town.

That is, his luck in every area save one. He dropped the deck and reached for the bottle of bourbon before him on the table, pouring himself a stiff drink. Over the rim, he watched Libby come downstairs, trailed by that young cowboy from the Rocking T.

Boone didn't know the boy's name and didn't care to know it. He did know what had been going on upstairs, even without seeing the boy's satisfied and slightly silly grin. Libby had a living to make, and how she chose to make it was her own business. It was nothing to him.

Or so he told himself, watching her smile at the boy and pat his arm. The boy frowned. "Please?" he said plaintively, but she shook her head, gave him another smile and turned toward Boone's table.

She really was a pretty woman, Boone admitted dispassionately. "It's late," she said in the soft voice that never demanded. "I thought you might be . . . ready to come upstairs?"

Boone nodded, tossed down the rest of the bourbon and stood up. Libby's cowboy had already disappeared into the night. In addition to Max, the bartender, there were only three others left in the Yellow Rose. All of them had heard what Libby said and were staring with avid interest.

Let them, Boone thought. Libby was generally acknowledged to be his girl, and it suited him fine not to disabuse anyone of that notion, false though it was. Standing, he slid his arm across her shoulder and hugged her against his side.

She gave him a quick, surprised glance but that was all. Once up the stairs and inside her room, however, she closed the door and faced him. Sliding her hands around his waist above his gun belt, she rose on tiptoe to press her lips to his jaw.

"Please?" she whispered.

For a long moment they stood thus. Boone's arms hung limply at his sides, even while he told himself he should curve them around her back and draw her closer. She whimpered and slid her lips from his cheek to his mouth and still he didn't respond.

If he did, he wouldn't be the first man she'd been with tonight, but that wasn't the reason he couldn't bring himself to act. He'd bedded prostitutes before and had never been all that squeamish about sharing.

In fact, none of this was Libby's fault. It was Rose's. Just letting her name slip into his mind brought a jolt to his system. A jolt Libby felt, for she looked up quickly with a hopeful question in her eyes.

Boone shook his head. "Go on to bed," he said roughly. "I'll sleep in the chair, as usual."

"Why, Boone? Am I so disgusting to you, then?"

"Ah, Libby." Ashamed, he did finally put his arms around her, but in a manner more brotherly than anything else. "You know that's not it."

"Then what is it?"

"Go to bed, Libby." He released her and turned away.

"Why are you still in Jones? You know the whole town's plotting against you and yet you stay."

"Let it go." It was an order. He sat down on the edge of the chaise longue and reached for his boots.

She looked as if it took every last ounce of her courage to ignore his ultimatum. "It's her."

He stared at Libby Bowman. She faced him bravely enough, but her lips trembled. "I think you've said enough," he growled.

She watched him kick off his boots and swing his legs up onto his makeshift bed. Finally she appeared to get up the nerve to continue.

"Do you plan on stoppin' the wedding?"

Her question stunned him. "What do you take me for?" He glared at her, then deliberately rolled away from her.

"Why else would you still be hangin' around? Once she's another man's wife—"

"Dammit, shut up and go to bed!" Boone slammed his body over so he could lend the force of his furious expression to the volume of his voice. "If you can't manage that, I know a nice, quiet livery stable where a man can get some sleep!"

She looked frightened, but hurried to do his bidding without further argument. Boone lay on her chaise longue cursing himself for forty kinds of a fool. But as his anger faded, her final words echoed in his mind.

Once she's another man's wife—

Rose and Jack. Jack and Rose. A week from tomorrow, she would become that other man's wife. That other man would have rights to her body no man but Boone had ever enjoyed before—no, not even Billy Curtis, who'd been first.

Jack would be last. Unless something happened, Jack would be last. For a moment, Boone thought of all the things that could happen to sabotage the wedding: illness, injury, death, an act of God, an act of man.

An act of mine.
No!

He might be able to stand by and watch Jack face any
number of grisly fates, but he couldn't be a party to hasten-
ing any of them. Jack Guthrie was a straight shooter; Boone
almost gave a bitter laugh. He'd never known Jack to fire a
weapon of any kind. Jack Guthrie was an honorable man.
Under different circumstances, they might have been
friends.

Hell, Jack seemed to think they were friends now. That's
all *he* knew.

Rose carried the basket of vegetables into Doc's kitchen
and set it on the table: tomatoes and string beans and a few
green onions, all fresh from her garden. There would still be
a lot more coming in after she and Jack left on their honeymoon—the melons and the corn and the peas. She'd have to
remember to invite Doc Beatty to help himself.

"Doc?" she called, turning toward the door to the parlor. "Doc, you in there?"

To her surprise, it wasn't Doc who appeared in the doorway but Libby Bowman. She was buttoning the sleeve of her
burgundy-colored dress around her wrist. She smiled nervously.

"Doc had an emergency and left rather suddenly," Libby
explained, adding, "it's nice to see you, Miss Rose."

Rose frowned. "Mrs. Bowman." She nodded politely. "I
hope you're not feeling poorly?"

Libby shrugged. "I have a...female complaint," she said
finally. "Doctor Beatty's been helping me with it for some
time now."

"I'm glad." Rose glanced at the bounty she'd placed on
the table. "I don't suppose you'd care to share my harvest?
I've brought far more than Doc will be able to use before it
goes bad."

"Why..." Libby's face lit up. "I'd be much obliged, if you're sure there's plenty."

Surprised and delighted, Rose returned the smile. "As you can see, there's more than enough. Here, we'll take out Doc's share and you can carry yours away in my basket."

"Oh, I couldn't. I'll just take a few tomatoes—"

"Nonsense." Busily Rose set about pulling out three or four tomatoes, a handful of onions and half the beans. "When these are gone, please feel free to help yourself to anything in my garden," she added impulsively. "Unless we have some rain soon, it won't last long after I leave but you're welcome to anything there."

Libby accepted the basket. "You're very kind."

"It's nothing." Rose brushed aside the pleasantry and turned toward the door.

"No, I mean it. You really *are* very kind."

Rose hesitated, blinking in surprise. Libby obviously meant what she was saying. "In that case," Rose said slowly, "I thank you. Now if you'll excuse me, I must hurry home. I have a hundred and one things to do before—"

"Miss Rose, please wait a minute."

Rose stopped in the doorway, turning around slowly. There had been something deadly serious in the other woman's tone. Rose wasn't sure she wanted to hear this. "What is it, Libby?" she forced herself to ask.

"It's Boone."

Rose reached blindly for a chair and sat down hard. Knowing Boone lived with this woman was one thing but being forced to confront that situation openly was quite another. "I..." She swallowed hard and continued in a faint voice. "I know about that."

"You do?" Libby frowned.

"I know he is—that the two of you are—"

"But we're not!"

The bottom dropped out of Rose's stomach and she felt the most blessed sense of relief. "You're not?"

"We are not lovers," Libby said, meeting Rose's questioning gaze. "That's what you heard, is it not? That's what you believed."

"W-well, yes. But it was only idle gossip—what he does and who he sees are no concern of mine." Rose lifted her chin, trying to ignore the hot blush the lie brought to her cheeks.

"That's not true," Libby said softly. She clutched one hand into a fist between her breasts. "Oh, Rose, everything is such a mess! Usually in a situation like this, someone wins and someone loses. But unless you come to your senses before Saturday there'll be nothing *but* losers."

Rose sprang to her feet, unable to remain seated another second. "What on earth are you talking about?" she exclaimed. "I'm getting married on Saturday!"

"Perhaps not." Libby took a step forward and her hand fell to her side, giving her a curiously defenseless air. "Did you ever wonder how Boone knew about Billy Curtis?"

"Of course— No!" Agitated, Rose pressed her hands against her cheeks. "I was engaged to Billy before his death. Everyone knew that. Anyone could have told Boone, although why he would care I can't imagine."

Libby shook her head in sharp denial. "I don't mean that. I mean what you and Billy…did. Please don't make me spell out," she added miserably, "although I could say it more easily than you could hear it."

Rose clenched her hands into fists. "You mean you knew about…*that?* How?"

"Billy told me, and I told Boone. It's weighed on my conscience ever since, because you have always been so kind to me. But Boone was kind to me, too. He saved my life that day when Mase—well, you know about that. And after-

ward, he treated me so . . . I don't know, as if I was as goo
as any other woman, and as deserving of consideration.''

Libby looked up, eyes burning. ''I think that's when I fe
in love with Boone Smith. That very night I offered mysel
to him but he—'' her head drooped again ''—he turned m
down. He's turned me down each time I've offered since—
and there have been many.''

A wild, fierce joy shot through Rose, a joy she couldn'
quell. She, too, had offered herself to Boone Smith—and h
had taken her. *Oh, God!*

''For your sake,'' she said in a strangled voice, ''I'r
sorry.'' *For my sake, I'm glad!*

Libby frowned. ''Don't you understand what I'm tellin
you?'' She spoke patiently, as if to a backward child. ''I'r
in love with Boone, but he's in love with you. Jack Guthri
loves you, too, but you don't love him in return—you lov
Boone.''

Libby spoke with absolute conviction. ''Rose Taggart, i
you go through with your marriage to the marshal Satur
day, you'll regret it for as long as you live. Because you'll b
condemning four people to misery, just as sure as God mad
little green apples.''

Chapter Eighteen

On Thursday, two days before the wedding, three hard-bitten strangers rode into Jones. Rose, stirring the iron wash kettle beside her cottage on the outskirts of town, looked up from her steamy task to watch them pass.

The man in the lead was both big and heavy—fat, actually. Following closely behind came a skinny individual who was probably just a boy, Rose judged from the narrowness of his shoulders. A big man lagged farther back, big as Boone, she realized with surprise, with the same broad shoulders and long legs. Shaggy black hair stuck out below his stained white hat.

But the resemblance ended there, she saw when the man's head swung around and he caught her staring. His face was pockmarked, his grin more closely resembling a leer than anything else. Shivering, she looked away until they'd passed and she could watch them without being caught at it.

All three packed heavy hardware and forked hard-used horses. They looked as if they'd ridden far and fast, without regard to such niceties as soap or water.

Rose wrinkled her nose in distaste, wondering what their business here might be. In all likelihood they were just passing through to pick up supplies. She certainly hoped none of the ranches around here had hired such a disreputable trio.

They passed out of sight and she turned her attention back to the task at hand. She wanted all her clothing and personal items clean and packed because James would be sending a wagon for her trunks before the ceremony day after tomorrow.

She and Jack would leave straight from the church, taking the Rocking T's light carriage to San Antonio, where their luggage would be waiting at the depot. They'd board a train to New Orleans for the honeymoon, then push on to Philadelphia, where he would present her to his family.

What happened next would be her choice, Jack had told her. They could move to Philadelphia, where he could enter his family's law firm, or return to Jones—or locate anywhere else she chose.

"You've made me the happiest man in the world," he'd murmured with that puppy-dog expression in his guileless blue eyes. "I'll spend the rest of my life trying to make you just as happy."

Rose stopped stirring the wash pot and leaned on the wooden paddle. Sudden tears stung her eyes and she dashed them away angrily.

Why had Libby said what she had about Boone? Just because he hadn't chosen to become intimate with her, did that mean he loved another?

At the thought of Boone, Rose swung around sharply and looked down the road the three strangers had taken. Boone had entered Jones in much the same way—worse, because he'd been wounded. Did he know these three men? Maybe that's why they'd come.

With fresh resolve, she turned to her task, banging the paddle down on the white cottons, sheets and underclothing swirling around in a mixture of lye soap and water.

Perhaps Boone would ride out with the three hard cases.

Perhaps he'd leave before Saturday.

Perhaps she'd never see him again.

Perhaps that was perspiration stinging her eyes, not tears.

Three strangers stood drinking in the Yellow Rose when
Boone entered at mid-afternoon, Tonio trailing along behind with his jaws flapping. Boone recognized them instantly for what they were, and he felt his hackles rise.

Warriors. The question now became, why were they here?

Choosing a table along the back wall, Boone sat down
facing the bar. Tonio placed his palms on the table and
leaned forward.

"Can I get you a beer?" he inquired eagerly.

Boone nodded, suppressing a grin. Tonio had been so
busy talking that he hadn't even noticed the three at the bar.
But he would—just about now!

Sure enough, Tonio turned to get the beer and his gaze
slammed into the three strangers. He stopped short. One
was fat, one was muscular and one was young; it was the
young one who raised Tonio's hackles.

Like two young bulls in the same pasture, they glared at
each other. Tonio's eagerness to please disappeared; he
swaggered up to the bar and snarled at Max, "Two beers
and get a move on."

Max raised a brow, shrugged and pulled the brews. The
kid at the bar never took his eyes off Tonio until the beers
were delivered. Then he turned to the fat man on his left and
said something.

The fat *dangerous* man on his left. The bulk didn't fool
Boone. There was nothing jolly about the mean little eyes all
but lost in the fleshy face, or brutal hands the size of hams.
Boone had immediately sensed that the big man was the
boss of this little expedition, whatever it might be.

The third man glanced around and Boone stiffened, rec-
ognizing the pockmarked countenance and silvery-blue eyes.
Coons! What the hell was a Colorado desperado doing this
deep in the heart of Texas?

Tonio leaned forward aggressively. "Whatta you figger?" he asked, jerking his head toward the bar.

Boone shrugged. "Damned if I know."

Tonio looked disappointed. "Think there'll be trouble?"

Privately, Boone thought trouble was probably inevitable, but again he simply shrugged, then lifted his glass of
beer.

Tonio grinned. "Would you tell me if you did?"

"Nope."

Libby walked down the stairs and hesitated at the bottom, checking out the clientele. Her glance caught Boone's
and when he gave no sign of recognition, she straightened
her shoulders and walked to the bar. The blue-eyed Coons
swung his head around; when he saw her, his glance grew
even colder.

Libby didn't falter. "Like some company?" she asked
brightly.

The fat man grinned at her. "Yes, ma'am, we surely
would. Come on in here and talk to ol' Hickey—"

Hickey. Where had Boone heard that name before?

Two hours later, he still hadn't solved the mystery. But he
hadn't given up; he continued to sit quietly at his table at the
back of the room, nursing his second beer. Tonio, with the
restlessness of youth, had finished his first and rambled off
someplace.

Boone just sat and watched the three strangers without
seeming to.

They were asking questions. Boone watched them split
up, the two older men moving with seeming casualness from
one drinker to another. After a few minutes, the kid went
out to lead the three horses away, no doubt to the livery
stable. They were going to be here for a while, Boone concluded.

None of the locals seemed eager to engage the strangers in conversation. It was only a matter of time before the two newcomers arrived at Boone's table.

"Boone."

"Coons."

The blue-eyed killer gestured to the fat man. "Meet my partner, Jim Hickey."

"Hickey." Still not sure why that name seemed vaguely familiar, Boone gestured to the empty chairs at the table. "Care to sit a spell?"

"Don't mind if I do." Hickey hooked a wooden chair with his toe and dragged it out. He heaved his bulk onto it and the chair squeaked a protest but held. He gave Boone an unctuous smile. "Coons says you two met back on the Platte."

"That's right." That had been shortly before Coons killed a lawman and took off at a run for Santa Fe. Must be paper out on him somewhere over that fracas, if a marshal had a mind to look.

Coons gave Boone a narrow-eyed glance. "Never rode together, though. Know 'im mostly by reputation."

Hickey nodded. "Kansas."

Boone waited. They were leading up to something, and he had no reason to rush them along. The two exchanged glances, and then Hickey leaned forward.

"I just come from San Antone, where they say you're a bad man to tangle with."

"Say that, do they?" Boone picked up his beer, keeping his free hand on the table.

"Yep. We just want you to know we got no quarrel with you whatsoever."

Boone's brows soared. "That right?"

Hickey nodded vigorously. "Unless you want to buy in on what's comin', we'll just forget we ever had this little pow-wow."

They were getting to the crux of the matter now. Boone felt the hair at the nape of his neck prickle a warning. "And what might be comin'?" he asked softly.

"Well..." Hickey leaned back in his chair, his expression closed and his little eyes shuttered. He sighed. "I used t' have this baby brother who had a weakness for hosses..."

It all clicked into place for Boone; the horse thief hanged by the Jones vigilantes a few months ago was Hickey's brother. Hickey had come to settle a score.

Coons grinned suddenly, his teeth surprisingly white against the dark, uneven texture of his pockmarked skin. "We here to get us a sheriff and a town," he crooned.

Boone nodded. "I heard about the hangin'. Vigilantes, so they say. You aware the marshal wasn't even hired until after?"

Coons laughed out loud. "We're aware, we just don't give a good goddamn. Do you? Like the man says, we got no quarrel with you unless... You buyin' in?"

Boone regarded the twosome through narrowed eyes. "Why should I? This town and the people in it are nothing to me." He said it negligently, as if they'd bored him with their story.

Hickey rubbed his pudgy hands together. "Good, that's real good," he said with satisfaction. He stood up. "Ready, Coons? We told Trig we'd meet 'im over to that café for some grub."

"Sure, I'm ready." Coons stood up more slowly, his gaze never leaving Boone's face. "Almost a shame, though."

Hickey frowned. "What is?" Now that he'd concluded his business, the big man was eager to go.

"That our friend ain't interested in gettin' involved. Ever since Denver I been wonderin' which one of us is fastest." His right hand caressed the pearl handle of the Colt .45 he wore strapped to his hip. "Figger we'll ever know for sure?"

Boone smiled with his mouth but not his eyes. "Happy to oblige any time curiosity gets the best of you, Coons."

For an instant the gunfighter hesitated, the temptation to say the single word "Now!" strong in his icy eyes. But then Hickey struck him a glancing blow on the shoulder and turned away.

Anger flared on the pockmarked face, then died. Coons touched the brim of his hat. "Glad to see we understand each other, Boone. Be seein' you." He swaggered after his partner.

Boone relaxed in his chair, surprised at the tension remaining from the brief encounter. No reason to feel jumpy, he argued with himself. He didn't owe anybody anything. It wasn't as if he gave a damn what happened to the residents of Jones, Texas.

Jack, Rose, James and Diana lingered at Rose's dinner table over coffee and cake. Despite the heat, the men had eaten heartily of the roast beef and mashed potatoes. Diana had eaten little, but then, she'd been suffering from morning sickness at all hours of the day and night.

Rose had pretended to eat but she wasn't sure she'd fooled anyone. The closer her wedding day approached, the more nervous and uncertain she became.

James leaned back and patted his stomach. "Good grub!" he announced with some surprise. "You marryin' her for her cookin', Jack?"

Jack laughed indulgently, reaching across the table to cover her hand with his. She tensed automatically, prepared to draw away. Then she thought better of it and forced herself to submit to his gentle touch.

"No, but it's all right with me if you want to think so," Jack said.

James laughed appreciatively. "It's still not too late to change your mind." His teasing was heavy-handed but affectionate. He glanced at his sister. "You, too, Rose. Getting cold feet runs in our family. Why, the day I married this lady—"

Diana slapped playfully at his hand. "Careful what you say, James Taggart! You could find your yourself sleeping in the bunkhouse with the hands."

Rose laughed along with the others but her heart had leaped at his words—*it's still not too late to change your mind.* Was she making the worst mistake of her life, as she'd begun to suspect, or was she grasping the last chance she'd ever have for a husband, children . . . happiness?

As the laughter died away, the quartet at the table became gradually aware of a pounding at the front door, then a voice calling, "Marshal? Jack Guthrie, you in there?"

Rose jumped to her feet. "Good heavens, that sounds like Mr. Curtis."

Jack caught her arm when she would have rushed to answer. "Let me handle this," he ordered.

With James on his heels, Jack headed toward the parlor. Rose and Diana exchanged perplexed glances, then followed.

A whole delegation of townsmen awaited them, led by George Curtis and the Reverend Salt. At Jack's appearance, everybody started talking at once.

The marshal held up his hands to quiet them. "Reverend, you go first," Jack decided. "To what do we owe this unexpected visit?"

"Fear," the preacher declared, "fear, pure and simple. We got three hard-lookin' strangers in town and they been seen talkin' to that mysterious gunfighter."

Jack frowned. "What mysterious gunfighter?"

The reverend looked flustered. "Why, Mr. Edwards, of course. Or Boone—whatever you want to call him. Folks was nervous enough about havin' one outsider of dubious character in our midst but now we got four and it's begin-nin' to look like they're in cahoots. So our question to you, Marshal, is this—what you gonna do about it?''

The mutter of agreement rose in volume until once again Jack had to gesture for quiet. James spoke into the resulting void.

"Who they talkin' about, Jack? You seen these men?''

Jack nodded. "They rode in mid-afternoon and stopped at the Yellow Rose.''

Rose tugged her brother's arm. "I saw them, too, James. They rode right past here.'' She shivered. "They're really scary. I can't imagine they're friends of Boone.''

Max, the bartender from the Yellow Rose, shook his head in disagreement. "I seen 'em talkin' together, actin' mighty chummy.''

"Did you hear what they were saying?'' Jack inquired. He didn't look worried, only perplexed.

"No, but when they left I heard one of 'em tell Boone he was glad they understood each other—them's the exact words, 'glad we understand each other.' That sound like strangers?''

Voices rose in consternation and it took a couple of minutes for Jack to restore order. When he had it, he spoke in a soothing tone. "Any of you hear any names connected with these strangers?''

Fred Loveless, toward the back of the pack, waved his arms to gain attention. "The youngest one brought the horses to my stable,'' he said importantly. "Told me to feed 'em, see they got rubbed down. And he said, 'Especially the bay—Coons is real particular about that hoss.'" Fred looked around smugly. "Coons—that must be one'a their names, right?''

Jack nodded. "Good work, Fred. Now I have something to go on.''

"You already had something to go on,'' George Curtis grumbled. "You've known that gunfighter Boone's name for days and you ain't found a thing on him. What if he's the reason they're here? What if they're part of—'' George glanced around for support ''—part of his gang?''

"Part of his gang—you don't suppose!" Fred marveled.

George warmed to the story he was apparently fabricating as he went along. "What if Boone's called his gang to town to—" He choked and turned pale, as if he'd just been speculating before but now had been confronted by irrevocable truth.

Everybody seemed to lean forward in anticipation.

"What if he's called his gang to town to stop the wedding?"

For a shocked moment they all stood there in horrified silence, then Rose cried, "No!" As everyone stared at her, she rushed on, "He'd have no reason to do a thing like that. Mr. Curtis, I *know* you're trying to build something up to steal attention from Crystal Springs, but this time you've gone too far!"

"You're wrong, missy. Think about the possibilities." George's eyes grew round with amazement. "That's the only possible explanation. You think we don't all know how taken he is with you?"

Diana slipped a supportive arm around her sister-in-law's waist. "That's ridiculous, Mr. Curtis!"

"Is it?" George was hitting his stride. "Who bought your box at the church social?"

A murmur of acknowledgment greeted this question.

"And when he beat up your brother and you slapped his face, what did he do?" George glanced around at his supporters. "What did he do?"

"Kissed you, is what he did," Fred Loveless chimed in. "Right there in front of—" he glanced at Reverend Salt, who had apparently not been previously informed of this breach of protocol "—in front of God and everybody!"

George nodded triumphantly. "Yep, that's it, all right. Boone's brought his gang to town to stop this weddin'. The question is, what we gonna do about it?"

He, and everyone else, swung around to confront the marshal.

Jack spoke with exaggerated patience. "I don't know who those strangers are or why they've come to our town," he said steadily, "but if we have anything to worry about it's not from Boone."

Rude and scornful noises greeted this pronouncement, but Jack shook his head with stubborn insistence. "Boone's my friend," he declared. "Now go on home. If any worrying needs to be done, I'll do it. Go on—I mean it now."

Still grumbling, the crowd dispersed, wandering toward town in disjointed and unhappy clumps. Jack turned to Rose.

"I meant every word I said," he told her calmly. "Boone's not involved with those men, I'd stake my life on it. He'd never do anything to bring you grief."

His serene acceptance of Boone's perceived concern for her shocked her to the core. She thought about it after he'd gone to town, after James and Diana had returned to the ranch.

Did Boone care for her? If he did, was it a selfish caring aimed only at his own gratification, or did he want to see her happy?

If Boone had brought those hard strangers to town, he could also send them away. If he hadn't brought them, he might still know why they were here. And if their reasons boded ill for Jack, Boone's mere presence at the marshal's side might be enough to discourage whatever plan they had in mind.

Without giving herself time to consider the consequences, Rose pulled the gray shawl from her closet and threw it around her shoulders. The night was hot and muggy

but the shawl would offer some slight protection against
being too easily recognized.

Letting herself out the back door, she started out, careful
to remain in the shadow of trees and houses as much a
possible. At the edge of town, she left Main Street and cu
over to the alley, proceeding with even greater caution.

Behind the Yellow Rose, she pressed herself into the
shadows and edged around the side toward the street. She
heard the doors in front flap open and the sound of stum
bling steps on the boardwalk, followed by the creak of sad
dle leather as someone mounted a horse, then thundered ou
of town.

How to get word to him that she was here? She needed a
messenger—

"Miss Rose! What in tarnation are you—"

Hands gripped her elbows and she must have jumped a
foot into the air. For a moment she couldn't imagine who
had sidled up behind her so noiselessly, and then she rec
ognized Tonio's shocked whisper.

"What are you doing out here in the middle of the
night?"

"Oh, Tonio! I didn't hear you!" She turned to him in re
lief, grabbing his shirt and hanging on. "Please, I need a
favor! It's very important"

She waited in the alley behind the saloon, her heart
pounding with fear and excitement and her hands like ice
despite the sullen heat of August. Was he there? Would he
come? Would he listen to her? Would he—

"Rose! What the hell do you think you're doing?"

He materialized out of the dark right beside her, and once
again her heart broke into a mad pounding. She wanted to
throw herself into his arms as she had with Tonio, but with
this man, she didn't dare.

He grabbed her upper arms and shook her. "I asked what the hell you think you're doing?"

"I—I..." Her mouth was dry and her voice scratchy. She swallowed hard and tried again. "I have to talk to you, Boone."

"Well, here I am." He set her down on her feet again and backed a few steps away, as if he didn't trust himself to be close to her. "Say your piece and go home."

His brusqueness hurt her but she reminded herself that she was here for reasons other than self-gratification. "It's about those men who rode into town today. There are rumors—"

"There are always rumors," he said with scorn. "What have you heard?"

"T-that these men are friends of yours, your g-gang if you will. Jack doesn't believe it."

"But you're not so sure."

His voice had dropped to a lower tone and it vibrated and pulsed around and through her. She felt her face flush and was grateful for the darkness.

"I'll be sure—if you tell me."

She heard him draw a quick breath. "I'm telling you. Those men are no friends of mine."

"Then why are they here?"

He was silent for a few moments and she wished she could see his face—see him at all, as other than a darker shadow.

"Remember when you told me about the town hangin' a horse thief?"

"Y-yes."

"Your horse thief had a brother, and he's out for blood."

"Oh, my God! B-but most of the men who did it are driving cattle somewhere between here and Kansas!"

"Yeah, well, that doesn't seem to concern them a hell of a lot. I think they figure the whole town's at fault and they'll take what revenge they can get—along with any loot they may happen to find layin' around.''

"There are three of them," Rose said slowly, thinking out loud. "If there's trouble, Jack won't have a chance." She looked up suddenly, trying to pierce the darkness to see Boone's expression. "Unless you help him."

"Not very damned likely." His voice sounded absolutely certain, and so far away. . . .

"Boone!" She stumbled forward to suddenly find herself hauled up hard against his chest. She brought her fists down on that hard, broad surface. "You've got to help him! Promise me!"

"The only thing I'll promise is that if you go through with that ceremony Saturday, it'll be the worst mistake of your life."

"But—"

"Shut up," he commanded, bringing his lips down on hers with a force at once bruising and exhilarating.

It seemed forever since he'd held her in his arms; she was dying with desire for him. Without hesitation she twisted her fingers in his hair and lifted on tiptoe, welcoming the hot exploration of his tongue in her mouth.

He was angry; she felt it in the driving violence of his kiss, the hard domination of his hands roving over her back and hips. But there was a deeper urgency there, too.

He had missed her as she had missed him.

Like her, he knew this was wrong.

Also like her, he seemed unable to help himself.

She wanted him—she loved him so much she couldn't think straight! If he swept her into his arms and carried her to some private place where they could make love, she could not fight him—but she must. She was promised to another man. Her honor was at stake.

Drawing back, she struggled to find her breath—and her resolve. "Don't!" She turned her face away to avoid his seeking mouth. "Promise me—"

His hand curved around her breast and she lost what little self-control she'd gained. "Promise me," she groaned, swaying toward him. "Promise me . . ."

Chapter Nineteen

Promise me you'll tell Jack why those three men are in town—and that you won't let anything happen to him!

Staring out her bedroom window Saturday at a hot and humid morning, Rose felt her stomach clench ominously. She had wrung the promise from him, but at what cost? He had looked at her with such disappointment...

Would she ever get past that final image of him walking away from her for what might prove to be the last time? When Diana arrived at half past eleven, Rose was still sitting at her kitchen table drinking coffee, still dressed in nightgown and wrapper, still miserable and depressed.

Diana threw up her hands in obvious dismay. "My word," she exclaimed, "haven't you even laid out your wedding dress?"

"There's plenty of time." Rose felt numb from head to toe; even Diana's arrival didn't shatter her sense of unreality.

"There certainly *isn't* plenty of time." Diana hustled her sister-in-law into the bedroom and pressed her down on the bench before the dressing table. "You sit right there while I do your hair. Gracious, Rose, you'd think you'd never been married before, the way you're acting!"

Diana's weak attempt at humor brought an equally weak attempt at a smile from Rose. "Did you come here straight from the ranch or have you already been to town this morning?" she asked.

Diana paused, holding the brush in one hand and hairpins in the other. "I stopped by the C and J to pick up the rice for the wedding, and then James and I popped in to say hello to the bridegroom." She spoke carefully, as if weighing her words.

"H-how is Jack?"

"Better than you are." Diana pulled the brush through Rose's hair with long, sweeping strokes. "He seemed fine," she amended more gently.

Rose frowned. Diana's furtive manner concealed something . . . but what? "Did you see anyone else? Mr. Curtis, perhaps?"

Diana stopped brushing. "Rose, what is it you're trying to find out? It'd be simpler if you'd just come out with it."

Rose looked at her sister-in-law in the mirror. "Is the town still as apprehensive as it was when those three strangers rode in yesterday?" she asked hesitantly. "Or has everybody settled down?"

"Everybody has *not* settled down. Half the population is hanging around the C and J gossiping." Diana resumed her efforts to tame Rose's wayward locks. "The general consensus still seems to be that those three strangers are somehow in cahoots with Boone."

"Oh, dear." Rose clasped her hands together in her lap. "They're not, Di."

"And how would you know that?" Diana demanded tartly.

"I . . . asked him straight out. He told me."

"And you believe everything he says to you?"

Rose thought about that and realized she did, indeed, believe everything Boone said to her. She nodded. "He also told me the real reason those men are here."

"Which is?" Diana's interest perked up.

"To get revenge for that hanging last spring."

"Hanging? You mean that horse thief?" Diana's eyes widened. "My word. You just never think of horse thieves having friends." Her mouth tightened into a disapproving line. "Still, that was a wrong thing the men did. James and your father took no part in it, of course, but some of the Rocking T cowboys did."

Diana parted off a section of hair and began twisting it into a fat loop atop Rose's head. "But in defense of the vigilantes, I must point out that they caught the man red-handed. And as we all know, there's nothing lower than a horse thief." She looked up and her gaze met Rose's in the mirror. "Does Jack know about this?"

Rose nodded. "I'm sure he does. Boone promised to tell him." Her lip trembled and she bit down on it. "Diana, am I doing the right thing? I went out of my mind all night with doubt and worry. I just don't love Jack the way I love . . . Boone."

There; she'd said it. She waited for shock and horror to appear on Diana's face. Instead she saw compassion—and sorrow.

"I know," Diana said softly. "Oh, Rose, I know! I feel so sorry for you, having to go through all this." She gave Rose a quick hug. "Are you absolutely sure Boone won't marry you?"

Rose nodded miserably, and the first loop of hair tumbled onto her shoulder again. "I think . . . perhaps he cares for me, but I don't believe he sees any way to escape what he's become . . . short of death."

"Then what are your options? We must be logical about this. You can remain single, an old maid growing more and more disillusioned with every passing year while you mourn your lost love."

Rose shivered. Who could face such a future?

"Or," Diana went on in a matter-of-fact tone, as if she was presenting irrefutable fact, "you can marry Jack Guthrie, a fine man with unlimited prospects who completely adores you." Her guise of impartiality fell away and she added passionately, "Rose, you must be practical. It's always left up to us women to be practical."

Diana was right and Rose knew it. Jack was her salvation. And it wasn't as if she'd lied to him, she reminded herself. He knew she wasn't madly in love with him. But he claimed to love her enough to make up for it. He'd take her away from here, away from all these memories; he'd give her the children for which she yearned, and a comfortable life wherever she chose.

Still, she had to admit at least to herself that none of that would count in the slightest if she could be with Boone. If only he was willing to try to make a life with her!

He wasn't; he considered himself a marked man, vulnerable to every reputation-hunting badman who crossed his trail.

And so, in the final analysis, Diana was right; Boone was right; Jack was right.

And the wedding would proceed as scheduled.

Boone leaned against the bar in the Yellow Rose and downed his second shot of bourbon. It didn't seem to help the raw ache in his gut so he signaled for Max to fill 'er up again.

Beside him, Tonio shifted restlessly. "You think you oughta be doin' that?" He jerked his chin toward the liquor. "Trouble's comin' and you ain't gonna be in any shape to meet it."

"It's already here." Boone picked up his glass and led the way to his usual table, the one against the far wall. Sitting down, he waited for the boy to do likewise.

With a final anxious glance toward the door, Tonio did. "You're sure actin' funny," he complained.

"Brace yourself. I'm about to act even funnier." Boone tossed down the liquor and slammed the small glass onto the table. "I'm gonna give you some free advice, kid."

"Yeah?" Tonio looked pleased, as if he thought he was about to be initiated into the brotherhood of the gun or some such foolishness.

"Yeah. This is it. The best thing you can do for yourself is to ride away from this town and that little gal who's got you all tied up in knots and never look back."

Tonio lunged halfway to his feet, hands flat on the table and young face filled with fury. "Why, because I'm dirty Mex or dirty Irish?" he flared.

"Because you're all man—or will be, if somebody don't cut the process short." Coolly Boone met the boy's impassioned glare.

"Like who?" Still angry, Tonio also looked hurt. "I know how to take care of myself." Gritting his teeth, he sat down.

"That's what you think. Listen to me. Sally Curtis is just another pretty girl. With that pa of hers, that's all she'll ever be. She's not woman enough to make a man happy in the long haul."

Not like Rose. Boone shoved back his chair and stood up. He'd made a promise to Rose—to tell Jack why the three hard strangers were in town. He'd keep that promise, but that's all he'd do. He hadn't promised to fight Jack Guthrie's battles for him, no matter what Rose might think.

Tonio looked up, face wrinkled in confusion. "That's it?" he demanded incredulously. "I'm supposed to take your word for it, just like that?"

Boone shrugged as if it didn't matter to him one way or the other. "Up to you. But if you're half as smart as I think ou are, it won't take a whole hell of a lot more for you to igure this out all by your lonesome."

He'd said his piece; the rest was up to Tonio. Without nother word, Boone walked out of the Yellow Rose and lown the boardwalk to the marshal's office. Pushing in-ide, he stopped short.

Marshal Jack Guthrie sat at his worktable, a wanted oster laying in front of him. Stepping closer, Boone looked lown at a rough drawing of himself.

"Well, well, well," he said dryly. Reading the type, he runted in disgust. "From that little fracas in San Antone, uh—fifty dollars for bringin' me in." He gave a short, bit-er laugh. "And me the aggrieved party."

"Were you?" Jack looked unperturbed. "If that's true, ou shouldn't have too much trouble getting this offer vithdrawn."

"Jesus Christ, man, we're talkin' about a little bitty al-ercation weeks past in a saloon in the worst part of a town vhere I'm unknown and therefore a suspicious character— nything about this sound familiar? The fact that there's aper out tells me something more is goin' on than I real-zed. Wouldn't be surprised if this was the work of the ancher who wanted to hire my gun. I'd been warned he lidn't like to ask twice."

Jack frowned. "You saying this isn't on the up and up?" Ie glanced at the reward poster. "If you'll go back and turn ourself in, I'll see to it you're treated fairly."

"Nah, you got it all wrong." Boone leaned over, his alms flat against the tabletop. "I've come to see *you* get reated fairly."

"I don't follow."

"Those three hard cases who rode into town yesterday are omin' after you."

"Me?" Jack slumped back in his chair, his astonishment plain. "I've never even met the gentlemen. What do they want *me* for?"

"That hangin' last spring."

"But—"

"I know, you weren't the law then and you had nothing to do with it. I pointed that out."

"Well, then." Jack shrugged as if that settled everything.

"They don't give a good goddamn."

"I beg your pardon?"

"*They do not give a good goddamn.* They're mad as hell at the entire town and they don't care who pays so long as somebody does. They plan to start with you—and they won't be any too particular who else gets hurt in the process."

Jack groaned; he looked like a man torn. "Then I'll have to delay my honeymoon," he said slowly. "Rose and I can't just climb on a train and leave others to—"

"Jesus!" Boone straightened, shaking his head with disgust at Jack's apparent inability to realize what the hell was going on here. "You don't seem to understand what I'm tryin' to tell you. These men have no intention of waiting until after the wedding or the honeymoon or any other damned thing. They're comin' after you *today.* It's time you strapped on a gun, Marshal. I'll be mightily surprised if you even make it to the church without lead flyin'."

"Impossible." Jack looked incredulous. "Nothing will happen today. No one is *that* devoid of humanity."

"Jack Guthrie," Boone said, "you're a fool. Pack a gun. You've been warned." He half turned toward the door before adding, "And don't look to me to bail you out."

"I won't," Jack promised. He stood up and walked around the corner of the table. "Boone Smith, I'm offering you my hand in friendship," he declared, doing so. "In spite of everything—" he glanced pointedly at the reward poster "—I believe you to be an honorable man."

Boone let out a scornful exclamation of disagreement. He stared at the other man's hand. "You're about to marry my woman," he snarled. "Just because I haven't shot you up to now doesn't make me your friend." He hesitated, a hopeful thought occurring to him. "Maybe someone else will do the job for me. That sure as hell would simplify matters."

Jack's face fell but he squared his shoulders with purpose. "Maybe so," he admitted, "but if they don't..." He looked and sounded sad. "The law will be coming after you, sooner or later. A smart man probably wouldn't hang around."

A smart man, Boone thought. For a moment he met the marshal's honest gaze, but Jack didn't falter. "Hell," Boone said, "nobody ever called me smart."

Turning, he walked onto the boardwalk. George Curtis and Fred Loveless hovered there, accompanied by a man Boone had never seen before.

George stepped into Boone's path, gave a tentative smile and gestured toward the stranger. "Mr. Boone, say hello to Phil Mossholder, editor and publisher of the *Crystal Springs Crusader.* He's visitin' our fair city for the nuptials."

Mossholder, a tall, gangly individual of about thirty-five, thrust out a bony hand. "The nuptials and anything else that might come along," he said with a sly grimace.

Boone looked at the man's hand. "By anything else, I take it you mean a shootin'."

Mossholder grinned. "Shooting, knifing, fistfight. Then there's always the chance that when the reverend asks if anyone knows any reason those two should not be joined together, someone will jump up and holler yes!"

"Holler yes!" Fred Loveless chimed in. "Whatta you think, Mr. Boone? We in for a bit of excitement today?"

Boone looked at the trio standing so hopefully befor
him. For his own reasons, each was anticipating the worst
George Curtis never forgot his primary concern—the feu
with Crystal Springs. Fred Loveless, as George's hench
man, obviously supported that vendetta.

And the editor, no doubt summoned by Curtis, would b
no different from others of his breed. Wielding a pen in
stead of a sword, he lived to chronicle the trials and tribu
lations of his betters, which as far as Boone was concerne
included just about everybody.

None of the three seemed to realize what they were deal
ing with. It wasn't Boone Smith who was about to go u
against duly appointed authority in Jones, Texas, but a gan
of badmen out for bloody revenge—and maybe a bit o
profit.

Mossholder pulled a small notebook from the folds of hi
jacket and felt around in his pants pocket, finally with
drawing a stub of a pencil. "My readers would like to kno
just what your interest is in all this, Mr. Boone," he an
nounced with pompous self-importance. "In fact, m
readers would like to know how a mysterious and fa
mous—or should I say infamous—" he glanced at his com
panions for accord, which was instantly forthcomin
"—Kansas gunman came to dwell in their midst at all."

Boone might have laughed if the situation hadn't bee
edging along toward life-and-death seriousness. If he wa
half as dangerous as they gave him credit for being, suc
temerity as that displayed by the three townsmen woul
probably earn them permanent residence in boot hill.

"Well, Mr. Editor," Boone drawled, "if you want to liv
long enough to satisfy all those readers, I suggest you but
ton your lip and get the hell off Main Street." To lend em
phasis to his warning, he patted his gun belt and rocked bac
on his bootheels. "And stay off."

"Is that a threat?" Mossholder took a quick step away, his thin face flushing and his full mustache quivering.

"Nope," Boone denied. "Just call it good advice from a man in a position to know."

He heard them twittering like a flock of birds as he walked away. Mossholder's voice rose above the others. "You heard him—whatever happens, he's in it up to his neck!"

James arrived promptly at one-thirty to drive the bride and her matron of honor to the church. Clad in her redecorated white gown, Rose climbed into the carriage and sat there numbly, barely aware of the sun beating mercilessly upon her head, which was swathed in Diana's beautiful white veil.

James lifted her down near the back door of the church. "You look beautiful, Sis," he said. "A little pale, but I guess that's normal."

"Pale?" Rose blinked, trying to force her raging emotions into some kind of order. She looked around, surprised to discover they'd reached their destination.

"To be expected," Diana said briskly. "Now James, as best man, I want you to go stand out front and when you see Jack, come warn us. Rose and I will wait in the church office until we hear from you."

James nodded and trotted off around the building just as Sally opened the back door and stepped outside. The girl looked lovely in a summer frock of soft green, with green ribbons twined through her blond hair.

"Oh, Rose, you're here." Sally skipped blithely down the few steps. She carried a small bouquet of flowers from her mother's garden, tied with white satin ribbons. "I've been waiting for you!"

"Are there many people here yet?" Diana asked anxiously.

"Not many, but they're starting to arrive. I came early because I wanted to give Rose her flowers—" Sally offered the bouquet along with her most ingratiating smile "—and maybe have a little talk?"

Diana sized up the situation in a flash. "Good heavens, girl, not now. It's Rose's wedding day, for goodness' sake!"

"I know that." Sally's tone was suspiciously close to a whine. "You don't mind, do you, Rose?"

Both of them turned expectantly toward Rose, who blinked hard and tried to think straight. Maybe dealing with Sally's problems would take her mind off her own, she decided. "N-no, I don't mind," she said.

"See?" Sally made a little face at Diana, then pointedly turned away.

Diana threw up her hands and shook her head as if disassociating herself from anything that might be said from this point forward. "In that case, I'll go inside and make sure everything's ready," she decided. "See you in a few minutes."

Rose stood there in her white wedding gown, her veil trailing out behind her, and watched her sister-in-law leave. Turning to Sally, she sighed. "What is it?" she asked.

"It's Tonio."

"I somehow thought it might be."

"Yes, well..." Sally twisted her fingers together. "When you found us in the alley, it wasn't exactly like it looked. I mean, it wasn't entirely Tonio's fault."

Rose pursed her lips. "I'm not sure I understand. It seemed perfectly obvious."

"Yes, well, I had agreed to meet him back there and I may have hinted I'd let him, but when the time came I started thinking about how my daddy is and—Miss Rose, I just got scared! When I heard footsteps I thought I was a gone gosling. Thank heavens it was only you and Marshal Guthrie, but the damage was done. Now Tonio's mad at me and I don't know what to do."

Rose touched the girl's arm gently. "Are you asking my advice, Sally?"

The girl nodded eagerly. "That's it exactly."

"Then I shall give it. Leave Tonio Ryan alone."

Sally blinked baby-blue eyes against the glitter of quick tears. "That's not the advice I wanted!" she wailed.

Rose shook her head wearily. "We seldom get the advice we want, dear. In fact, we so rarely get it that I wonder we keep asking."

"But you don't understand. I want you to tell me how I can get my papa to accept Tonio."

"Accept him as what?"

"Why, my husband, of course! What kind of girl do you think I am?" The rosy cheeks flushed brighter still.

"There is no way," Rose said as gently as she could.

Sally stomped one dainty foot. "There has to be!"

"I'm sorry, but in this case, there isn't. I wanted to believe so, when I first realized you two young people were enamored of each other, but now I firmly believe that the best you can hope for is that your father and Tonio don't kill each other."

"But I want him!" Sally cried petulantly. "He's so handsome. When he kisses me . . ."

"He wants more from you than kisses. If he doesn't get it the romance will not survive. If he does get it, your father will kill him—certainly he'll try. And you'll be ruined—listen to me, Sally!"

Rose caught one of the girl's hands and squeezed hard. "Do you understand what that means? Your father will never let you marry Tonio Ryan, not if he's the last man on earth. You know that as well as I do. Unless you're prepared to give up everything and run away with him—"

Sally's face blanched. "Give up everything? I could never do that!"

"Then why don't you do the good and honest thing and set Tonio free before you ruin both your lives?"

Sally began to cry in earnest. "I love him!" she wailed. "I can't live without him! You're old, you don't understand—"

"Oh, do I not?" Rose felt weary beyond even the years attributed to her by Sally. "If you love him, you must want what's best for him. And what's best for him is *not* risking his future and his very life on a girl who—"

Rose bit off her words, realizing she was about to say something so blunt it was sure to be hurtful. But say it she must; there was no time left for polite little euphemisms. "When all is said and done, Sally, you will always choose your papa first."

Sally threw off Rose's hand. "I won't!" she cried. "I swear I won't!"

"Sally, dear, you already have, time and again." Rose slid her arm across the quivering shoulders. "Let's go inside now. Perhaps it was wrong of me to speak so frankly but this may be the last opportunity I have." A shiver darted down her spine as if she'd just prophesied the future.

"Don't be silly." Sally snuffled. "I guess a bride has to be honest on her wedding day—even if she's wrong!"

Even if she's wrong, Rose thought.

Or even if she's waiting for the wrong man.

Boone stood on the boardwalk in front of the Yellow Rose, looking north toward Jack's small frame house. As if on cue, the front door opened and Jack stepped out.

Even at a distance, Boone could see the marshal was all duded up for the occasion in black broadcloth suit and white shirt. His Stetson gleamed in the midday glare, white and new. He walked confidently, a spring in his step.

There was no bulge of a holster around his hips, no flash of a revolver when his coat swung open. The marshal wasn't wearing a gun. Swearing, Boone turned into the Yellow Rose.

Tonio stood at the bar talking to Libby, a glass of beer in his hand. Boone barged between them. "Let me have your hardware, kid," he ordered brusquely.

Puzzled, Tonio pulled the Colt .45 from his holster, spun it around in his hand and offered it, butt first, to Boone.

Boone took the pistol and stuffed it in the waistband of his pants and turned away.

The boy reached out and grabbed Boone's arm, his face flushing angrily. "What the hell you think you're doin'?"

"Two things," Boone said.

"Which are?"

"Makin' damn sure you won't be able to horn in on somebody else's troubles."

The kid's square jaw jutted out. "What else?"

"Teachin' you not to give up your weapons to *anybody,* you young jackass." Boone shook his head as if saddened by the boy's stupidity. "Stay out of the way, kid. You've been warned."

Inside the church on the hill south of town, Sally rushed into the minister's office. "He's coming!" she exclaimed, her eyes bright and excited.

Rose's pulse leaped and she pressed one fist between her breasts. "Who's coming?"

"The groom, of course." Sally laughed. "Your brother, James, just told me to come let you know everything's right on schedule. Most of the women are already here but the men and boys are following along with Marshal Jack. Men! Can't just come in and sit down like they're supposed to."

Rose and Diana exchanged anxious glances. Had something happened? Was that why the men and boys were escorting Jack to the church?

"I have to see," Rose decided suddenly, starting toward the door.

"No! You can't do that!" Sally, standing in Rose's path, flung wide her arms. "You can't let anyone see you in your wedding gown before the ceremony. It's bad luck."

"That only applies to the groom, and you said yourself, he's not here yet."

Still Sally blocked the way, her face rebellious. "You're making that up. It means everybody—doesn't it?" She glanced at Diana for support.

Diana seemed torn. "Rose, do you really think you should—"

"I've got to know what's going on." Rose fought back the sudden welling of tears that threatened to spill down her cheeks. She was on the ragged edge of collapse, and she knew it but felt helpless to control her wildly fluctuating emotions.

"Then you shall," Diana decided. She took Sally's arms and drew her aside. "Take care," she added to Rose in warning.

Rose nodded and swept past, lifting her skirts above her ankles. Emerging from behind the altar, she was only dimly aware of the gasps of surprise and disapproval led by Reverend Salt as she flew down the aisle toward the door.

James, standing on the front step, looked equally surprised by her precipitous arrival. "What are you doing out here, Rose? Jack's coming."

"I just want to be sure," she said breathlessly.

Her brother cast her a suspicious frown, and Rose turned away so he couldn't see her face and guess how agitated she was.

"Where's Di?" he asked suddenly. "She's feeling all right, isn't she?"

"Oh, for heaven's sake." Rose, tired of James's over-blown concern now that his wife was expecting a baby, realized somewhat belatedly the opportunity he'd just presented. Despite the fact that Diana hadn't uttered a single word of complaint, Rose lied without compunction. "Actually, I think she is feeling a little peaked. Maybe you could—"

She didn't have to spell it out; James was gone in a flash. Relieved to be rid of him, she turned her attention toward town. Men and boys did indeed line the street. And there was Jack, coming from the opposite direction, walking right down the middle of the thoroughfare.

Shading her eyes, she strained to make out what was going on. An unearthly quiet seemed to hang over the town; then behind her in the church, someone began to play the piano.

As if responding to a signal she knew they couldn't hear, three figures stepped out from between the buildings on the far end of town.

Three figures—one massive, one thin, one straight and strong and menacing—almost slinking into the middle of the street where they stopped, slowly turning toward the north.

"Now who do you suppose—" Sally's voice was filled with idle conjecture.

Fear choked Rose and she felt her world tilt crazily. Unlike Sally, she knew who was waiting down below for Marshal Jack Guthrie—and she knew why.

Chapter Twenty

Boone lounged on the steps in front of the Yellow Rose, hi face a careful mask of indifference while he watched th marshal's approach. Coming even with the saloon, Jac glanced Boone's way and dipped his head in greeting.

Boone grunted with disgust and turned deliberately to ward the three gunmen spreading out across the street t intercept the marshal. Their wide-legged stances and aler expressions proclaimed their intentions.

Jack approached a few steps toward the trio, his smil pleasant if a little questioning. "Afternoon, gentlemen. Yo in town for the wedding? You're welcome—a lot of ou friends from Crystal Springs are joining us."

Coons, two paces to the right of big Hickey, laughed. sounded a little crazy and sent warning prickles dow Boone's back.

"Nah," Coons demurred. "I ain't here to see you ge hitched, Marshal, I'm here to settle your hash." H crouched, arms swinging out so his hands could hover nea the butts of his pistols.

Nice and easy, Jack spread his coattails wide. "I'm afrai I can't oblige you at the moment," he said, sounding ge uinely sorry. "As you can see, I dressed for a wedding, n a killing. I'm unarmed and I know that means something gentlemen such as yourself."

"Ha!" Jim Hickey patted his massive gun belt. "What it means is, it'll be even easier than we figgered to do what we come to do."

"I heard about that," Jack said, looking sympathetic. "I don't blame you for being angry about your brother. But the truth is—"

"We know what the truth is!" Hickey glowered around him; men and boys lining the boardwalk fell back before his fury. "Somebody's gotta pay for the death of my brother, and we ain't too particular who that is. We'll start with you, then tree this town and gun down anybody who gets in our way."

Boone, intent on the confrontation before him, felt a tug on his sleeve. Glancing around irritably, he saw that Tonio had come up soundlessly.

"*Do something!*" the boy muttered, his dark eyes wide with disbelief. "You can't stand here and watch them—"

Boone had no intention of doing a damned thing, nor did he intend to let Tonio get involved. The marshal had made his bed. Looking at Jack, Boone saw that the truth of his predicament was finally beginning to dawn.

Jack Guthrie was going to die. Unless something completely unanticipated occurred . . .

It did, in the form of little Emmett Cox and his puppy, Tige. The little yellow mutt bolted into the street with his pint-size master in hot pursuit—directly between the two opposing factions.

Coons went wild. With an oath, he jerked his pistol from the holster and pumped three quick shots at the animal. The bullets slammed into the dog, knocking him off his feet. Tige landed in front of Jack and lay there twitching. Shrieking, Emmett threw himself on the animal's body.

Coons grimaced and took a staggering step sideways, as if the boy's shrill cries were more than he could bear. Swearing, he raised his pistol and took deliberate aim.

It all happened in the blink of an eye, freezing the on-lookers with horror. Tonio reacted first, hurling himself down the few steps into the street to fling his own body between Emmett and the gunman.

Coons fired once. Tonio jerked like a fish on a line and collapsed on top of the sobbing boy and the dead dog. Then he lay still.

For an split second, the shocked silence was absolute and total. Then Boone moved.

On top of the hill south of town, Rose threw herself off the church steps and came down running. Clutching her flowers, she lifted her white wedding gown indecently high to keep from tripping over it. Her veil floated behind like a streamer.

She had too far to go—she'd never make it! But she must try. Despite the shouts behind her, despite fear of what awaited her, she must try!

"Jack!"

Responding to Boone's shout of command, Jack whirled. The lawman's white, shocked face registered in the split second it took Boone to grab Tonio's pistol from his waistband and toss it, left-handed. In the same smooth movement, he drew his own weapon and threw a shot at Coons.

Jack caught the revolver on the fly, spun around and fired without hesitation. The report echoed right behind Boone's.

People screamed and fought to get off the street. Boone ignored them; they shouldn't have been there anyway.

A bullet kicked up dust inches from Tonio's inert body. Jack stepped over the huddled figures and knelt to shield them. Trying to draw fire, Boone yelled above the tumult, "Hickey, Coons! Over here, you sons of bitches!"

They swung toward him, pistols leaping in all three hands. A bullet pierced Boone's hat and grazed his scalp; another plucked at his sleeve. He crouched lower and started forward, firing with cold precision.

Hickey went down, flopping in the dust and dirt like a butchered hog. The youngster, Trig, staggered back a few steps and then he, too, fell, his head bouncing crazily on the hard-packed surface of the street.

Coons managed to reach the horses pulling frantically against the restraint of reins wrapped around the hitching post. He popped up over the rump of an animal and snapped a shot toward Jack; a soft splat announced a hit. Jack grunted and sagged forward, clutching his arm.

Out of ammunition, Boone could only watch Coons free one of the horses and swing up into the saddle. Brutally sawing on the reins, he forced the animal around so he could get a clear shot at the marshal.

The hammer fell on an empty chamber.

Sagging with relief, Boone watched Coons work his spurs, trying to force the horse to trample the huddled threesome. But the skittish animal jumped that hurdle neatly, and the gunman thundered north out of town.

Reloaded at last, Boone threw a final shot after Coons, but horse and rider were too far away.

In the strained, unnatural silence following those few seconds of hell, Boone glared around for fresh targets. The killing rage had not yet left him. Acrid gun smoke curled around him, along with the aroma of fresh blood—smells all too familiar.

It had all happened in little more than a heartbeat.

Doc Beatty hurried into the street to kneel beside Tonio and Jack. Junius Cox hauled his sobbing son away, giving the boy hell with every step.

"Take care of Tonio," Jack said thickly, holding his arm. He rocked back and forth, fighting his own pain.

Boone walked over to glower at Jack. "God dammit, I told you to wear your gun." He holstered his own with unnecessary force. "Maybe next time—"

Jack howled and struggled to his feet, his face turning red with the effort. "You two-bit, no-good gun-slinging owl hoot, there won't *be* a next—"

Involved in their own quarrel, the two men had no time to get set for the impact of Rose, barreling into them. Her arms opened wide to embrace them both. She was laughing and crying all at once, her veil hanging haphazardly over one eye and dark hair tumbling around her shoulders.

She had never looked so good to Boone. For once he didn't even try to conceal his longing, just stared at her with stark hunger. She belonged to another man, dammit; he knew that, but the freshness of her beauty and the magnitude of her relief overpowered him—that and the force of his love for her. Without pausing to consider, he slid an arm around her slim waist and hung on.

Rose gave him a quick startled glance before turning to Jack. "How badly are you hurt?"

He grimaced. "Just nicked me but it smarts like hell—Hades."

"Thank God you're all right." She looked from Jack to Boone, her eyes awash with tears. "And you, too. Thank you, Boone. Without you, this would have been a tragedy."

"I don't want your thanks," he said in a thick voice. He wanted her love. Now that it was too late, he realized that.

"I know you don't," she whispered. Her lips trembled. "I never thought it was possible to love two men at the same time," she said brokenly, "but I do. God help me, I do."

Jack's smile was lopsided. "I knew I'd hear those words someday," he said, "but I never expected it would be under circumstances such as these."

Rose smiled and leaned toward Jack. Boone felt his chest tighten with a kind of pain he'd never felt before. He had faced the blaze of gunfire with greater ease than he did the sure and certain knowledge that she was about to affirm her commitment to another man. Toward Boone, she felt only gratitude for his role in saving Jack's life.

He didn't have to wait around and watch this. He turned toward the hitching rail and the buckskin.

Pausing beside Doc and Tonio, Boone asked a question without words. The boy stared up stoically but his eyes were dark with pain and his mouth a tight line.

Doc paused in his labors. "Young scalawag's tough," he said, "no doubt about it. Took a clean hit in the shoulder but the slug passed on through. He's gonna be all right."

Boone nodded. "You're sure about that, I reckon."

"God willin' and the creeks don't rise," the doctor said, turning to his patient.

Tonio started to say something but a groan came out instead. Boone's grin felt stiff and unnatural after all that had happened, but he managed it anyway.

"Hell of a life I lead, ain't it, kid. At some future date, you might want to think about how much fun you've had here today."

Boone unhitched his horse and swung up into the saddle. For a moment he hesitated; then he turned the gelding's head toward Rose and Jack, still standing in the middle of the street.

He saw her look into Jack's eyes. "I have to do this," she said in a low, firm voice.

Jack's jaw worked as if he couldn't get words out. Fresh pain washed over his face and he swallowed hard. "I know you do," he said tightly. "Perhaps I always knew."

Rose drew a deep breath and squared her shoulders. Kicking her train out of her way, she swung around to confront the mounted man who'd come up behind her. Dropping her raggedy bridal bouquet in the dust, she grabbed hold of the saddle strings and stared up at him.

"I love you, Boone Smith!" She said it fiercely, decisively. "If you think you're getting out of here without me, you've got another think comin'. I don't care if you marry me or not—I mean I do, but I'll go with you regardless, anywhere—''

Leaning down, Boone caught her beneath the arms and swung her onto the saddle before him. He refused to consider all the reasons this wasn't going to work; he refused to consider anything except the joy her declaration brought to him. His heart swelled with such happiness that it felt about to burst.

"I love you, too," he said in a low, incredulous voice. The buckskin danced beneath them but still Boone held the animal back. He had to be sure Rose understood. "But it won't be easy," he forced himself to add. "You know that."

She twisted on the pommel until she could slide her arms around his waist. If she said now that she'd changed her mind, he didn't think he'd be able to let her go.

But she hadn't changed her mind; he saw the resolve in her clear, beautiful eyes. He lifted the reins—

"Wait!" Jack Guthrie stepped up to the horse's shoulder. Reaching into his pocket, he withdrew a folded sheet of paper. Boone recognized it immediately—the wanted poster. Slowly and deliberately, Jack crumpled that symbol of Boone's past and dropped it into the street.

"It may be easier to make a new start than you think," the marshal said. "*Vaya con dios,* my friend."

Not for the first time, a glance filled with respect and understanding passed between the two men. Boone lifted one hand to touch the brim of his hat, a salute to a gallant adversary. Setting spurs lightly to the buckskin, he carried his love north out of town at a gallop.

The train and veil of Rose's bridal ensemble floated out behind them as if borne by a zephyr. Tonio, who had seen and heard the whole exchange, thought he had never seen anything more beautiful or romantic.

Tonio watched Jack strap on an ammunition belt and reach for a revolver. The marshal, moving stiffly because of the wound in his left arm, snapped open the cylinder to check the load.

"I don't like guns and have rarely found them necessary," Jack said grimly, "but in this instance, I don't seem to have much choice."

Damn right, Tonio thought irritably, since Jack was about to lead a posse after a badman—a very bad man, indeed. The marshal's failure to recognize the seriousness of the threat sooner had nearly got Tonio's head shot off.

Boots clomping on the boardwalk announced company. Both men glanced around as George Curtis, Fred Loveless and the newspaper man from Crystal Springs entered the law office.

"You plannin' to take out after 'em anytime soon?" Curtis demanded, his tone caustic. "Our town was shot to ribbons hours ago, one of our finest young men lies near death—"

Obviously George hadn't noticed Tonio, bandaged but upright in a chair against the far wall; the fine young man nearly choked at the storekeeper's phony outrage on his behalf.

Jack stared at Curtis if he'd lost his mind for sure this time. "You mean Tonio Ryan?"

Curtis finally noticed Tonio's presence and had the good grace to redden beneath his ruddy complexion. "So maybe I exaggerate a little, but that outlaw and his friends did shoot up our town," he insisted. "We can't let him get away—or the other one, either."

Jack slipped the revolver into the holster and reached for a rifle from the gun rack. "What other one?"

"Boone, the mysterious gunman who's been hangin' around all these weeks."

"All these weeks," Loveless agreed, nodding vigorously. "Looks to me you'd be hot on his trail, him carryin' away your bride and all."

Jack's face had taken on a new hardness. "I've got no quarrel with Boone," he said shortly. "If he hadn't stepped in when he did, I'd be dead and I sure as hell wouldn't be the only one."

Phil Mossholder, the newspaperman, cleared his throat. "I beg to differ, Marshal. As an officer of the court, I believe you *do* have a quarrel with the man Boone." Officiously he pulled a crumpled ball of paper from his pocket and spread it out on the marshal's worktable.

Tonio gritted his teeth and heaved himself onto his feet. Lurching a bit, he managed to make his way to the table where he stared down at the sheet of paper.

It was a wanted poster bearing Boone's likeness. *What the hell?* Tonio swung on Jack, seeking answers.

The marshal looked taken aback; he licked his lips, apparently at a loss for words. Tonio's anger threatened to explode. Damn these town-bound busybodies, anyway! Where were they when there was a man's job to be done?

The door opened and James stuck his head inside. He took in the situation at a glance, then ignored it. "You ready, Marshal?" he snarled, apparently still bent out of shape because he'd missed the showdown. "We're saddled up and waitin' out here."

"I'm ready," Jack said grimly.

"I'm goin', too." Tonio licked his lips and steeled himself for the walk to the door. His injury wasn't that bad but his shoulder hurt like hell.

Jack frowned. "You sure you're up to this?"

"Hell, I ain't hurt any worse than you are."

The marshal nodded. "In that case, get a move on. We've got a lot of ground to cover."

Tonio followed Jack through the door. The three townsmen lingered behind, although George Curtis did call out a challenge.

"Bring that gunfighter Boone back dead or alive or we'll find somebody who can, Marshal!"

* * *

By the close of the fourth day of fruitless pursuit, only three members of the posse remained dedicated to the search: Marshal Guthrie, James Taggart and Tonio Ryan. Stiff, sore, recovering from injuries of various types, still each had vowed that hell would freeze over before they called off this manhunt.

Sitting their horses atop a ridge, the three men stared out morosely over an unidentified river, each lost in his own thoughts.

They'd been moving with deliberate speed on the trail of Coons, which seemed to cross and recross those of Boone and Rose. Worried, Tonio shifted in his saddle.

"Has Coons dropped back to trail Miss Rose and Boone now?" he wondered aloud.

James appeared equally disgruntled. "Looks that way," he admitted. "Now whatta you suppose—"

Tonio supposed Coons knew whose horse was making those tracks, and he further supposed Coons had a score to settle with Boone. Without another word he kicked his horse on down the slope and into the river. There was no time to waste.

They didn't stop until it was too dark to go on, and then reluctantly. Over tin cups of coffee, they sat in sullen silence around a smoldering camp fire. Tonio spoke first, bringing up a subject that had been preying on his mind since they'd ridden out.

"Why'd you let George Curtis get away with that?" he asked Jack.

The marshal reached for the coffeepot on the edge of the coals. "Get away with what?"

"Accusing Boone of being no better than the killer we're chasin'." It was a relief for Tonio to get it out; it had been eating at him like a saddle sore.

Jack sighed. "I started to set him straight, but why bother? Everybody who was there that day has their own idea as to what happened and why. Frankly, I don't much care what anybody thinks.''

"But Boone's no criminal." Tonio flung his cup onto the ground in frustration. "I don't give a damn how many reward posters you find on him.''

James shifted on his log. "There may be a new one out soon—for kidnapping. My sister—''

Jack's impatience surpassed even Tonio's. "God dammit, James, I told you she made her choice! I don't like it any better than you do but—''

James surged to his feet. He had been touchy as a bear for the past four days and his bad temper seemed about to be unleashed. "And I told you, I'll believe it when I hear it from her own lips! He forced her—I don't know how but somehow he forced her. Don't you want to—''

"All I want to do is bring Coons in to face the full penalty of the law!'' Magnificent in his righteous fury, Jack uncoiled his lean frame and stood up. "Then I want to shake the dust of Jones, Texas, off my boots forever.''

He strode toward the dark, outside the circle of light cast by the feeble fire. His anger seemed to dissipate as quickly as it had come, for he threw over his shoulder, "I'm heading home to Philadelphia once this is settled. So much for the romance of the West.''

They found the body just before noon the next day, laid out beside the trail. A bullet had smashed into the man's face, obliterating his features. It could have been any big, black-haired man—any big, black-haired man with Boone's gun belt and pistol lying beside his lifeless body.

Tonio's stomach plummeted down somewhere into his boots. Swearing, he almost fell out of his saddle in his haste to reach the corpse.

Jesus, it wasn't Boone, it was Coons! Weak with relief, Tonio sat down hard in the weeds beside the trail. He didn't even notice the note until James plucked it from the bloody

:hirt, pinned there by Rose's cameo brooch—the one she'd vorn on the high collar of her wedding gown.

With shaking hands, James unfolded a rumpled piece of)aper, which looked as if it had been ripped from a tally)ook. Drawing a deep breath, he began to read:

"Dearest James and Jack, for I'm sure you will be the ones who persevere and find this note—
Please believe me when I tell you that my husband (yes, we were married by a preacher in San Angelo) killed this man Coons in self-defense. We want no further trouble, only to be left alone. If that wish be granted, you'll never see nor hear from us again, for we plan to go as far away from here as we can possibly get.

As a token of our good faith, you will find Boone's gun belt and revolver. He has no further use for them in the new life we hope to build together.

James, my love to you and Diana and the niece or nephew I will never see. And to you, Jack dearest, I offer my deep affection with a firm conviction that you will find a woman who is worthy of you, for I never was.

Goodbye. In spite of everything, I am the happiest of women for I am beside the man I love more than life itself.

Rose

P.S. Boone says he would like Tonio Ryan to have his gun as a reminder."

James looked up, his eyes glittering suspiciously. He :leared his throat. "A reminder of what?" he demanded ;ruffly.

Tonio swallowed hard and shrugged. He wasn't sure iimself, but perhaps some day when he needed it, it would ome to him. He glanced at Jack. "You think folks back in ones will let it lay here?" he asked plaintively.

Jack, too, seemed moved by Rose's message. "I don't know," he said, "unless..."

Tonio and James turned as one, and Tonio felt an unexpected surge of blind hope.

"You know," Jack mused, "Coons is a big man—damn near big as Boone. If we hauled him back and planted him in the Jones cemetery..."

A broad grin split James's face. "We even got Boone's pistol," he agreed. "Everybody knows the only way to get a gunfighter's weapon is to shoot him dead."

Jack's lips twitched with the ghost of a smile and he nodded. "We could put up a marker...something on the order of, 'Here lies Boone, the baddest hombre of them all.'" He held out one hand, flat, palm up. "If we did that, it occurs to me that Rose and her husband just might find the trail a bit easier to travel. Are you with me?"

With a rebel yell, Tonio brought his fist down on Jack's palm. "Hell, yes!"

Tonio and Jack turned expectantly to James, who rolled his eyes and shrugged. "Why the hell not?" he asked rhetorically. "We can at least try. We'll have to get our stories straight, though. How the hell we'll get away with it, I don't know, since so many people saw what happened."

Tonio felt his hackles rise at James's gloomy attitude, but Jack didn't look perturbed.

"One thing I've learned," he said slowly, "is that people usually believe what they want to believe. Let's go back and find out what that is...."

Epilogue

Showdown, Texas—today

Showdown Days—the annual Fourth of July recreation of the famous Texas legend of the gunfighter and the lady, which gave the town its name—was coming up in a few weeks. Ever alert for a human interest story, a San Antonio newspaper dispatched a writer-photographer team to the Rocking T Ranch to interview old Thom T., the eighty-something-year-old patriarch of the Taggart family.

"Get the *real* story," the editor instructed his young staffers, sending them out to deal with the wily old grandson of James and Diana Taggart and grand-nephew of the famed Rose Taggart, the lady of the legend.

Like sendin' baby chicks after the chicken hawk, Thom T. thought as he greeted the pair. This bored little snip of a reporter wasn't interested in the *real* story. Being from California, she hadn't even known there *was* a legend until her editor told her.

Hell, she didn't even know the town of Showdown had been called Jones prior to 1876. Before Thom T. would negotiate with her on the *real* story, he'd have to fill her in on what *they say*.

And so he began, "They say that in 1876, Rose Taggart was the best-lookin' gal in three counties, maybe the whole state of Texas."

Almost two hours later, he neared the conclusion of the yarn.

"And they say the brave marshal outdrew the gunfighter Boone and shot him down like a yellow dog on Main Street. Then, with the help of the brave citizens of the town, he cleaned up the rest of Boone's outlaw gang. Finally Rose and Jack were married and they moved to Philadelphia, where he took up the practice of law again. They never came back to Texas.

"The gunfighter Boone was buried in the graveyard over yonder where everybody would forever after know the caliber of folks in this neck of the woods. George Curtis and the boys promptly changed the name of the town from Jones to Showdown, and within a year, it was chosen county seat."

Thom T. paused for breath and darted a quick glance at his rapt audience. Both reporter and photographer had been hanging on every word, their expressions awed.

Thom T. figured he ought to be ashamed of himself, tellin' all those lies about his Great-Aunt Rose and Great-Uncle Boone, but he wasn't.

These young whippersnappers didn't want the *real* story, they wanted the legend, just like everyone else. A few—maybe most—thought the legend *was* the truth.

So be it. All that could be gained by the truth at this late date was economic ruin for the city of Showdown, Texas, which relied upon the annual celebration of Showdown Days for financial stability.

That's why Thom T., as the oldest living descendant of the Taggart clan, occasionally made himself available to spin yarns for public consumption. So what if everything he said wasn't strictly true—what were they gonna do if they caught him in a lie, throw him in the hoosegow? He laughed.

The girl reporter sighed. "Thanks for telling us what really happened," she said as the photographer grabbed a few final shots. "Wow—just like a fairy tale, everyone living happily ever after." She grimaced. "Except that gunman Boone. At least he got what he deserved."

"He sure as shootin' did," Thom T. agreed innocently, following his guests out into the ranch yard to wave them on their way. For a moment he stood there alone, watching their car disappear over a hill. Then he sighed and turned toward the quiet house.

Tomorrow the Rocking T would erupt into chaos. Tomorrow all the known descendants of both James Taggart and Virginia Rose Taggart Smith—Jesse, Boone, Trey, their assorted wives and children—would gather at the Rocking T for a family reunion. The whole kit and caboodle, Thom T. thought with satisfaction.

He wasn't any too sure at this point he'd even bring up the things he'd learned about their forebears since the last family gathering.

Sometimes it was better to leave well enough alone.

Instant fame as the final resting place of a renowned desperado brought rewards to the town in the form of growth, just as George Curtis had hoped. What he hadn't anticipated was that increased population would mean increased competition. In 1888, he gave up, declared bankruptcy and moved back east, a broken man.

His daughter, Sally, did not go with him. Two years after the gunfight, she married a farmer. She managed to make her husband's life a living hell by deferring always to her father, but once George moved away things appeared to gradually improve. She bore five children and, at the age of thirty-seven, shocked the entire county by running away with a drummer.

Jack Guthrie returned east, a better man for his adventures in wild and woolly Texas. To his surprise, a young

woman he'd much admired before his departure—but who
had never so much as glanced his way—fell instantly in love
with this new, more masterful Jack Guthrie. They married
and quickly became the parents of twin boys. Jack entered
his father's law firm and eventually became famous in legal
circles by successfully arguing the controversial case of
Belsnapper vs. the State of Pennsylvania before the Su-
preme Court.

Everyone in town agreed that Tonio Ryan took the gunfighter's death hard; he left town shortly after the burying
in the company of the prostitute, Libby Bowman. Where he
went and what he did, nobody really knew.

The Rocking T Ranch prospered, as did James and Diana. They named their firstborn son Boone, justifying this
peculiar choice to the townspeople by explaining that Diana was distantly related to Daniel Boone, of frontier fame,
on her mother's side. This was, of course, a barefaced lie.

On a visit to San Francisco in 1886, James and Diana were
astonished and delighted to run into Mr. and Mrs. Jeb Smith
while attending the opera. At the conclusion of a delightful
reunion, they agreed that discretion being the better part of
valor, it would be best for all concerned if they henceforth
communicated only by letter, which the two women proceeded to do in great, if frequently cryptic, detail.

Therefore Diana was aware that Virginia Rose Taggart
and Jeremy Edward Boone Smith, now called Virginia and
Jeb, had relocated in California where he invested the proceeds from the sale of his Colorado holdings in land, making a fortune before turning to politics. Elected to the state
legislature, he was widely rumored as a potential candidate
for governor when he suddenly withdrew from public life
and moved with his wife and children to a sprawling ranch
near Stockton.

Seems he'd decided that "happily ever after" with the woman he loved would be more rewarding than high office.

* * * * *

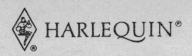

THE TAGGARTS OF TEXAS!

Harlequin's Ruth Jean Dale brings you
THE TAGGARTS OF TEXAS!

Those Taggart men—strong, sexy and hard to resist...

You've met Jesse James Taggart in FIREWORKS!
Harlequin Romance #3205 (July 1992)

And Trey Smith—he's THE RED-BLOODED YANKEE!
Harlequin Temptation #413 (October 1992)

And the unforgettable Daniel Boone Taggart in SHOWDOWN!
Harlequin Romance #3242 (January 1993)

**Now meet Boone Smith and the Taggarts who started it all—
in LEGEND!
Harlequin Historical #168 (April 1993)**

Read all the Taggart romances!
Meet all the Taggart men!

Available wherever Harlequin Books are sold.